Making the List

Aiden Murray

May the magic of the holidays be yours year round!

Aiden M.

Copyright @ 2024 by Aiden Murray

Title: Making the List

All Rights Reserved

No part of this book may be reproduced or used in any manner without the express written permission of the author except for the use of brief quotations in a book review. This includes, stored in any retrieval system, or transmitted in any form by any means—electronic, mechanical, photocopy, recording, or otherwise

This is a work of fiction. Names, characters, businesses, places, events, locales, and incidents are either the products of the author's imagination or used in a fictitious manner. Any resemblance to actual persons, living or dead, or actual events is purely coincidental.

This book is licensed for your personal enjoyment only. This book may not be re-sold or given away to other people. If you would like to share this book with another person, please purchase an additional copy for each recipient. If you're reading this book and did not purchase it, or it was not purchased for your use only, then please return to Amazon and purchase your own copy.

Thank you for respecting the hard work of this author.

Cover Design: Belle Ames Designs

Editing: Belle Ames Designs

Formatting: Belle Ames Designs

DEDICATION

For all the believers. Never stop believing in the magic of the season. For my wife Joey, whose infectious love of all things Christmas inspired me to write this story. Thank you for reminding me of the wonder, the reason, and the magic that the holiday brings.

Prologue

We all know the story of Santa Claus, the jolly old elf, that brings Christmas toys to children around the world. Or at least we know what we have been led to believe. What if the story of Nicholas hadn't started out as such a happy tale?

On Nicholas's twenty-fifth birthday, he left his workshop early to buy a ring for the woman he had been seeing for over a year. When he reached her home, he knocked but she didn't answer, so Nicholas tried the door. Finding the door unlocked, he entered to see the woman he loved kissing another man.

Overcome with grief, Nicholas decided to take a walk in the woods. As tears filled his eyes, he lost his way and wandered deep into the forest, stumbling upon a small home. Tired and unsure of which way the village was, he knocked on the door, hoping that whoever resided within could help him find his way.

A tall, thin man with pointed ears and a crooked smile answered the door and welcomed Nicholas in. The man offered him a drink, asking Nicholas why he had been wandering in the woods. Nicholas confessed to being quite lost, since he'd never seen the man's house during his previous wanderings. Then he told him of his broken heart.

"If only one could see the true nature of others before they opened their heart to them," the man offered.

"Yes. That would be helpful. I wish there was a way to know if someone was nice or not," Nicholas replied.

"Perhaps there is," the host answered. "I could help you. You just have to say the word."

"That's impossible. There's no way to be able to tell the true nature of someone without getting to know them," Nicholas said.

"Ah. But there is. If it's what you truly desire, you just have to ask," the man answered.

"You can do that? You could help me see who people really are? I'm rather skeptical, but it's been a terrible day and I need something to wish for. Can you please help me to see people as they are?" Nicholas asked.

The man laughed and snapped his fingers. Nicholas wiped his eyes as the cottage, the man, and the forest disappeared, and he found himself back in his village. Had he imagined all of that? No, he'd definitely been in the woods. Nicholas decided to walk to the tavern to try and clear his head. However, when he walked through the doors, he found that he instantly knew how good or how bad every person in the room was.

Nicholas tried to blink away the label that he saw above every person's head, but try as he might, he couldn't make them go away. Somehow that strange man had given him the gift to see people's true nature. As much as Nicholas thought he had wanted this, he was now finding it very hard to see anything else, making it impossible to be around people.

Nicholas withdrew to his workshop, where he spent several days creating wooden toys. When he ran out of wood, he placed the toys in a bag, loaded them on his sled, and walked into the village with plans to give the toys to the children. Unfortunately, as he entered the town, he found that he could still see the tags above each of the children. Discovering that all the children in the square were naughty, he turned and walked towards the forest, hoping to find the strange man and ask him to undo what he had done.

After hours of wandering the woods, Nicholas saw no signs of the cottage or the strange man. Defeated, he stopped walking and sat on his sled, placing his head in his hands and sobbing. If he couldn't stop seeing the bad in people from a distance, how was he ever supposed to be surrounded by them?

"Excuse me, sir, are you lost?" a small voice asked, pulling Nicholas from his thoughts.

He looked up to see a tall, thin woman with slightly pointed ears, similar in appearance to the man who had cursed him. Maybe she could help him. "Hi, I'm looking for someone. He looks a little like you. Maybe you can help," Nicholas said.

"Perhaps you can tell me about him?" the woman offered.

"Yeah, he, wait," Nicholas stood and took a better look at the woman, staring at the space above her head. "Why can't I see if you're good or bad?" he asked.

"If I'm what? I don't understand," the woman replied.

"The man who looked like you gave me the ability to see the truth in people. I can see if people are good or if they are bad when I look at them and I can't unsee it. I need it to go away. Can you help me?" Nicholas asked.

"I fear you've been tricked. It sounds to me like you were cursed and I fear that I'm unable to break it. However, I can take you to be around people like me where you can live your life in peace," the woman offered.

As you may have guessed, the woman who found Nicholas in the woods was an elf. She took him with her to the North Pole, where he eventually became a part of their community. In time he fell in love with one of the elves and married her. Through the years he taught the elves to make toys and, with support and help from the elves, he returned to his village to deliver toys to all of the nice children.

For the rest of his life, Nicholas continued this tradition of visiting the village on the same day each year, celebrating the anniversary of when he came to live with the elves, and giving gifts to all of the good boys and girls. This could have been where the legend of Santa Claus ended, but the curse set upon him by the evil elf was passed down to his children, who continued Nicholas' tradition.

Over the years, as the Christmas family grew, more and more children experienced the joy of gifts on the holiday. Eventually there were so many descendants of Nicholas that only a few remained in the North Pole. The rest of the family strategically moved around the world to help compile a list of naughty and nice children so that their relatives who remained in the North Pole knew which children to deliver toys to.

Because they had to live everywhere and surround themselves with the people whose names they put on the lists, they created the legend of Santa Claus that we all know to help protect them from any repercussions from those that were naughty. For most, being a Christmas was a point of pride, and they taught their children about it from an early age. However, some of them began to take on human tendencies as they became more and more removed from the elven part of their heritage and found themselves on the naughty list as well as using their abilities for their own purposes. As a result, there are some that walk among us not knowing the gift they have until it is upon them.

Chapter 1

Sam sat on a stool in the city's only lesbian bar and looked out at the dance floor, running their hand through their thick, messy short brown hair. As they felt their phone vibrate, they reached into the pocket of their skinny jeans retrieving it. Sam sighed as they realized it wasn't a message but just a reminder to meet at the bar. Silencing their phone, they returned it to their pocket and resumed watching the crowd, tapping their foot to the music as they waited.

They weren't sure why they held onto this tradition, especially since their best friend hadn't been single for years and they had no real interest in meeting anyone. But tonight was their twenty-fifth birthday and they had been coming to this bar with Faith to celebrate their birthday since they turned nineteen. However, now they were sitting by themselves, sipping a beer while they waited for Faith to meet them because she was having dinner with her partner before joining them.

Faith had invited Sam to her house to have dinner instead of going to the bar, but Sam had always been oddly fond of tradition, even if it was something as silly as meeting at a bar. This was what they did. It was one of the few things that Sam could count on and one of the few things they looked forward to all year. Sam wasn't big on holidays as they tended to be full of disappointment. Their father had left their mother on Valentine's Day when she had told him that she was pregnant. As a result, Sam didn't even know who their father was, but if he was anything like the long list of men that their mother had introduced them to over the years, he wasn't a good man. Sam had lost count of the number of men that her mother had dated. None of them had been father material or, for that matter, husband material.

Watching their mother date - paired with their own romantic mishaps over the years - made Sam believe that love was as made up and useless as the Easter Bunny and Santa Claus. There was one year when Sam was six that their mother had a boyfriend in December who tried to get Sam excited about Christmas. He'd promised a trip to see Santa and a Christmas morning filled with gifts, and for the briefest of moments, Sam had been a normal child and not a cynical small human forced to adult way too early. That all came crashing down as the man broke up with their mother the very day they were supposed to take Sam to the mall to visit Santa. That was the day that Sam stopped believing in people and realized that holidays would always serve as a reminder that some people had and some people didn't.

Sam was one of the people who didn't and, though they swore to grow up and be one of the people that had it good, they also vowed to never forget where they came from. Sam spent their youth taking care of their mother, who struggled to keep a job and moved them from place to place, as they often lived with whoever the current fling happened to be. Now that Sam was an adult in their twenties, they barely spoke to their mother. They had put that life behind them, settling into their career as an accountant for one of the country's largest retailers. It was a steady job that paid well, allowing them to move away from their hometown and put the past in the past. It also kept them very busy in the last three months of the year, so they didn't have to pay attention to foolish holiday nonsense.

That last part was something that caused their best friend a great deal of distress, as Faith forced Sam to celebrate both Thanksgiving and Christmas with her and her partner every year. Sam tried desperately to avoid those holidays and always made sure to work the majority of both, allowing no more than an hour of either day to spend with Faith. It wasn't that Sam didn't want to spend the day with their friend, but they despised the holidays and Faith loved them. Sam couldn't watch Christmas movies, sing Christmas carols, eat Christmas cookies, or decorate a Christmas tree. All of those things filled them with rage and brought on a spiraling depression that they fought very hard to prevent. Which sadly meant that they spent a few months every year desperately trying to evade the one person that they actually truly liked.

Faith and Sam were roommates in college and despite Sam's best efforts, Faith quickly became their best friend - or rather their only friend - as Sam had never found it easy to trust others with their feelings. Every time they had opened their heart to anyone - family, friend, or potential romantic interest - it had always ended with Sam all alone and brokenhearted. Somehow Faith had pushed past Sam's walls and forced her way into their heart.

It hadn't hurt that Faith had opened Sam's eyes to a whole new world of possibilities as Sam was learning about their sexual identity and gender. Faith was more than happy to have a friend to go with her to every gay/lesbian/queer activity in the city. Sam moved around so much with their mom that they never really took the time to make friends. Instead, they focused on their school work and spent all of their free time at home. This caused them to live a very sheltered life, which gave them little exposure to the people their mother deemed "sexual deviants," a list that consisted of anyone who wasn't living a completely heteronormative lifestyle.

Their mother was appalled when she learned that Sam's roommate was dating another woman, suggesting that Sam ask to move to a new room. Instead, Sam took that opportunity to tell their mother that they, too, had been on several dates with girls and had no intention of dating men. Their mother was still praying that Sam would come back to the path of "the Lord" and settle down with a nice man, something that she was certain could happen since Faith had given up her life of sin when she had started dating Xavier.

Sam had been so enraged by this declaration that they decided to officially move out, spending the rest of their freshman year working so that they would have enough money to get an apartment with Faith and Xavier. After they moved out, they rarely spoke with their mother, except on holidays when she thought it was necessary to call. This was just another reason that Sam hated holidays, their birthday included. In fact, that was the reason they were at the bar an hour early. After speaking with their mother, Sam needed a strong drink and a pretty distraction, but the second part would have to wait until Faith arrived.

As Sam finished their second drink, they noticed a woman sitting by herself, sipping on a hard cider, checking them out. When Sam smiled at her, she blushed, her face turning a shade of red that matched her curly auburn hair. The woman looked away as she was joined by her friends. Sam shook their head, turning back to the bar. That girl was adorable and definitely not the type of woman that they should approach for a fling. She was far too wholesome looking, wearing a sweater and jeans when most of the women in the club were barely clothed. If Sam wanted to have an evening forgetting about everything, those were probably the women they should be choosing. They glanced back towards the redhead as they heard a melodic laugh come from the table. The woman was smiling and giggling with her friends, revealing a dimple in the cheek that Sam could see, and making her green eyes sparkle. Although that might have been the light reflecting off of the woman's glasses, it definitely looked like there was a twinkle in her eye.

"See something you like?" a snarky and very recognizable voice said, pulling Sam's gaze from the impossibly cute girl.

"Faith! It's been the longest day. I was starting to think that X was going to keep you all night," Sam said, standing to hug their best friend.

"You know that I would never leave you hanging, especially tonight. Happy Birthday, Sam!" Faith said, sitting on the barstool beside them. "Xavier might have won my heart, but it was yours first and you will always be my number one."

"Thanks, Faith. You look incredible! I'm surprised X let you leave the house like that. I guarantee you leave with more numbers than I do tonight," Sam laughed.

Faith shook her head at Sam, her long blue hair falling over her shoulders as she did. Her perfectly tanned shoulders were bare, as was her collarbone. Faith was wearing a strapless black dress that barely covered her, leaving little to the imagination. "X doesn't **let** me do anything. You know better than that," she answered.

"Fair point. What do you say we get sloppy drunk and forget about the rest of the world for a few hours?" Sam asked, laughing as they waved the bartender over.

"Two shots of peppermint schnapps, please, and two gin and cranberries," Faith ordered. "For someone who hates Christmas, you drink like an elf," Faith said, sticking her tongue out at Sam.

"You drink with elves often?" Sam asked. "I can't help it if I have very specific tastes. And I don't think it's fair for Christmas to claim ownership over peppermints or cranberries."

"You just sit there in denial. I know deep down you love Christmas just as much as I do," Faith laughed, grabbing the shots from the bartender and handing one to Sam.

"I assure you that the only thing Christmasy about me is my last name." Sam rolled their eyes. Because the universe and fate had a twisted sense of humor, Sam's last name was Christmas, something that drove their hatred of the holiday even more. They shook their head at their friend as they grabbed for their shot glass. "Shall we toast to what we always do?" Sam asked.

"No. You only turn twenty-five once. This one needs to be special. Let me think. To my best friend, my sibling by choice, happy birthday. May twenty-five be your best year yet, bringing success and happiness. And may this be the year that you let love back into your heart," Faith said. "To twenty-five." Faith tapped her shot glass on Sam's before downing the shot.

"I love you, Faith. Isn't that enough for you?" Sam said as they lowered their shot glass. "You're the only person in my life that's never let me down."

"Alright. You actually answered her call today, didn't you? That's why you want to get plastered," Faith said. "What did she have to say today?"

"Aside from repeatedly calling me her daughter? She asked how you were doing and if you were still living without sin with your husband," Sam answered.

"You still haven't told her that Xavier is trans, have you?" Faith asked.

"Do you want to explain that to her? Because I don't have the energy. Besides, she hated you until you started dating a man. At least this way she likes one of us," Sam replied.

"Like I care if your mother likes me. I don't like **her**. The only good thing she's ever done is give birth to you. And the fact that she can't bring herself to love you for the amazing person that you are fills me with rage every time I think about it. Why did you answer her call?" Faith asked.

"She called six times. And I know I should ignore her, but she's my mother. I keep hoping that she'll come around. I don't want to talk about her anymore tonight. This is supposed to be my birthday celebration," Sam answered.

"From the person who doesn't believe in celebrating birthdays. But yeah, I get it. Let's talk about that cutie over there in the sweater instead," Faith laughed.

"Her? No. She is far too pure for the kind of distraction I'm looking for tonight. She looks like the kind of girl you take home to meet your mom and, while I have no plans to subject anyone to that kind of hell, she seems like the kind of girl that deserves a relationship. You and I both know I don't do relationships so I can steer clear of the evil L word," Sam replied.

"What word would that be? Lame?" Faith asked, rolling her eyes.

"You know damn well what word I'm talking about. Just because you believe in romance, doesn't mean it's real," Sam said.

"Fine. But this is going to be the year that you start to believe in something. If it isn't going to be love, I guess it's going to be the spirit of Christmas," Faith declared.

"Fat chance. Christmas exists for one reason and one reason only and that's so companies like the one I work for can make as much money in three months as they do the rest of the year combined," Sam argued.

"My dear, sweet cynical friend, you couldn't be more wrong and one of these years I'm going to prove it to you. Why not this year? I think twenty-five is going to be life changing. Here's to seeing things through a different light and opening your heart to the wonders of love and holiday cheer," Faith raised her glass to Sam.

As Sam's alarm beeped on their phone, signaling the time of their birth, they raised their glass and nodded to Faith. "Here's to twenty-five. May it suck less than the previous twenty-four years," Sam said before tilting their glass back and finishing their beverage.

Chapter 2

Sam put down their glass and closed their eyes, inhaling deeply and trying to make sense of what they had just seen. They opened their eyes slowly and the bar's crowded dance floor came back into view. Sam rubbed their eyes in disbelief. What was in that drink? Had someone drugged them? That was the only logical explanation for the incredibly bizarre hallucination they were currently having.

"Are you alright, Sam?" Faith asked.

"I, um. Yeah. I gotta go to the bathroom. Be right back," Sam answered, standing and looking over the sea of people to where the restrooms were. Seeing past the crowded dance floor was proving almost impossible with the addition of Sam's current hallucination. That was the only possible explanation for what they were seeing. Sam blinked rapidly trying to make things return to normal as they approached the dance floor. When that didn't work, they lowered their gaze to the floor as they pushed through the dancing women on their way to the bathroom.

Sam leaned over the bathroom sink, turning on the faucet and splashing their face with water. The ice cold water caused a chill to run through them as they looked up at their reflection in the mirror. Water dripped from their chin, spraying the mirror when Sam smacked themselves in the face. "Come on Sam. You didn't have that much to drink. What the hell is wrong with you? Snap out of it," they scolded themselves, smacking both of their cheeks and closing their eyes tightly.

"Hey, you okay, friend?" a voice from behind Sam, caused them to open their eyes and turn around.

A young woman, probably not old enough to drink yet, was standing behind them. She was gorgeous - definitely the type of girl that Sam would have been interested in spending the night with - but as she stood there staring at them with a concerned look in her eyes, all that Sam could see was the white bubble above her head with the word "naughty" in gray letters. What was going on? Why had everyone turned into a walking SIMS character? That was the only way that Sam could describe what they were seeing as they ran from the bathroom and back through the bar. Everyone, even Faith, had a bubble over their head with the word "naughty" or "nice" in black or gray above their head. How was that even possible?

As Sam looked to the bar and their best friend, with "Nice" in dark shade of gray floating above her head, they knew they couldn't spend another minute in the bar. Faith was not looking in their direction as they turned and walked to the exit. Pulling their phone from their pocket, Sam quickly sent an apology text, saying that they must have eaten something bad and they weren't feeling well. Faith would be disappointed, but she would understand. Birthdays were hard for Sam and this wasn't the first time that, despite their fondness for this tradition, Sam was bailing early.

Still, they felt guilty as they entered their apartment building. Sam was walking with their head down, trying to avoid seeing other people, as the words hadn't disappeared. They also were staring at their phone, trying to figure out how to respond to Faith. She had understood, but she also saw right through Sam's story about food poisoning, which meant Faith wanted to know what was actually going on. Sam wanted to know that as well and had no idea what they should tell Faith, as everything they had tried to type made them sound like they were crazy. Perhaps they were.

Sam stepped on the elevator, pressing the button for the 4th floor before leaning back against the wall. They let out a relieved sigh as the elevator began to move. For the first time since they had left the bar, Sam was completely alone. The walk home had been difficult. Not only did every person they pass let Sam know what their character was by the word above their head, but Sam found that they also knew each person's name and to what degree each of them was naughty or nice. That was impossible, of course. Sam knew this. There was no way that this was anything other than some insane hallucination and everything would be better after they got some sleep.

At least that was what Sam was telling themselves as they exited the elevator and walked to their apartment. Faith had wanted twenty-five to be life-changing, but Sam was pretty sure that their friend didn't want it to be the year that they went insane. There had to be an explanation. Maybe someone had slipped something in their drink. They were normally so careful about that, but Sam had been so caught up in their thoughts from their call with their mother that they hadn't been as vigilant as usual. If someone had attempted to drug them, that person hadn't followed them. There was thankfully still no sign of another person as they walked down the hallway towards their home.

Once Sam was back in their apartment, they sent one more quick apology text to Faith before collapsing in their bed. "Alright twenty-five, you win. But it isn't some grand competition. You didn't have to make this year suck worse than the rest as soon as you began. It would have been alright to wait at least a few days," Sam sighed as they kicked off their shoes. In bed by nine, they thought. Guess they were officially waving farewell to their youth. Can't stay out late and sleep with strange women when your brain is short-circuiting.

Sam closed their eyes and said a quick wish for tomorrow to be a better day. They intended to get themselves ready for bed and make themselves a hot cider before falling asleep, but as their head sunk into their pillow and the images of the night began to play in their mind, Sam nodded off to sleep. Their dreams were filled with strange images of a snowy village of people dressed in red and green.

In the dream, Sam found themselves walking through the village with snow covered streets. The buildings were all decorated for the holidays with twinkling lights and Christmas trees. Seeing as it was only September, it seemed rather odd to Sam that this town was so festive. Maybe though, it wasn't September here. The bright colored ribbons and bows that adorned the streetlights sure made it seem like December. As Sam stood looking at their surroundings, several deer-like animals ran towards them, causing them to jump to the side. As they dodged the approaching animals, Sam fell into the snow, landing on their backside. A woman with long blonde hair so light that it appeared white, wearing a red and green hat that rested on her pointed ears, reached a hand down to help Sam to their feet. Was she an elf? Sam shot up in bed, wide awake and annoyed that Faith's love for Christmas had invaded their dreams.

They groaned as they grabbed their phone to check the time. It wasn't even eleven. They really should go back to sleep, but since they were awake, they might as well actually change for bed. Sam walked to their chest of drawers, passing the window as they did. There were people walking around on the street below. Sam tried to fight the urge to look as they really wanted to be back in bed, but they had to know if whatever had happened at the bar had run its course. Sam punched the wall beside the window when they watched a couple walk by each with a line of text above their heads. Sam couldn't read the words from where they stood, but the fact that the labels still appeared concerned them.

Nothing about this made any sense. As they continued to look at the street below them, they thought they saw a streak of red and green go by, heading for the apartment building. Whatever it was moved too quickly to be a person. Most likely it was just another piece of this strange hallucination they were having. Sam turned from the window, forgetting about changing for bed as they walked from their bedroom to the kitchen.

They opened the fridge hoping to find something alcoholic. Unfortunately, they desperately needed to go shopping and the only beverages they had were milk, cider (the non-alcoholic kind), and water. With a heavy sigh, they grabbed the jug of cider, filling a large mug and placing it in the microwave. Sam loved cider but drinking the beverage cold had always felt wrong to them. It was why they didn't drink hard ciders. Their affinity for warm cider and hot cocoa was something that Faith often called into question whenever Sam spoke ill of Christmas.

Ugh, Faith. What were they going to do if they couldn't figure out what was wrong with them? Sam promised her they would meet for lunch to make up for bailing at the bar. Why were they thinking about that? It would be fine. Whatever this was would pass. They just needed to sleep it off. As soon as they finished their cider, they were going back to bed.

The microwave beeped, pulling them from their thoughts. Sam retrieved their beverage and leaned against the kitchen counter, holding the warm mug in their hands and inhaling the sweet apple scent. They were just about to take their first sip when there was a knock at their door. "Faith, I told you I don't feel good and I just want to be left alone," Sam called towards the door, not moving from the kitchen.

Assuming that had solved their problem and that Faith would give up and go home, Sam lifted the piping hot mug, the warm steam hitting their face as they inhaled the scent. The mug was almost too hot to hold but they were in need of the calming effect hot cider had on them. Blowing on the beverage once to cool it, they brought the mug to their lips. "Shit!" they yelled as they jumped from the now louder knock on their door, causing them to spill cider on their hands, the shock of the hot liquid causing them to drop their mug, which shattered as it hit the ground. As they looked down at the broken mug, whoever was waiting outside began to pound on the door. Hot cider began to soak through Sam's socks, burning their feet that were much more sensitive to the hot liquid than their hands that held mugs of hot cider regularly. They stepped away from the spilled beverage and peeled their socks off, throwing them in anger as they walked to the door.

Sam had no idea who would be knocking on their door at this hour if it wasn't Faith. They were confident that it wasn't their best friend, as she would have either given up or let herself in by now. Whoever it was, they'd better have a damn good reason to be disturbing them this late at night, because they were in no mood to deal with anyone. Annoyed and in pain, Sam threw open their front door, only to slam it shut after they saw the person standing in the hallway.

Chapter 3

"Nope. Nope. Absolutely not. Wake up, Sam," they said as they stared at their closed door. There was no way they had seen that. There had to be an explanation. Maybe they just weren't awake yet. Sam took a few deep breaths before reaching for the doorknob and opening the door once again.

Standing in the hallway was a woman with light blonde hair that almost looked white at first glance. She was tall and thin and wearing a red and green sweater covered in snowflakes with a red skirt. Her long pointed ears were resting under a red hat similar to the Santa Claus hats everyone wears at Christmas. Sam lowered their gaze and wiped their eyes, noticing her green boots with red laces as they did. This really couldn't be happening. There were no explanations for the elf-like woman in the hallway.

"Samantha Christmas?" the woman asked in a small, child-like voice.

"Sam. Sam Christmas," Sam answered. "And you are?"

"Candycane Tinseltree at your service. It's a pleasure to meet you," the woman responded.

"I'm sorry. Candycane? You have to be joking. How much money is Faith paying you to do this to me?" Sam asked.

"I don't know who this Faith is. I'm here on behalf of the Christmas line. Today is your twenty-fifth birthday, is it not?" Candycane asked in return.

"The Christmas line? So you're implying that my deadbeat father was waiting for me to turn twenty-five to have a relationship with me?" Sam questioned.

"Oh, no. I have no idea who your father is. I'm here as a representative of the family. It appears you know nothing of your family's history. May I come in? I have much I need to tell you," Candycane answered.

"Look, I have had arguably the worst day of my life and having a conversation with what I can only assume is supposed to be a Christmas elf is not making it any better. I don't know who sent you, but I really just want to go back to bed and forget today ever happened," Sam answered, starting to close the door. "So I'm truly sorry, but if you still feel the need to talk to me, come back tomorrow."

"Wait. Am I naughty or nice?" Candycane asked, putting their boot in the doorway to block Sam from closing the door.

"Clearly you aren't nice," Sam huffed.

"No. Look above my head. What does it say?" Candycane asked.

"What do you mean, look above your head?" Sam asked as they looked at the woman again. "There isn't anything above your head." Sam opened their eyes wide and blinked as they realized that the annoying words had disappeared. "Oh, thank you whoever answered my prayer," Sam mumbled as they glanced skyward.

"So, you were seeing the tags, then?" Candycane asked.

"The hallucinations? Yeah, but as you so kindly pointed out, they seem to be gone now, so if you don't mind, I'm very, very tired," Sam replied, once again trying to close the door.

"Your gift only works on humans. It won't work on me. I assure you that, were I human, you would still very much see a word above my head," Candycane said. "I know that what you experienced tonight has you very confused, but that's why I'm here. I'll explain all of it to you, but please let me come inside."

Sam heard the sound of the elevator ding and glanced down the hallway. They didn't want to let this woman in, but they also didn't really want anyone to see them talking to someone dressed as a Christmas elf in September, either. "Fine, come in," Sam said as they stepped aside.

"Thank you," Candycane said as she looked around the apartment. "Is that apple cider I smell?" Her face lit up as she inhaled the scent.

"It is, but unfortunately I dropped it on the ground when you knocked. I wasn't expecting company this late," Sam answered. "About all I have to offer is water if you're thirsty."

"That'd be fine. Thank you. And I'll make it up to you for the cider after I've explained things to you," Candycane answered.

"I really just want to go to bed, so whatever you have to say, please make it quick," Sam said, walking over to the window and glancing down at the street. As they watched, a cab stopped in front of the building and a couple stepped out. "Dammit," Sam mumbled, slamming their fists down on the windowsill as they could clearly read that the girl was naughty, while the man's tag was switching back and forth between the two. Sam turned from the window and looked at the woman sitting on their couch. "Why don't you have anything written above your head? And why did you know that I was seeing these things? Are you part of this ridiculous hallucination?"

"Please sit. I'll try to keep my explanation short, but you need to understand where you come from and how Christmas as we know it came about," Candycane answered.

"I can't sit. There's a Christmas elf in my living room and I can't look at other people without instantly knowing who and what kind of person they are. I .... no, nope. This is it. I've finally snapped. My therapist is going to love this story," Sam said, looking at Candycane. "You aren't real. I'm going to bed. You'll be gone in the morning." The elf replied, but Sam didn't hear her as they walked from the room and slammed their bedroom door.

The blaring sound of Sam's alarm came far too early, causing them to knock their phone on the ground as they tried to silence it. They sat up with a groan as they leaned down to pick it up. There was a message on their phone from Faith asking if they were feeling better. Were they? Last night was going to go down as one of the strangest, if not **the** "strangest," night of their life. Today, however, was a new day and it was going to be a better day. It had to be.

Sam stood and stretched their arms above their head, inhaling deeply as they did. The sweet smells of chocolate and maple syrup assaulted their senses, causing their stomach to growl. That smelled amazing, but how was it a thing? Nobody else was there. Sam inhaled again, making sure they weren't dreaming, and their mouth watered at the smell.

"Faith? When did you get here?" Sam called as they exited their room.

Sam stopped short as they caught sight of the person standing in their kitchen. "Good morning, Sam Christmas. I hope you don't mind that I made breakfast. I felt terrible for intruding last night," Candycane said, smiling at them.

"No, no, no, no. You aren't supposed to be here. You were supposed to be a dream, a hallucination," Sam said, slapping their face to make sure that they were still awake.

"I assure you that I'm real. I know this is confusing. Here, eat. I'll tell you who I am," Candycane said.

Sam hesitantly walked forward and sat at their kitchen island in front of a plate covered in pancakes and a large mug of hot chocolate. "I don't want any of this to be real, except for maybe the food. It smells amazing and I'm starving," Sam said, picking up utensils and cutting into the stack of maple syrup-covered pancakes.

If Sam had thought that the food smelled amazing, there wasn't a word to describe how it tasted. These were the best pancakes that they'd ever had - light, fluffy, and buttery. It was perfection paired with the richest, sweetest, creamiest hot cocoa that Sam had ever consumed. This food was too good to be true. "Okay. Now I know I'm dreaming. There's no way that food should taste this good," Sam said, shoveling another forkful into their mouth.

"I'm flattered, but there's nothing special about my cooking. Your senses were awakened when you turned twenty-five. It wasn't just your sight that received a boost. You'll find that all of your senses have been amplified. You'll taste and smell things more fully. You'll be able to hear whispers across a crowded room and, as you already know, you can see who people truly are just by looking at them," Candycane answered.

"How? How is any of that possible? And you still haven't told me why I can't see anything when I look at you," Sam replied.

"The simple answer is magic, but there's little that's simple when it comes to magic. For instance, your magic only works on humans, which is why you're unable to see my nature. I'm an elf," Candycane answered.

"Magic isn't real and elves don't exist. I got very little sleep last night and I'm in no mood for games," Sam replied.

"You are a Christmas. How can you say that magic doesn't exist?" Candycane asked.

"I knew it. Faith did send you. Look, no amount of trickery is going to make me believe in the magic of a holiday that has brought me nothing but pain. I'm sure Christmas is great for people who have loving families and money, but for those of us who don't, it's nothing more than a constant reminder that we'll never be enough," Sam answered.

"What? No. That's not what Christmas means at all. It's a time to celebrate the good in people. It's a time of joy," Candycane responded.

"Good in people? You have to be kidding me," Sam laughed. "I gave up looking for that a long time ago. Humans are self-serving and awful. In my experience, there are very few people that aren't like that," Sam said, standing and walking to the window to look out at the city. The street was full of people beginning their day and, to prove Sam's point, many of them had a text block with the word "naughty" displayed above their heads. "Look, I'm not buying into this whole magic thing, but please tell me that you can make the words go away," Sam said, turning back to face Candycane.

"It doesn't work that way. I don't think you're going to believe me until you see it, are you?" Candycane asked.

"There's no possible way that you can prove to me that magic exists, especially if it has anything to do with that fat man in a red suit that ruins the last three months of the year," Sam said, crossing their arms.

"Oh, boy. I'm gonna regret this, but I think this may constitute an emergency," Candycane said, snapping her fingers.

Chapter 4

Sam wiped their eyes as their kitchen faded around them, replaced by a snow-covered lane with buildings decorated for Christmas on either side. They shivered, crossing their arms and rubbing their hands on the bare skin of their forearms trying to get warm. "Wh, wh, where are we?" Sam asked, their teeth shattering. "Huh, huh, how da,da, did you da, da, do that?"

"I used magic, which is very real and brought you to the most magical place on Earth," Candycane replied, snapping her fingers again and transporting them to a small room with a large fireplace and two armchairs.

Sam ran to the fire and began warming their hands. "The most magical place on Earth? I have been to Disneyland and I don't recall freezing my ass off when I was there. Where are we?"

Candycane rolled her eyes as she sat, gesturing to the seat beside her. "The North Pole, obviously. Sit down so we can finish our conversation that was so rudely interrupted by your inability to just believe," she answered.

No longer shivering, Sam was able to focus on their surroundings. They appeared to be in the living room of a small apartment as there was a small kitchen to their right and a short hallway with a door on either side leading to what Sam presumed was the entrance behind the chairs. "Look. Whatever you just did was a really cool party trick, but there is no way this is the North Pole. For starters, there is nothing at the North Pole. Secondly, this is just a typical apartment. If you really are an elf, wouldn't you live in something more impressive or at least unique?" Sam asked.

"Oh. You thought all elves lived in gingerbread houses or something? We reserve those homes for the elves who bake, obviously," Candycane answered, rolling her eyes. "We don't live that differently from your kind. We live with our family when we are young. We go to school. We grow up, get jobs, and live on our own until we start our own family."

"I'm sorry. I didn't mean to offend you, but if this was supposed to convince me that Santa Claus really does exist, it isn't working," Sam replied.

"First assignment and I get a Christmas who doesn't believe. Perfect," Candycane mumbled, reaching into her pocket and grabbing her phone. "I need to make a call. I have an idea, but it could cost me my job." Candycane sighed as she stood and walked out of the room, leaving Sam alone.

Sam walked to the window and glanced out. The street was covered in snow and bright colored lights hung from rooftops and balconies. Sam didn't believe in magic, but how had they gone from their apartment in the city to a strange home in a snow-covered landscape? Sam closed their eyes and placed their head in their hands. "Come on, Sam. Snap out of it. Wake up. Wake up. Wake up," Sam muttered to themselves.

Opening their eyes, Sam focused on the individuals that were starting to exit the buildings. They were all dressed in outfits similar to what Candycane was wearing, though they were not all red and green. The street that had been empty moments before was now full of people wearing bright colored clothing and long stocking caps with bright colored pom poms at the tip. "Well at least I have stopped seeing words above people's heads," Sam muttered as they wiped their eyes, trying to make sense of what they were looking at.

"Of course you don't see any words. We're at the North Pole. You are surrounded by elves. I told you that your magic doesn't work on us," Candycane said as she entered the room.

"I don't have magic," Sam replied. "What I have is a headache. Seriously, where are we?"

"I really thought bringing you here was going to be enough. I have never met anyone with such a strongly rooted disbelief in the magic of Christmas," Candycane said, placing her hands on her hips and shaking her head at Sam. "You really are leaving me no other option."

"No other option than what? Taking me back home and leaving me alone? That sounds like a pretty great option to me," Sam said, reaching for their pockets to grab their phone. "Shit! What time is it?" they asked as they realized that they were still in their pajama pants and their phone was at home.

"Your time?" Candycane asked, closing her eyes and counting on her fingers as she silently did math. "I think it is like eight thirty in the morning."

"I'm going to be late for work. You have to take me back," Sam demanded.

"No, you aren't. You called out of work last night or rather I did for you. Trust me you are in no way ready to return to work and face the fact that many of those you work with and for are on the naughty list," Candycane replied.

"You did what?" Sam asked. "I never miss work. There is no way that they believed whatever excuse you gave them."

"They did. I can be very convincing. Well most of the time," Candycane said with a sigh as she looked at Sam. "People tend to believe me."

"I guess you have never met a realist before," Sam offered with a shrug. "Life isn't candy canes and rainbows for all of us. Some of us have had to work very hard to get to where we are without any magic or happy endings along the way."

"I'm not sure how humans manage to live without magic, but the vast majority still believe in it, even if they don't have any of their own. You actually possess magic and yet you can't accept that it is real. It really is quite a puzzle, one I don't believe I can solve on my own," Candycane replied, walking towards the front door, stopping at the coat rack. "Here, put this on. I don't think I have shoes that will fit you, but I will at least find you some socks." Candycane handed Sam a green and red striped scarf and matching knit hat as she walked past them, heading for another room.

When Candycane reappeared, she could not help but laugh at Sam who looked rather ridiculous pairing a thick scarf and warm hat with sweatpants, a t-shirt, and a pair of birkenstocks. What made it even funnier to the elf was the sour expression on Sam's face as they held the large green pom pom in their hand, released it so that it fell to their knee, and picked it up to repeat the action. "This is the most ridiculous hat I have ever seen," Sam complained as they scowled at Candycane.

"That is one of my favorite hats," Candycane snapped back, throwing a balled up pair of socks at Sam. "Put those on so your toes don't completely freeze off. It is a long walk to the workshop."

Sam caught the green and red striped socks, sighing as they unrolled them to realize that they were very high knee socks. "You are determined to make me look every bit as ridiculous as you, aren't you?" Sam asked as they pulled on the socks.

"I'm so very sorry that you find my clothing to be absurd. You will find that everyone here dresses this way," Candycane huffed as she opened the door. "Now come quickly. The faster we walk the less likely you are to catch your death from the cold. I will already be in trouble for bringing you to the workshop. I can't imagine what they would do to me if you died on the way."

"If you are going to get into so much trouble, why don't you just take me back home and let me go to work?" Sam asked, running to catch up to Candycane as she was already walking down the sidewalk.

"I would be happy to, but it is my job to prepare you for your life as a Christmas and I cannot do that if you have a severe mental break dealing with your new found gift," Candycane replied.

"Great. Even my delusions are calling me crazy," Sam mumbled. "This has to be the strangest damn dream I have ever had."

"For the last time. This is not a dream. Myself and everything around you is very real," Candycane explained, bending down to grab a pile of snow between her hands.

Before Sam had a chance to argue or even realize what it was that the elf was doing, a snowball smacked them in their face, icy tendrils of pain wrapping from their nose back to their ears. "Ouch. What the hell did you do that for?" Sam asked, wiping the snow from their face.

"To prove to you that it isn't a dream. Now come on. We have wasted enough time. Let's go," Candycane answered, turning and continuing down the street.

Sam followed Candycane in silence, trying to figure out how they were in an arctic climate and make sense of this not being a dream.

There was no making sense of that, though. Magic wasn't real and elves and Santa Claus were most definitely not real, but Sam was running out of ways to explain what was happening. That snowball had definitely hurt and there was no denying the burning sensation in their toes as the snow soaked through the socks they were wearing. Believe it or not, Sam was certain that they were awake. Quite possibly on the verge of a complete mental collapse, but awake.

Trying to figure this out was getting them nowhere, so Sam decided that they might as well try to be present in whatever this was they were experiencing. Taking a deep breath and centering themselves, Sam attempted to keep up with the fast pace of the so-called elf in front of them. As they ran to catch up, they looked around at the festive buildings surrounding them. Many of the buildings looked similar to that of the small apartment that belonged to Candycane, but mixed in there were coffee shops, bookstores, clothing stores, and even hardware shops. If it wasn't for the Christmas lights, wreaths, trees, and other assorted decor, it would have seemed like a normal town. As they had continued the walk, it had only furthered what they had seen when they looked out of the window back in the apartment. Each and every person they saw was dressed in brightly colored striped or polka dotted outfits similar to that of what Candycane was wearing.

Sam was so focused on looking around them that they failed to notice that the elf had stopped walking and ran directly into her back. "Hey. Pay attention. We're turning onto Sugarplum Lane. This is where all of the candy and baked goods that you are used to seeing around the holidays originate from," Candycane explained.

"I'm quite sure that there are a good number of companies that manufacture the bulk of the candies, cookies, and fruitcakes that are consumed at Christmas time that prove that to be false," Sam said.

"I didn't say that we make all of it here, not anymore, but the ideas all began here. Except for fruitcake. That is just gross. I'm not sure who thought that was a good idea," Candycane explained. "I would love to show you some of the kitchens, but there is no time. We have to get to the workshop in time, and oh dear, you look like you are absolutely frozen." Candycane shook her head, mumbling to herself as she snapped her fingers.

The sweet smells of baked goods faded along with the buildings themselves as Sam watched the scenery around them blink out of existence. It was replaced by a similar looking street filled with large buildings. Each of the six buildings had a large red and white striped number on it. At the end of the street sat what appeared to be a hotel as it was a massive building. "Wh, where are we?" Sam asked, their teeth beginning to shatter from the cold.

"This is Tinker Avenue, home to Santa's workshop, more accurately Santa's six workshops and the house where the members of the Christmas family that are fortunate enough to earn the title of Santa live," Candycane explained.

"Those fortunate enough to be called Santa? Why not just say where Santa Claus lives?" Sam asked.

"Because there is more than one person with that title at a time," Candycane answered.

"What? Not that I believe in any of this nonsense, but I'm pretty sure there is only one fat man in a red suit," Sam replied.

"Actually there are zero Santas that fit that description," Candycane laughed. "There are over one hundred names for Santa Claus across the globe, which means that there are billions of children who expect gifts from St. Nicholas every year. It would be impossible for one human to do that all on their own, so instead we divide the workload. There are a total of six people working in the role of Santa at a time, each of them assigned to a continent with Australia and Antarctica sharing a Santa. If we hurry, you may get to meet all six of them," Candycane explained, grabbing Sam's hand and dragging them behind her as she walked toward the residence at the end of the street.

Chapter 5

Sam sat in a plush red chair, their cold bare feet propped on an ottoman in front of a warm fire and a piping hot cup of hot cocoa in their hands as they waited for Candycane to return. The elf who had greeted them when they reached the building had been genuinely concerned for Sam's health and rather angry at Candycane for allowing them to walk in the snow without proper winter attire on. As such, Sam found themselves thawing in front of the fire while they waited for Candycane to return from what Sam could only assume was a reprimand for her behavior. For some reason, Sam felt a little guilty about that. Sure they wanted nothing to do with this bizarre North Pole nonsense, but aside from pelting them with a snowball, Candycane had been kind to them and it seemed unfair for her to be in trouble when she was only trying to help.

"Do you mind if I join you?" a man who looked to be in his mid to late fifties with salt and pepper hair and a short beard asked as they sat in the chair beside Sam.

"Um. No. I would welcome the company," Sam answered, taking notice of the khaki pants and black flannel shirt the man was wearing. "It's nice to see someone who is dressed in normal clothing. Maybe you could tell me where we are and what is really going on."

"Ah. A non-believer," the man shook his head. "I wasn't that different from you when my gift manifested over thirty years ago."

"Your gift? Do you mean the weird thing with the naughty and nice descriptions above people's heads? Because I wouldn't call that gift. Also, you don't have one, but you also don't look like an elf," Sam replied.

"I'm sadly not an elf. I'm just another Christmas, perhaps a distant cousin of yours. I can tell you are Christmas because I cannot read your behavior either or for that matter discern your name. Oh my. Where are my manners? I should have introduced myself. My name is Peter. I'm the Keeper of the List, something that you are about to become a very important part of," the man said, smiling at Sam.

"I'm Sam. What do you mean by keeper of the list?" Sam asked.

"I'm the one who compiles all of the information gathered by our family throughout the world to create the list. I add and subtract names as well as being the final say on people who tend to find themselves resting in the middle," Peter replied.

"I didn't sleep much last night and I'm still trying to wrap my brain around where I am, but I feel like I missed something. What list are you talking about?" Sam asked.

"Why, the list of course. Santa's list, the one that shows who is naughty and who is nice," Peter answered.

"Ugh. You, too? I thought with how you were dressed that you might be normal," Sam sighed.

"Normal is relative. You will find that believing in Santa and the magic of Christmas is quite normal here," Peter answered. "I understand, though. As I said, I was a skeptic once, too, before I embraced my gift."

"There you go calling it a gift again. Maybe you enjoy vacationing in crazy town, but I would prefer to return to the land of rational thinking," Sam replied.

The sound of a door opening caused both of them to look towards the hallway. As two figures exited a room and began walking towards then, Peter stood. "Well, Sam, it was a pleasure meeting you. Open your mind to the possibility that magic exists and enjoy your visit. I'm sure we will meet again," Peter said, nodding at Sam before he turned and walked away.

"Sam Christmas, sorry to keep you waiting," a female elf with brown hair in braided pigtails wearing a green jumper with red and white tights and a matching red and white hat said as they approached Sam. "I do hope that the fire has helped to take some of the chill off. Though Candycane meant well, it was not wise for her to let you walk here without proper footwear and a coat. My name is Peppermint Gumdrop. Welcome to the workshop, home of the six Santas and the Keeper of the List."

"I'm sorry. Did you say Peppermint Gumdrop? That name is even more absurd than Candycane Tinseltree. What silly name generator app did you all use to come up with these?" Sam laughed.

"I come from a long line of Gumdrops and we have proudly served the Christmas family, in particular those selected to be Santa Claus for hundreds of years. I do not see the humor in my family name or that of the Tinseltree line." Peppermint huffed.

"Right. Look. I'm sorry. I didn't mean to offend. I just. You two don't seriously expect me to believe in all of this North Pole Santa Claus nonsense, do you?" Sam asked.

"Nonsense? Hmmph. You were right to bring them here, Candycane. I will speak with the Santas and see if they will be willing to meet with Sam. Please wait here," Peppermint instructed before turning and hurrying back down the hall.

"I really hope you didn't get into too much trouble," Sam said once it was just the two of them.

"Peppermint wasn't pleased that I let you walk here. Though the fact that you still don't believe after seeing everything you have seen and after meeting the Keeper proves that it was necessary," Candycane replied.

"You thought meeting that crazy old man was going to convince me that this was all real and I wasn't losing my mind?" Sam asked. "He is convinced that he holds some power over who is perceived as naughty or nice on a made-up list from a children's story."

"His job is extremely important. He is responsible for placing those who do not lean enough towards naughty or nice. The Keeper must be the one to decide which way the needle points on the scale. He makes the final decision that puts them on the nice list or the naughty list," Candycane explained.

"Right, because that seems fair. What qualifies him to pass judgement on people he doesn't know?" Sam asked. "If you are trying to open my heart to Christmas, showing me the things that are inherently wrong with the system are not going to help your case."

"How can you have opinions about the way that Christmas works when you don't even believe in Santa Claus or the list?" Candycane asked. "Unless you do believe and are just upset because you never experienced the joy of the holiday either as a child or an adult."

"It is true that I never received gifts from the fictional fat man, but I assure you that my best friend has forced me to participate in many silly Christmas traditions. Quite honestly if Faith hasn't been able to get me to embrace the Christmas spirit, it isn't going to happen. So why don't we just end this nonsense? You can take me home, wipe my memory, and fix my brain so I never see the words naughty or nice again," Sam replied, standing up and crossing their arms.

"As I have told you more than once, I cannot take away your ability to see what you do in other humans. No one can. What I can do is help you learn to live with it while I teach you about your role here," Candycane answered. "Here comes Peppermint. Hopefully she has some good news."

"It wasn't easy, but a meeting has been arranged," Peppermint announced as she entered the space. "Judging by the way things look here, meeting with the Keeper didn't sway your opinion, Sam. Am I right?"

"Look, I really appreciate all of the effort that you are both going through, but Christmas really isn't for me. I applaud you for the effects and the elaborate buildings. If this was a movie, it would be very impressive." Sam paused as realization dawned on them. "Wait. That's it. This is a movie set. Isn't it? I still don't understand how I got here, but my head is so foggy that I'm guessing I'm still coming off of the effects of whatever was slipped into my drink last night. Wow. Faith has officially gone too far. Don't worry. I'm sure she will still pay you both," Sam said, looking around the room for their friend. "Faith, you can come out now. Great try but it isn't going to work," Sam called.

"Ugh. Stop trying to rationalize this and turn it into something your brain can process without having to deal with what it actually is," Candycane yelled, stomping her foot and putting her hands on her hips. "It isn't going to make any of it go away. The sooner you embrace who you are and what it means, the sooner you can go home, and I can get paired with a Christmas that actually believes and sees the importance of what we do."

"Woah. Woah. Who said anything about you getting reassigned Candycane? It is customary for elven companions to stay with their Christmas for at least two years and I have a feeling that this one may require a longer commitment," Peppermint said, nodding her head towards Sam.

"I'm sorry. Did you just say years? I have a job, a normal boring quiet life, that I need to get back to. It might not be exciting and I don't have a family or a romantic partner to return to, but I do enjoy the company of a woman every so often and I cannot have a weirdo in an elf costume hanging around me if I expect that to ever happen again," Sam said, deflating as they sat back down in the chair. "My life is never going to be the same again, is it?"

"I'm afraid not, but once you come to terms with who you are, I think you will find that your life will have a purpose that might just turn that cynical lump of coal in your chest into an actual beating heart," Peppermint replied, rolling their eyes and turning their attention to Candycane. "The Santas have agreed to meet with Sam at lunch, which means that you have a few hours to show Sam around. Please make Bobbin's shop your first stop so that Sam doesn't catch their death walking around here in those ridiculous clothes. I will see you both back here at twelve twenty-five on the dot." Peppermint turned and marched back to their office.

"Twelve twenty-five? You have got to be kidding me. Really?" Sam asked.

"Yes, really. Christmas is taken very seriously around here. It is our way of life and our purpose. Now we need to get you some suitable clothing. Grab your useless shoes, so that they don't end up as fuel for the fire," Candycane answered.

Sam had barely grabbed their shoes when Candycane snapped her fingers and the room around them disappeared, replaced by the snow-covered street that Sam had found themselves walking down earlier that morning on route to the workshop.

Chapter 6

Sam's teeth were already shattering as they read the sign on the door of the shop in front of them, Bobbin's: Clothes for Every Occasion. As they squinted through the snow-covered windows, Candycane opened the door, causing a pile of snow that had settled on the awning above to fall directly onto Sam's head. Sam shook their head and glared at Candycane as the snow fell to their shoulders.

"That is why we wear hats," Candycane offered with a shrug, stepping aside so that Sam could enter.

"I'm wearing your hat. It didn't save my face from the impact of the snow or keep the icy cold water from dripping down my back," Sam growled, pulling the hat off of their head and shaking the remaining snow onto the floor of the shop.

"That was just rude. Stay here while I go find a mop," Candycane scolded as they turned and walked towards the back of the store.

Sam slid their bare feet into their birkenstocks and walked further into the store. There were racks upon racks of brightly colored pants, skirts, dresses, jumpers, overalls, shirts, and sweaters surrounding them. Sam could also see displays containing socks, hats and scarves in the same bright colors and loud patterns. Along the back wall was a display showing a variety of boots. There was little in this shop that Sam would be caught dead in if they had a choice, but their feet were very much frozen and if they were forced to stay in this place any longer, they would need a pair of boots, so they walked to the back to take a closer look at the brightly colored shoes.

Sam stood at the wall, holding a bright blue leather boot in one hand and a bright orange boot in the other, turning them as they tried to decide which one was least offensive. They weren't drawn to them for the color, but these were the only two options that didn't have bells, or ribbon, or toes that curled upward in a completely useless manner. In fact, had these shoes not been so bright, they might have passed for regular Doc Martens. They were so focused on the boots that they didn't hear the approaching footsteps or the conversation behind them, causing them to jump and drop both shoes when they heard their name.

"Sam Christmas, it is a pleasure to meet you," a small male sounding voice said. "Oh. Oh my. I didn't mean to startle you. Oh dear."

Sam reached down and picked up the boots, turning to smile at the short, portly elf with a long brown beard that almost reached the ground. "It is quite alright. I'm sorry that I dropped these," Sam answered.

"Oh! Oh no, that is quite alright. Quite alright indeed. And those are both fine choices. Allow me to introduce myself. My name is Bobbin Threadweaver and this is my shop. I'm lucky enough to be the exclusive designer of clothing for all six Santas currently living in the workshop and I'm sure that we can find something here that will suit your needs while you are visiting," Bobbin said, extending a hand to shake with Sam.

Sam clumsily balanced the shoe in their right hand and the crook of their left arm as they took Bobbin's hand and shook. "Thank you, sir. It appears you have a lovely shop, but you wouldn't happen to have anything a little less bright would you? I find that blacks, browns, and grays are more my thing," Sam said as they released his hand.

"Hmmm. Perhaps, but sadly no. I think with your skin tone and light brown hair, blues would do nicely. Why don't we start with the blue boots there and build an outfit from that?" Bobbin asked.

"I was afraid this bright blue would be the most tame color you had here. I'd like to stay out of stripes and polka dots if possible," Sam said as they followed Bobbin into the racks of clothing.

"What about these?" Candycane offered, holding up a pair of sea foam green denim overalls.

"Ah. Yes. I think that would go quite nicely with the boots. Now we just need a blue shirt to go underneath," Bobbin said, flipping through the button up flannel shirts in front of him, pausing on one that was a plaid design of bright blue and navy blue, with thin teal green lines. "Yes, yes. I think this will do quite nicely." He handed everything to Sam, instructing them to go put it on as they handed them a pair of blue and green polka dotted knee socks.

Sam rolled their eyes as they took the socks, but smiled at Bobbin and thanked him before turning and walking to the fitting room. When they emerged five minutes later, Sam felt like they looked like a farmer on a children's television show for toddlers. Though the farmer idea was quickly replaced as they were handed a bright blue stocking cap with a large green pom pom on the end that fell to the middle of their back.

"It is perfect, Bobbin!" Candycane squealed as she looked at Sam.

"It is cold out there, much colder than Sam will be used to," Bobbin said as they handed Candycane a deep blue puffy coat and a scarf.

"Make sure they bundle up out there. I would hate to think what would happen if Sam fell ill before getting to meet with the Santas."

"We will be careful. Thank you," Candycane replied. "Here, put these on Sam. We have a bit of a walk to our next location, but I promise we will stop for cider on the way."

Stop for cider they did. The delicious cinnamon apple beverage that Sam was sipping on as they trudged through the snow was almost enough for them to forgive Candycane for the intrusion into their life. "If heightened senses means that everything is going to taste as amazing as this cider, I might be able to get used to dealing with reading annoying words over everyone's heads," Sam said as they stopped in front of a large red barn.

"Good, because that ability isn't going away, so whatever it takes for you to find peace with it," Candycane replied. "So Scroogey McScroogerson who doesn't believe in Santa Claus, what do you think is in this barn?"

"Not believing doesn't mean that I'm uneducated when it comes to this ridiculous world. I would presume that this is where Rudolph and all of his friends live," Sam answered.

"Yes. That is mostly right. There is a Rudolf but he isn't a magical reindeer with a red nose." Candycane smiled as she mentioned Rudolf. "This is where we take care of and train the reindeer that will aid in the delivery of the toys on Christmas night," Candycane replied. "Reindeer are very sensitive creatures and will not respond well to your lack of Christmas spirit."

"Right, right. Christmas spirit makes them fly or whatever. I have seen my share of Christmas movies," Sam replied.

"No. The reindeer are served a very specific diet which is enhanced with elven magic. The combination is what allows them to fly. When

I say they are sensitive, what I mean is that they may well bite you if you try to touch them," Candycane answered.

"Somehow I feel like you would get great enjoyment from that," Sam mumbled as they followed Candycane around to the front of the barn.

"Candycane! I wasn't expecting you today," a tall thin elf with light brown skin and curly black hair smiled warmly at them as they entered the barn. "And who is your friend?"

Sam thought they caught a slight blush on Candycane's face as she answered. "Hi Rudolf. Sorry for the unannounced visit. I hadn't planned on being here today, but there were some complications with my assignment. This is Sam Christmas. They just turned twenty-five yesterday and I have been assigned to help them adjust to their new gift."

"You are welcome to drop by here anytime that you want," Rudolf smiled at Candycane and this time Sam was positive that she was blushing.

"Um, thanks Rudolf. Sam, this is Rudolf Skysong. His family has been breeding, raising, and training the reindeer here since the very first Santa took flight," Candycane explained.

Sam looked between Candycane and Rudolf who both now had the faintest bit of a blush on their cheeks, though Rudolf's was much harder to see. Sam did their best to contain a giggle as they extended a hand toward Rudolf. "It's nice to meet you. You have very impressive animals here," Sam said looking behind him at the pens that housed large deer with impressive antlers.

"Would you like to meet one?" Rudolf asked.

"That isn't a good idea. Sam here doesn't believe in the magic of Christmas," Candycane replied.

"Well I bet Sam hasn't seen a reindeer fly then," Rudolf offered, his face lighting up at the prospect of showing off one his reindeer.

"I'm not saying that would make me a believer but it could go a long way in getting me to lean in that direction," Sam replied

"Excellent. Candycane, can you take Sam out to the training field? I will be there shortly with Blizzard," Rudolf said, turning and jogging towards the back stalls.

Sam followed Candycane to a large field with obstacles both on the ground and in the air for the reindeer to practice. "We can sit over here and watch Blizzard run through the course. He is in the running to lead one of the teams this year so it should be an impressive run," Candycane said, walking toward a bench. Sam sat down beside Candycane, looking at her with a goofy grin on their face. "What is wrong with you?" Candycane asked. "Why are you smiling like that?"

"First you got mad at me for being a cranky scrooge and now I can't smile? You should really make up your mind," Sam laughed.

"What? No. That isn't what I meant. It just... Why are you smiling?" Candycane asked.

"You think I'm smiling? You should see the way you look at Rudolf," Sam replied.

"We went on a couple of dates, but he is way too busy training the reindeer and I'm about to spend months away, living with you, so he is nice but nothing is going to come from it," Candycane answered.

"Why not? His face lit up when he saw you. He is totally into you and you are definitely feeling him. I don't need a babysitter. You could stay here and pursue this," Sam said, nodding towards Rudolf as he walked into the center of the training course with a reindeer.

"No. No, I cannot. The rules are very clear. I'm to accompany you as you learn to navigate your new gift, which is infinitely harder since you refuse to admit that the magic of Christmas exists," Candycane answered. "I really hope this helps." Candycane turned her attention to the field in front of them as Blizzard began to run towards the first obstacle."

Sam gasped as Blizzard leapt over the first fence and soared into the air towards a large hoop that was about fifteen feet in the air. The reindeer flew above the ring before diving downward to go through it. Sam looked on in amazement as Blizzard zigged and zagged through the many hoops in the air, returning to the ground to jump over fences and walls varying in height from two to eight feet before returning to the sky. It was possibly the most amazing thing that Sam had ever seen and there was no way for them to explain it away. Blizzard really was flying.

Once Blizzard had completed the course a few times, he returned to the field to stand beside Rudolf. Sam jumped to their feet and began applauding. "That was awesome!" Sam declared, a smile spreading across their face.

"Would you like to come meet him now?" Rudolf called to them. "I know he is very excited to see you, Candycane."

The blush returned to Candycane's face as she stood and nodded at Sam before walking towards Rudolf. "Are you starting to believe?" she asked as they approached the field.

"In Christmas?" Sam asked, shaking their head. "No, but I'm not sure if there is an explanation outside of magic for what I just witnessed."

"Well that is a start, I guess," Candycane sighed. "Let me go first. Blizzard knows me and it will make him less likely to be on the defensive with you."

Once Candycane was close, Blizzard walked to her, tilting his head so that Candycane could scratch under his chin. She lowered her face to his, so that he could nuzzle into her cheek. She wrapped her arms around his neck and hugged him as he did. "You were spectacular, Blizzard. I think that was the best I have seen you, yet," she said, giving the deer a kiss on the top of the head before stepping back from him. "My friend would like to meet you. Is that alright with you?"

Blizzard looked at Sam, tilting their head from side to side as they did. After what felt like an eternity to Sam, the reindeer slowly walked towards Sam. Cautiously Sam extended their hand towards the animal so that he could smell them. After a few sniffs, Blizzard turned their head and rubbed in against Sam's hand, asking them to pet him.

"I think he likes you," Rudolf laughed. "I have never seen him warm up to someone that quickly."

"He is beautiful and so very soft. I'm not sure what I thought he would feel like, but his fur is much softer than I had imagined," Sam said, continuing to pet Blizzard.

"He needs that thick warm coat to be able to deal with the temperatures in the high altitudes when he is flying," Rudolf said.

"Not for the extreme temperatures here?" Sam asked.

"Oh no. I suppose this seems cold to you, but we're all rather used to it. This is a pretty pleasant day here in the North Pole," Rudolf said, smiling. "Are the two of you able to stay for lunch?" he asked.

"We would love to, but we're meeting the Santas for lunch," Candycane said, looking at her watch. "Oh! We need to go. Can't keep them waiting. Thanks for letting us see Blizzard. He really is improving. Sam, are you ready? We don't have time to walk." Candycane waited for Sam to step away from the reindeer before snapping her fingers and returning them to the front door of the Santas' home.

Chapter 7

Peppermint Gumdrop was waiting for them as they entered the home, a smile on her face as she took notice of Sam's new attire. "Sam, that outfit looks wonderful on you. I do hope that you are warmer," she said.

"Yes. Much. Although I do feel a bit ridiculous," Sam answered.

"Nonsense. You look wonderful, like a true Christmas," Peppermint replied.

"Unfortunately that is the only thing about Sam that is Christmas like. They still don't believe. I'm really hoping that meeting with the Santas will change their thoughts," Candycane said.

"As am I. If anyone can erase the doubts Sam is having it will be them," Peppermint answered. "I'm afraid you will have to wait here, Candycane. We can dine together once I have escorted Sam to the dining room. The Santas wish for this to be a family only meeting."

Sam followed Peppermint down the hall as Candycane anxiously paced in front of the fire behind them. "Why wouldn't she be allowed to eat with us?" Sam asked as they walked down the hallway.

"It has been a long time since a non-believer had their gift unlocked. The Santas feel it is best that they speak to you without the distractions of elven magic or Christmas spirit," Peppermint answered.

"Everything about this place screams Christmas. How can they possibly remove that from the equation?" Sam asked as they stopped in front of two large doors.

"We are about to enter the residence of the Christmas family. They try to live the same as they would if they lived in the normal world and not surrounded by magic," Peppermint answered as they opened the doors. "Not many get to see this part of the house."

True to Peppermint's word, once they stepped through the doors the holiday decor and festive music ceased. The walls were adorned with portraits of members of the Christmas family. As Sam took a closer look, they realized that these were all Christmases that had served as Santas. "Wow, there have been a lot of Santas. Who would have thought? I would have guessed he was an elf. Don't you all live forever?" Sam asked.

"No. No one lives forever. We do have much longer lives than humans but we are not immortal. Most Santas live here until they are in their sixties. Then they retire and choose to either spend the rest of their days in one of the chateaus in the hills here or back in whichever country they once resided in," Peppermint answered, stopping at a small table with an old rotary phone sitting on it.

Peppermint picked up the phone and dialed the number one, two, two, five as they brought the receiver to their face. "Sam Christmas is here," she said to whoever was on the other end. "Very well. I will have them wait here for you." Peppermint hung up the phone, turning to face Sam. "This is where I leave you. Santa Wyatt will be here shortly to take you the rest of the way."

Sam stood staring down the hallway watching Peppermint walk away. This had by far been the strangest day of their life. Were they really standing in a hallway waiting for a Santa Claus to take them to lunch where they would meet with not one but six Santas? They had seen a flying reindeer and Candycane was somehow transporting them from place to place with a snap of her fingers, so maybe that wasn't so weird afterall. None of it made sense and the fact that they were beginning to rationalize it could only mean they were fully slipping into the delusion themselves. Definitely hadn't seen a full on mental break coming at twenty-five, but here they were. Sam sighed, bringing their hand to their temple and massaging it as they closed their eyes.

"Just ride it out, Sam," they mumbled to themselves. "You have to return to rational thought eventually."

"I assure you that everything you have experienced today is very real my friend," a kind voice with a strong southern drawl said, causing Sam to open their eyes and look at the newcomer.

Sam found themselves staring at a man that couldn't have been much more than thirty. He was wearing faded green jeans and a green and orange checked button up shirt, along with the orange boots that Sam had almost picked out earlier. He was also wearing a bright green cowboy hat and Sam could not help themselves from laughing at the way the green hat contrasted with their bright red hair. "I assume you are Wyatt?" Sam asked.

"Sure am," he smiled at them. "Wyatt Christmas," he said, extending his hand for a handshake. "Welcome to the Workshop."

"Um. Thanks," Sam said, shaking his hand. "I'm sorry, I'm having a hard time wrapping my brain around you being a Santa Claus. You are tall and lanky and young. Hell, you look younger than me," Sam said.

"Well, I appreciate that. I'm twenty-eight. My grandfather was a Santa so I kind of always knew I wanted to be one. But Santas can look like anything. You weren't honestly expecting the jolly fat man with a white beard and red suit, were you?" Wyatt asked.

"I mean. Until a few hours ago, I didn't believe that any of this could possibly exist, so I'm not sure what I was expecting. I only know what I'm forced to see for months back home as the holidays draw close," Sam answered. "Also, how are we related? Are we cousins, like extremely distant ones?"

"Most likely. The Christmas family is incredibly large. As the descendants of Nicholas started moving away from the North Pole, they branched out until there were Christmases living across the globe. There are now Christmases living in every country in the world. As such, many of our cousins don't look like us. In fact I look nothing like any of the other Santas. You ready to meet 'em?" Wyatt asked.

"I don't really know. This has been a really wild day. I woke up in my apartment in the city in September where it was seventy degrees outside and ended up here in the snow freezing because the elf that was in my kitchen making me breakfast was trying to get me to believe in Santa Claus. On top of that, I just saw a reindeer fly. I don't know how much more I can take, if I'm being honest with you," Sam replied.

"I can't imagine what it was like to grow up not knowing what your destiny was. I always knew that I would be a Santa. And I believe most Christmas children learn about their gift well before they have it. Your parents should have prepared you. Look, everybody is waiting to meet you. We haven't had a non-believer up here since Peter and well the only Santa from his awakening that is still here is Galina, but she was just barely twenty-five herself when Peter arrived," Wyatt explained. "I would love to give you more time, but as you said it is already September. We need to start compiling the list and to do that, we're going to need your help."

"Right? Because I know who is naughty and nice and which kids deserve presents. Unless they have the misfortune of being born a Christmas destined to never know the joy of presents under the tree on Christmas morning but forced to ensure that others enjoy what they could not. Does that system make sense to you?" Sam asked, folding their arms and shaking their head.

"You should have had presents under the tree and holidays filled with the joy that Christmas brings. This is why the full council of Santas wishes to meet with you. We need to figure out what went wrong and how you were allowed to slip through the cracks until the arrival of your gift," Wyatt answered. "Please, I'm the youngest of those lucky enough to earn the rank of Claus. I can't answer your questions, but perhaps the others will be able to. All I'm asking is that you give us a chance."

"I don't really have a choice, do I? I mean from everything I have been told, I'm stuck with this curse that you keep calling a gift. It isn't like I can just go back to my normal life, is it? Because either I will be driven crazy as a result of never being able to look at other people with knowing who they are and if they are good humans or not or it is all in my head and I'm already crazy. So why not continue this ride to crazy town? It can't possibly get any weirder," Sam replied.

"After everything you have seen today, you still have doubts? How is that even possible? You have been surrounded by the magic of Christmas all day long. How can you ignore it? Please, come with me. Meet the rest of the Santas and let us help you become a believer or at the very least let us teach you about how to navigate life with your new found magic," Wyatt pleaded.

"I already said I would go. You don't have to beg. Just don't expect me to become a tree decorating, carol singing, cookie baking Christmas freak. Even if I accept what you say I am, it doesn't mean that I will ever like the holidays or buy into the magic of the season. Nothing good has ever happened to me in the month of December and I don't see that changing now that I will have to take an active role in the ridiculous commercial holiday. All I have ever gotten for Christmas is heartache, depression, and a need for therapy," Sam answered.

"It breaks my heart that a holiday that should have so much to do with love and joy has caused you so much pain. I know we can't take that hurt away but I hope that over time you can start to see Christmas for what it is meant to be," Wyatt replied.

"Let's just get this over with so I can get back home. You might get to hang out here all day and make toys or whatever it is that you do, but some of us have actual real jobs that we need to pay for things like rent so can we hurry this along?" Sam asked as they walked past Wyatt, continuing down the hall.

"Slow down. You are gonna pass the dining room. And could you try to go in there with a little less hostility? We really are just trying to help you," Wyatt said, rushing past Sam to a door on the right. He placed his hand on the doorknob and looked Sam in the eyes. "Please. I know you are angry and upset with your experiences but we had nothing to do with that and we just want your current situation to be something that you can live with and possibly even grow to enjoy."

"Yeah. Fat chance of that happening," Sam rolled their eyes. "But. yeah I will try to be nice to your friends in there and I'm sorry that I'm taking this all out on you. I just really wish I could go back to yesterday before all of this started. I really am not the right person for this job," Sam replied. They closed their eyes and took a deep breath in an attempt to calm themselves and settle some of the rage that was building within them. Sam exhaled and looked at Wyatt, forcing a smile. "Alright. I'm ready. Let's do this."

Chapter 8

Wyatt smiled at Sam as he opened the door behind him. "Allow me to introduce you to the rest of the Christmas Council," he said, stepping aside for Sam to enter.

Gathered around a round table were five very different looking people, of all ages and races. Each of them smiled warmly at Sam as they approached the table with Wyatt. "We were beginning to wonder if you were going to keep them all to yourselves, Wyatt," a woman with long blonde hair and an Australian accent laughed. "Please, Sam, join us." She pointed to one of the empty chairs indicating that Sam should sit.

Wyatt sat in the other empty chair, shaking his head at the woman who had spoken. "Come on Harper. You know I wouldn't do that. Sam, here, just needed a little time. Time I wish I had been given before meeting you all for the first time," Wyatt laughed.

"Don't scare them, Wyatt. You have known some of us since you were a tiny tot," the oldest of those gathered at the table scolded, though she had a kind smile on her wrinkled face as she looked at Wyatt with affection.

"A room full of Santas is still rather intimidating," Wyatt replied. "Now then. You all seem to already know who our guest is, but perhaps you would each like to introduce yourselves."

"Yes. Of course. Sam, it is a pleasure to meet you. My name is Galina and I have the honor of being the Santa with the most experience," the older woman who had scolded Wyatt introduced herself. She was a kind looking woman who appeared to Sam to be in her sixties. Of everyone in the room, she looked like she belonged there the most. With white hair, a red and green dress, and a plump frame, she could have easily passed for the Mrs. Claus to the jolly fat man in the red suit that children flocked to in shopping malls to give their Christmas wish lists.

"If we're going to mention years served, I rather imagine that I should go next," an Indian man with a thick black mustache wearing a purple and blue sweater said with a nod. "My name is Arjun and I have had the great honor of being a Santa for almost as long as Galina."

"Konichiwa, Sam," a Japanese gentleman in a red sweater who was probably around forty greeted Sam. "I'm Benjiro. We are honored to have you join us."

"You can call him Benji. We all do," the blonde with the Australian accent said.

"I would rather you didn't," Benjiro grumbled.

"Oh, don't be a grump, Benji. My name is Harper. I'm the Santa from down under," she laughed, tossing her long blonde hair over her shoulder. Dressed in pink and blue overalls with a pink shirt and her sun kissed skin, Harper could have been sixteen or thirty-two. Sam really wasn't sure.

"Wyatt would be next by a month or two," the last of the council spoke. They had dark skin and wore their hair in short afro. "My name is Kamara and my pronouns are they/them, something that my counterparts neglected to share with you though I have told them repeatedly that gender should never be assumed."

Sam smiled at Kamara, before looking around the table at the rest of the council. "It is nice to meet all of you. As you already know, my name is Sam and my pronouns are they/them. Thank you Kamara for sharing yours as well."

The rest of the council looked ashamed as Sam offered their pronouns. After an awkward few seconds of silence Harper loudly announced that her pronouns were she/her just like Galina and Wyatt, Benjiro, and Arjun all used he/him.

"Yes, thank you, Harper," Galina said as she focused her attention on Sam. "Candycane tells us that you do not believe in the magic of Christmas even though that very magic resides within you. Why is that?"

"Um, well. Christmas has never been kind to me. I didn't grow up knowing the joy of the holiday, and I didn't know my father. My mother gave me his last name because she hoped that he would come back one day, but he never did. So if he happily adjusted to a life as a Christmas, he did so by leaving me behind and forgetting that I exist," Sam answered.

"Hmmm. Kamara, were you able to find any information on Sam's family?" Galina asked.

"I did, and it is most unusual. Sam's father is a man named Steven. His mother was a Christmas, but she died giving birth to Steven before her magic awoke. I do believe that she was aware of her magic and her duties as a Christmas because both of her parents had the gift," Kamara answered.

"Wait. Are you implying that my paternal grandmother was the product of inbreeding?" Sam asked.

"No," Kamara smiled. "The Christmas line has been around for hundreds of years. Yes we are all descendants of the same man, but there are millions of Christmases across the globe. For instance you and I are very far removed from one another when it comes to the family tree. There would have been the smallest fraction of shared dna. Your great grandparents met by chance while your great grandmother was vacationing in Ireland. She was from a small town in Tennessee and your great grandfather was an Irishman, so they were not even remotely related. It does not happen often that two members of the Christmas line end up together, but it has happened. What makes your case particularly unusual is that from what I can tell, your father does not have the gift. It seems to have skipped him. As such, he was not on our radar. If he had been, you would have experienced the joys of Christmas even if he had not stayed because we would have known that a child with the gift had been born," Kamara explained.

"Thank you, Kamara. That explains a lot," Galina said. "As I'm sure you have noticed, you are unable to see if we're naughty or nice. This is because of the magic that we all carry inside. Because of this when the Christmas who was assigned to the towns that you were a child in would not have reported your status back to the Keeper, meaning that your Santa, Wyatt's grandfather, didn't know that you should have received presents. Typically children with the gift are automatically placed on the nice list so that they are not forgotten. I'm deeply sorry that you managed to slip through the cracks, but I do not believe the gift has skipped a generation in over a hundred years."

"So what does that mean for me? I already knew that my father wasn't anything special and I'm used to being forgotten. In fact if it is all the same to you, I would just as soon go back to my normal life," Sam replied.

"I'm quite certain that your elven companion has already explained to you that the gift cannot be taken away," Benjiro said.

"Also, your father might not have been special, but you are. You have a gift and a chance to help spread Christmas cheer because of it. You did not get to grow up knowing the pure happiness that a child feels on Christmas morning, but you do have the ability to ensure that other children don't miss out on that feeling," Harper added.

"But you said there are millions of people with the gift. Surely there is someone else living where I do that can report back to the Keeper or whatever. I mean, you all didn't even know I existed a few days ago," Sam countered.

"Ah, but we did. We may not have known who was going to unlock their potential, but we knew to be on the lookout in your city that night. A ripple had been sent through the stars. Candycane simply had to follow the trail of your magic once she arrived. You are an important part of what we do here and we need you," Arjun answered.

"Look, this is a responsibility I neither want or believe in. I do not like Christmas. Even if you all can sit here and prove to me that Santa in some form is real, it doesn't mean that I'm going to start to celebrate a holiday that has caused me so much pain in my life," Sam responded. "However, I'm not my father and never have been. I'm not one to walk away from my responsibilities even if they are inconvenient and unwanted. If you really need me to make this system work, I will play my part."

"At the end of the day, that is all we can ask," Benjiro said.

"This is true, but I hope that as you learn to use your gift, the spirit of Christmas will work its way into your heart," Galina said, smiling at Sam.

"It is settled then. Wyatt has himself a new set of eyes on the street. Now let's eat. I'm starving," Harper announced, reaching for a tray in the center of the table and removing the lid to reveal a maple glazed spiral ham. As lids were removed from other trays, Sam found themselves looking at a Christmas feast complete with cranberry sauce and sweet potato casserole.

"I hope you are hungry, Sam. The way they feed us around here, it is a wonder we don't all look like the Santa Claus from popular culture," Wyatt laughed.

"This looks amazing," Sam said as they filled their plate with food. "I feel a little guilty eating this feast while Candycane anxiously waits for me, though."

"Don't worry about her. I assure you that she is eating a feast every bit as grand as this with Peppermint," Kamara said. "Like Wyatt said, one does not go hungry here."

"So you all live here year round?" Sam asked. "You don't return to your homes?"

"This is our home. When we made the commitment to be Santas, we made this our home. We have everything we could ever want here," Benjiro answered.

"And we can visit our old homes whenever we want to," Harper said. "I just came back from a few days surfing the coast. I love my life as a Santa but I will always be drawn to the beach."

"That explains your perfect tan," Sam laughed. "I'm curious. How does one become a Santa? I know Wyatt said he took over for his grandfather, but what makes a Christmas more that just a person gathering names for a list?"

"We were each picked by the Santa before us. It is a great honor to be asked, but we could have declined if we had wished," Galina answered. "I don't believe that has happened often, though. Being a Santa allows one to really live in the true spirit of Christmas, to become one with the magic."

"Speaking of magic, I think it is perhaps time that Sam learns how their magic works. If you all would excuse us, Peter has agreed to show Sam the list," Wyatt announced as he stood.

"You must have made quite the impression on him. Peter tends to keep to himself and doesn't share the list with outsiders," Arjun said.

"Outsiders? I'm a Christmas, aren't I?" Sam asked.

"You are, but you don't work in the Listiary," Kamara said. "You should consider yourself lucky."

"It was indeed a pleasure meeting you, Sam. Thank you for being open to what we had to tell you," Galina said. "Now, go. Peter does not like to be kept waiting."

Chapter 9

The Listiary was located on the upper most floor of the Workshop. Where the other floors were divided into rooms, the fifth floor was one giant room with bookshelves recessed in every wall. The shelves that contained archived lists were the backdrop for the rows of desks that filled the space. Each desk was home to a computer and a printer and as Sam and Wyatt entered the room, the sound of hundreds of printers all printing at the same time filled the space with an electronic buzzing. It was unlike anything that Sam had ever seen, despite spending a large portion of their adult life working in a cubicle.

"Sam, welcome! I told you I was sure I would see you again," Peter said from the large desk in the center of the room.

"What is this place?" Sam asked, looking around at the long sheets of paper coming from the many printers.

"Welcome to the Listiary," Peter said, his face lighting up with pride. "This is where we make Santa's list."

"But, how?' Sam asked.

"Each of those computers compiles the information collected by Christmases like you and sorts the names into two lists. Nice lists print to my right and naughty lists to my left. Once the lists are printed, we feed them into the main computer or as I like to call it the Master Generator. Once a week, a master list is printed with every name and sent to the Santas so that they can make the work orders for toys and other gifts in their respective workshops," Peter answered.

"And what does that computer do?" Sam asked, pointing to the monitor that was flashing on Peter's desk.

"Ah, that one houses the list of names that are on the fence. Those are the ones that I have to investigate to determine which list they belong on. That is my favorite part," Peter answered.

"Ok, but how does the information get from someone like me to you? Because I definitely don't have time to record the name and character of every person I see throughout the day," Sam asked.

"That is the beauty of it. You don't have to do anything, other than observe. The things that you see travel through the stars collecting in the aurora borealis. It is the magic of Christmas that causes the beautiful colors that dance in the night sky. We have satellites positioned in the northern lights that collect the information and submit it to these computers. It really is an amazing collaboration between magic and technology," Peter explained.

"So all that nonsense about how important I am was a lie. I literally just have to exist and what I see gets transmitted here?" Sam asked.

"Yes and no. What you see is incredibly important. If you were to only pass the same people every day, it wouldn't give us enough information to be useful. So, if your normal routine was just to go to work and go home every day, you will need to change your daily routine," Peter answered.

"Yes. It is important that you find yourself in places frequented by large crowds of people," Wyatt added.

"Perfect. I loathe people and social events," Sam sighed.

"Candycane can help you figure out how to navigate the sorts of places we need you to frequent as well as teach you ways to make the clutter of the nice and naughty tags easier to navigate," Wyatt said. "Trust me. I know it is a lot to take in. I was expecting it, and it still made me turn into a hermit for a few months."

"Speaking of research. I do believe it is time that our friend here returns home and begins learning how to use their gift," Peter said. "Good luck, Sam. I do hope that our paths cross again."

"Thank you for sharing this with us, Peter. I always enjoy a visit to the Listiary," Wyatt smiled.

"I can't say that I fully grasp how all of this works, but I guess knowing how my talents will be used makes this slightly more tolerable," Sam said. "Before we go, I'm curious about one of the things that you said."

"I would be happy to answer any questions that you have," Peter replied.

"About the people who are neither naughty or nice. First, how does that happen and then how do you decide where to put their name?" Sam asked.

"Ah. I thought I had seen a question in your eyes when I told you about that. As a whole, people are not inherently naughty or nice. There are exceptions, but most of us float between the two as we navigate life, our decisions dictating which way the needle points. Some people will have naughty and nice actions that cancel each other out. Basically they do the same amount of good as they do bad. It is then my job to investigate the actions that would have moved the needle and see which actions appear to be greater. For instance if they stole something but then they donated money to charity, they would probably end up on the naughty list," Peter answered.

"I guess that explains things. I'm doing my best to look at this with an open mind, but my cynicism for the holiday is not making this easy. But I really do appreciate you all taking the time to try and make me a believer," Sam said. "I suppose we should get back to Candycane. If nothing else, I'm anxious to return home."

"Yes. Thank you again, Peter," Wyatt said, turning and walking to the exit.

Back in the foyer, Candycane stood talking with Peppermint. She smiled brightly at Sam as they entered the room with Wyatt. "Welcome back, Sam. How was lunch?" she asked.

"Enlightening, I guess," Sam answered.

"Our friend here is going to be a hard one to crack, Candycane, but if anyone can show them the spirit of the holiday, it is you," Wyatt said, giving Candycane's shoulder a squeeze.

"Thank you, Santa. I will do my best," Candycane answered. "I guess we should head back now. You ready, Sam?" Candycane didn't wait for a response as she snapped her fingers, the smells of the fireplace and cinnamon fading away as the white walls of Sam's home appeared around them.

"Holy fuck! Where did you just come from?" Faith screamed as Sam and Candycane appeared in the apartment.

"Faith!" Sam exclaimed. "What are you doing here?"

"What? What am I doing here? You weren't answering your phone and after last night, I was worried. You just appeared out of thin air. What the actual hell?" Faith asked.

"Oh boy. I'm going to lose my job," Candycane mumbled. "I assumed that your home would be empty, Sam."

"It should have been. I, um, what do we do now?" Sam asked.

"How about you tell me what the fuck is going on?" Faith demanded.

"You are probably gonna want to sit down for this," Sam answered. "Would you believe I was in the North Pole?"

"Sam! You can't tell her!" Candycane yelled, placing her hands on her hips.

"What am I supposed to do? We can't explain away blinking into existence. Magic doesn't exist here," Sam replied.

"There are rules, Sam. I already broke so many of them when I took you with me," Candycane countered.

"To hell with your rules. Faith is my best friend and also she has been trying to get me to believe in the magic of Christmas for the last seven years so the two of you are on the same side," Sam answered.

"Um, Hi. Still here. You can fight about this later, but you damn near gave me a heart attack. I deserve answers," Faith interrupted.

Chapter 10

"Fine," Candycane said through gritted teeth. "I'm making hot cocoa. You can let her know what happened when you turned twenty-five."

"You mean when they ditched me to hang out with someone dressed like a Christmas elf. Sam, that wasn't exactly what I meant when I said this was the year you would start to feel the magic of Christmas," Faith shook their head.

"I can assure you that whatever image just popped into that dirty little mind of yours is not what is going on here," Sam said, rolling their eyes. "Although that would be so much easier to explain."

"Well I hope you have something a little bit better than trying to convince me you were at the North Pole, Sam," Faith laughed.

"I'm not sure cocoa is gonna be strong enough, Candycane," Sam called to the kitchen as they sat down next to their friend. "You remember how I left after our toast last night? I didn't leave because I met someone or got a message to go meet some hook-up. I would never do you like that. I mean, I might have once, maybe twice, but that was years ago and not what happened last night."

Faith raised an eyebrow as she looked at Sam and then at Candycane. "Right? I mean she is real cute, Sam. I get it. The elf thing is a little weird but to each their own. I'm not here to judge your roleplay," Faith replied.

"Faith, for the last time. That's not what's going on," Sam said as they reached for a mug of cocoa from Candycane. The elf handed Faith a cup as well before sitting down across from them. "Thanks. Cocoa always calms my nerves." Sam smiled at Candycane, taking a sip of the warm chocolate beverage.

"I'm sorry. Candycane? Really? I feel like you are trying to have a serious conversation with me, but it is really hard when you keep calling her that," Faith said.

"That is her name. I'm not sure what else you would like me to call her. Candycane is an elf from the North Pole which if you will just listen, I'll explain," Sam replied.

"Sure. Fine. Enlighten me," Faith said, sitting back in the chair and looking at Sam expectantly.

"Okay. Here goes. As you are well aware my last name is Christmas, something I have hated for my entire life. I had always assumed that it was just an unfortunate bit of irony. Turns out there is a bit more to it than that. This is going to sound crazy and I fully expect that you won't believe me, but when I turned twenty-five, I was hit with the ability to be able to tell if someone is naughty or nice just by looking at them," Sam sighed. "I'm not completely sure how to explain this. What I can say is that I know that you are on the nice list at least for now."

"What do you mean by that? Of course I'm on the nice list," Faith said, bringing her hand to her chest and doing her best to look offended that Sam would imply otherwise.

"I'm not saying that you aren't nice. What I'm saying is that, I can read the word nice above your head. It is gray which means, it could turn if you did something wrong, I think. Help me out here, Candycane," Sam said, looking to the elf for help.

"You are right about the color of the word. As someone moves more toward nice or naughty the word becomes more bold, until it is eventually a dark black color. So yes, Faith, who would have to do something really bad to tilt to naughty if it clearly says nice, could still end up on the naughty list," Candycane answered.

"I'm sorry. Are you trying to tell me that you just became Santa Claus? I get it. I pushed too hard about you believing in the spirit of Christmas. Great joke. I still have no idea how I didn't see you when I entered your apartment, but you must have been here. People don't just appear," Faith said. "You got me. I will lay off if you want me to. I just want to see you find happiness, Sam."

"When Candycane first showed up at my door, I was pretty sure that you sent her, so I get it if you think this is a joke, but I'm telling you the truth. I can really look at people and see if they are naughty or nice. I wish I couldn't but apparently it comes with being a Christmas. I'm not Santa. I just help make Santa's list," Sam answered.

"Look, I'm all for you believing in Santa Claus and Christmas, but this is a bit much, Sam," Faith said, sitting forward and looking at Candycane. "What did you do to my friend?"

"This is why we don't let people outside of the Christmas family know about this. It is too unbelievable for people who don't have the gift. I have an idea that might help but I'm not sure that Sam is ready to be around a lot of people yet," Candycane offered.

"If it will make Faith stop looking at me like I have eight heads, I'm all for it," Sam said.

"Alright, but we should both probably change," Candycane said. "Judging from the shorts and tank top your friend is wearing, I don't think we need the warm clothing from the North Pole."

"Right. I don't think I have anything that will fit you, properly," Sam said. "I'm sure I have a t-shirt or something. Faith, did you leave anything here that she can maybe wear?"

"Yeah. I have a few things in your room, I think. Check my drawer," Faith answered.

"I knew there was a reason that I let you leave clothes here, even if it makes for awkward conversation when I'm lucky enough to have a woman spend the night," Sam laughed. "Come on Candycane, let's make you look like a human.

"Sam, we don't have to do this," Candycane said once they were in their room, looking for clothes.

"We do, though. I don't have a family, not really. I have Faith. She is all I have ever had. If you expect me to be able to navigate this curse, I'm going to need her support," Sam answered, handing Candycane a pair of jeans and an old t-shirt from their college days.

"It is going to be a lot of information to process and it is all going to come at you really fast. Faith won't be able to see what you are seeing, but she will be able to see how you react and I think that will help her realize that you are telling the truth. I will be there to help you filter through it all and give you methods to silence the noise in your head," Candycane said as she finished changing. "Do you have a pair of shoes? I don't think my boots go with these jeans."

Sam couldn't keep themselves from laughing as they looked at the ridiculous boots. "Maybe, I think there might be a pair of flip flops in the closet that will fit you," Sam said walking to the closet. "Without your hat, your ears are very noticeable. Anything you can do about that?" Sam handed her shoes as they walked past her to the door, heading for the living room.

Candycane followed once they had stepped into the flip-flops. "How do you walk in these things?" she asked, tripping and catching herself on the back of the couch.

"Seriously? You have never worn flip flops?" Faith asked, helping Candycane stand upright.

"Why would I have worn these silly shoes? It snows all the time where I live," Candycane answered.

"You really are committed to this whole elf thing aren't you?" Faith asked.

"Because she is an elf, Faith. Look at her ears. Those aren't fake," Sam said.

"Sorry, Sam. I know you asked me to do something with them," Candycane said, closing her eyes and wrinkling her face tight in concentration. As Faith and Sam looked on, Candycane's ears began to shrink, the pointed tips rounding to look like the ears of a human. "Is that better?" she asked, opening her eyes.

Faith rubbed her eyes before lowering her hands and blinking rapidly. "How did you just do that?" she asked, staring at Candycane.

"Magic. I told you I was an elf," Candycane answered.

"Alright. That paired with the way the two of you showed up here might make me start to believe there could be some truth to your story. I mean I really want to believe in Santa and Christmas elves. I love Christmas, but everyone knows it is just a myth," Faith said. "It can't be real, can it?"

"You actually believe in this stuff. It should be a lot easier for you to come around to this. It is very real. I have been to the North Pole and seen Santa's Workshop and a reindeer fly. I know it sounds crazy, but

I'm telling you the truth," Sam said. "Look at me. Have I ever lied to you when it was something important?"

"Alright, you have me there. But, you have to understand why I'm finding this hard to believe, right?" Faith asked.

"I completely get it. I'm not entirely sure what Candycane has planned, but I know it is her job to make sure that I'm able to do mine, so I trust her if she says this is going to work," Sam answered.

"It will work. I'm sure of it. Faith, Sam can't look at other people without their brain processing who that person is and what kind of person they are, and Sam hasn't been around a lot of people since they left the bar that night before they knew what they were seeing. I don't think their magic was even fully working when they were there, so Sam might seem a little bit off. I'm going to do my best to help them with it, but there is going to be a ton of information running through their brain very quickly," Candycane explained. "I just want you to be prepared if Sam looks pained or anything. It will take them some time to get used to it."

"This doesn't sound like the best idea ever if it is going to hurt them," Faith said.

"I don't think it will actually hurt me. It might just give me a headache. At least now, I know that I'm not suffering delusions or going crazy, which was how I felt when I left the bar," Sam explained. "Let's get this over with. I can't live in my apartment forever."

Chapter 11

Sam was not prepared for what Candycane had in mind. When they left Sam's apartment, they hopped into a cab. Candycane gave the driver a destination, but Sam was too distracted by the people around them to hear what she said. When the car came to a stop and they exited, Sam found themselves struggling to breathe as they found that they were standing in front of the mall. There were people everywhere, their names and naughty or nice designation bombarding Sam's thoughts. Sam brought their hands to their head and closed their eyes as they tried to focus on their breathing.

"Sam, take a deep breath. Think about something that makes you happy, the day you met Faith, maybe. Focus on that. And breathe," Candycane said as she placed a hand on Sam's back.

"Sam? You, alright, buddy? I'm here," Faith asked, reaching out and placing a hand on Sam's shoulder.

The noise in Sam's head had faded away as they were no longer receiving new information with their eyes closed. They could hear Candycane and Faith and the sounds of their voices provided a calming presence that allowed Sam's breathing to return to normal. They slowly dropped their hands from their head and cautiously opened their eyes. "Alright, Candycane, you win. I was not prepared for that. Can we maybe go somewhere with less people while I try to adapt to this?" Sam asked.

"If you can learn to navigate here, you will be fine anywhere we go," Candycane replied. "If it becomes too much we can find somewhere quiet and reset."

"Maybe it would help if you told me what you were seeing? I know it would help me to understand what you are going through," Faith offered.

"Okay. I can try that. But I'm not sure if I can carry on a conversation while I'm looking around. It may be more like reading a list than anything else," Sam answered, raising their head so that they could see the people around them for the first time since they had closed their eyes. "Joseph Long, nice. Marcus King, naughty, Wanda King, nice, Winston King, nice. Claire Miller, naughty, Justin Gordon, naughty, Lindsey Gordon, nice. Kevin Gordon, naughty." Sam rattled off the names of each person who walked past them to enter the mall.

"Wow. You see that for every single person?" Faith asked.

"Yeah," Sam said, looking over Faith's shoulder at a bus that was pulling up to the front of the mall. "Could we maybe go in before that bus unloads? I would rather not have to deal with that."

"Of course. Let's go inside," Candycane said, walking to the door and holding it open for Faith and Sam.

"Are you sure you want to do this, Sam?" Faith asked as they entered the mall.

"I have to. I can't unsee it, so I need to learn to live with it, but hey if I ever see you slipping over to the naughty list, I will be sure to let you know," Sam said with a laugh, their eyes scanning the mass of people in front of them. Thankfully Sam couldn't process the information until they were closer so they didn't get hit with the hundred or so names from the crowd that was walking through the mall.

"How dare you imply that I would ever be on the naughty list?" Faith said, playfully hipchecking Sam. "Since we are here, I desperately need a new pair of jeans and I think we need to do some shopping for your friend there." Faith pointed to Candycane.

"That isn't a bad idea. I'm sure we can find some clothes that are more fitting to your style. What do you say Candycane?" Sam asked.

"I would actually like that a lot. Are you sure?" she asked.

"I haven't given you the easiest couple of days and for that I really am sorry. Let me do this for you," Sam answered.

"Thank you. That is really very kind of you," Candycane said. "And thank you, Faith, for suggesting it."

"No problem CC. I got you," Faith said.

"CC?" both Sam and Candycane asked in unison.

"Well we can't very well walk around calling you Candycane, can we?" Faith laughed.

"I suppose not," Candycane answered. "Thank you."

As Faith and Candycane shopped for clothes, Sam watched people, names flooding their brain. When they reached the center of the mall, the number of people seemed to quadruple. There was a large atrium with benches and a stage that housed Santa Claus as soon as Halloween was over. To the right was the food court, arcade, and movie theater. Forward, behind the stage, was another long corridor filled with shops, similar to the one they had walked down to get there and to the left was the largest store in the mall.

Mercers, the largest retailer in the country, had stores in every mall and major city. This one, however, was the largest. Richfield was home to the corporate office and the flagship store that was five stories of clothing, home goods, and toys. Mercers also happened to be Sam's employer. Sam worked at the corporate office in the accounting department, a thankless job that kept them incredibly busy but allowed them to live comfortably and had allowed them to avoid relationships and the holidays for the past few years.

Avoiding Christmas, something Sam had become very good at, was no longer an option. This year and every year from here out, Sam would at least have to acknowledge the holiday. As Sam looked at the pumpkins and hay bales on the stage, they laughed. It wasn't even October yet and they were concerned about Christmas. They shook their head as they turned towards Mercers with Candycane and Faith, their best friends' voices pulling them from their thoughts.

"And this is where Sam works, well kind of. They work for the corporate office which is a few miles down the road," Faith explained. "Mercers is the best. If you can't find what you need here, you don't need it. They have everything, and you should see the way the decorate for Christmas. You are going to love it."

"Yeah, it is really amazing," Sam said, an image of the store packed with customers flashing in their brain. "And absolutely full of people for two solid months, two months that I refuse to step foot in that store or this mall. I guess that will have to change this year, huh?"

"Shopping malls do tend to be great places to gather information on a large chunk of the population," Candycane answered. "I think we will probably visit here often."

Faith began to laugh, a full body laugh that had her holding her stomach and trying to catch her breath. "I'm pretty sure you just described Sam's biggest nightmare," she said. "Guess you can't be a recluse for the next few months. That means you are coming to my Halloween party this year."

"It, what? How does that have anything to do with Christmas and my unfortunate fate?" Sam asked.

"Because I'm going to make you be social so that you are prepared for November and December when CC here drags you all over town," Faith answered.

"That sounds like a wonderful idea! I have alway thought that the idea of Halloween was fascinating. Might I be allowed to attend this party as well?" Candycane asked.

"Of course. I sort of figured that you and Sam were a package deal," Faith replied, winking at Sam.

"Ugh. For the millionth time, we are not dating. She is involved with someone and I don't do relationships, remember?" Sam said.

"You don't do Christmas either, but here we are," Faith laughed. "Anyhow, CC, come on. Let's finish working on your wardrobe." Faith grabbed Candycane's hand and began walking towards Mercers.

"Um, you know what. Why don't the two of you go ahead and text me when you are ready to check out. I think I need to step outside for a second and get some fresh air," Sam said, stopping short of the entrance and staring into the very crowded store.

"Do you need me to go with you?" Candycane asked.

"No. No. Go, shop. I just need a few minutes away from the mall. I will be back before you know it," Sam answered.

"Are you sure you will be alright, Sam? I didn't think about how crowded Mercers would be. We can always come back another time," Faith offered.

"Really. I'm fine. I just need a few less people at the moment. I can meet you both at the check out, but seriously take your time. Show CC the entire store. I really think she will like it," Sam replied, turning and walking towards the exit on the far side of the food court.

Chapter 12

Sam walked past the patrons in the food court as quickly as they could, trying their best to process as few of them as possible as they made their way to the exit. The time in the mall had given them a massive headache and they were desperate for somewhere secluded. Exiting the mall, Sam turned to the left and walked a few blocks before crossing the street and entering Richfield's Old Town, an eight block section of Old Richfield Road that was home to bars, restaurants, and unique shops. Typically it would be quite crowded, but many of the businesses were closed on Mondays so Sam found the street to be rather empty.

Sam let out a relieved sigh as they walked past the closed storefronts. Since they had returned to the city, this was the first time that the noise in their head had ceased. Sam found themselves smiling at the few people that they passed as they slowly strolled down the street, allowing the names and behaviors to register one at a time instead of the massive intake of data they had experienced in the mall.

With the stress of the crowds gone, Sam was enjoying the cool autumn breeze as they looked at the fall displays in the shop windows. This street, like all of downtown Richfield, would become covered in bright lights and Christmas decor in November, but for now this quiet corner of the city with pumpkins and fallen leaves was far removed from Christmas and the holiday season. It was almost enough to make Sam briefly forget about their crazy day and newly acquired responsibility. They would have to come back here often in the next month to find their calm as the world around them prepared for the holiday that Sam had spent the majority of their life hating. They knew by the middle of October the mall would already be full of red and green signs in store windows, but Old Town celebrated every holiday, which meant that autumn decor would last until Thanksgiving.

Yes, this part of the city would be Sam's perfect escape, devoid of the bright colors of Christmas and Santa Claus. Santa Claus, why had they just thought of the jolly old elf in a red suit when they were trying so hard to purge their mind of Christmas for a few minutes. Sam stopped and blinked rapidly as they looked in the window of the store they were passing, The Christmas Claus-it. The small Christmas store featured a Santa Claus blow mold in the window that was wearing a pumpkin costume. Painted in Green on the glass were the words "Have A Merry Halloween,"

How had someone managed to ruin Sam's peaceful getaway with a Christmas shop? They didn't remember that being here, but then again it had been a few years since they had visited Old Town. Their twenty-second birthday had brought Sam and Faith to Old Richfield where they had attempted to complete a bar crawl of the seven bars or taverns located there. Sam had been in a particularly poor mood after talking with their mother and spent the night trying to forget about it in the arms of attractive women everywhere they stopped. They were only at the third bar when Sam was thrown out by the owner for distracting the bartender by means of making out with her in the alley behind the bar. The bartender in question had been the owner's girlfriend, which had made for a rather hostile exchange as they had been physically removed from the bar. After that Faith had taken Sam home and they had vowed to steer clear of Old Town for a while.

Sam shook their head as they remembered that night, glancing down the street to the location of the bar and that terrrible night. They smiled as they saw that the space was now a cafe. Perhaps if they could stay away from the Christmas store, this street would still prove a sanctuary. They stepped back from the window ready to walk away when they spotted a curvy woman with red curly hair and glasses wearing a Christmas sweater stocking the shelves.

It was the woman with the impossibly cute laugh from the bar. She looked up and caught sight of Sam, smiling at them making her dimple appear, and Sam couldn't help but smile back. Despite their better judgment, Sam found themselves entering the store so that they could talk to the beautiful woman with the crimson locks.

As they entered the store, they heard a soft voice offer them a greeting. Looking towards the sound they saw the word nice in very solid bold black letters. Was it possible for someone to be that nice? Sam pondered that as her name found its way into their mind, Holley Daye. Seriously? How was that possible and how did that make her even more adorable? Sam closed their eyes for a moment trying to make sense of things. That couldn't really be right. It was just Candycane and the events of their day getting to them.

When they opened their eyes, they found Holley Daye, the name still making its way through to Sam's brain, standing in front of them and smiling a warm welcoming look on her face. "Hi. Welcome to the Christmas Claus-it. Can I help you find anything?" she asked.

"Um, hi," was the best that Sam could muster as they looked into her emerald green eyes. "I, uh, I'm not really sure why I came in," Sam said, running their hand through their hair as they looked around the shop.

"I have seen you before," Holley said. "At the bar. I was going to come talk to you, but you left before I worked up the nerve. I'm Holley."

"Sam," they said, smiling at her. "Last night was a bad night, but I'm sorry I left before I got to meet you."

"It would seem that fate is giving us a second chance," Holley replied.

"Yeah, I guess so," Sam agreed. "So, a Christmas shop? You do know it is September, right?"

"Yes. Only ninety-nine days until Christmas," Holley answered.

"What? How would you even know something like that?" Sam asked.

"Because Christmas is the most magical time of the year. I keep a running countdown all year, and yesterday was one hundred days from my favorite day of the year as well as being three months from my birthday," Holley answered.

"Oh. Well happy really early birthday," Sam laughed. "I can't imagine counting down to a holiday or my birthday, but if that is a thing, only three hundred and sixty four more days to go." Sam shrugged.

"Yesterday was your birthday? I would have had an excuse to buy you a drink," Holley said, sighing as she frowned or at least tried to frown. From Sam's perspective it looked like an adorable attempt at pouting, causing them to laugh.

"Last night was a really strange night. It is probably just as well that you didn't talk to me," Sam replied.

"Happy belated birthday. I'm about to close up, and this might be a little forward, but I would love to still buy you a birthday drink," Holley said, smiling hopefully at Sam.

Sam's phone started ringing as Holley finished speaking. "I gotta take this, sorry," Sam said walking away from Holley as they answered their phone.

"Sam, where are you?" Faith asked as soon as Sam answered.

"In a Christmas store in Old Town," Sam answered. "I didn't plan on walking so far, but it was really quiet over here and exactly what I needed. I might need a favor. I will explain when I get there. See you in a few."

Sam hung up the phone and turned back to Holley who was trying her best to look like she was focused on rearranging ornaments on a tree. "Look, I have to go meet a couple of friends. But, um, I would love to have that drink," Sam said, offering their phone to her. "Can I have your number? I will text you."

Holley handed the phone back to Sam, brushing their hand as she did, causing both of them to blush. "I guess you shouldn't keep your friends waiting," Holley said. "It was nice meeting you, Sam."

Sam hit the call button on their phone, not bringing it to their ear. White Christmas began playing from a phone on the shop's counter. "It's September," Sam said. "Anyhow, that's me. Text me and we will see about that drink." Sam turned and left before Holley could reply.

As Sam walked back towards the mall, they couldn't help but smile. They didn't even let the increase in people and the influx of information bombarding their brain distract them from thoughts of the cute girl who loved Christmas. She wasn't like anyone that Sam had ever gone out with, and they weren't even sure that they could go out with anyone now with their gift, but there was something about her that made them want to try. Something that Sam didn't quite understand. They had spent the last several years of their life avoiding all things Christmas and straying away from women, unless it was for a one night stand, something that they were certain Holley wasn't. Why then were they on their way to ask Candycane about the rules regarding dating and the logistics of going on a date when they couldn't shut off the part of their brain that would spend the night processing data for the list?

What was happening to them? Two days ago, they were sure that Christmas was a hoax and Santa Claus wasn't real. And they stayed far away from nice girls who looked like relationship material, because love was even more made up than the man in the red suit. But that was all before they had been to the North Pole. There was no denying that Christmas was real and that Santa existed, even if it took six people to fill that role. That knowledge didn't make them hate the holiday any less, but if Christmas was real, it meant that love might actually exist as well. Not that they would go looking for it, because love, just like the magic of Christmas, was probably not meant for Sam.

Maybe that was why they were drawn to Holley. It was destined to fail, so there were no strings attached. Sam despised Christmas and Holley lit up like the sun reflecting off of a fresh snowfall when she talked about the holiday. There was no way that this would ever be more than just one drink, but it would be worth it if they got to see her smile again. Sam pulled out their phone as they approached the entrance to the mall and sent a quick message to Holley.

The Spectrum at 8? We can have a redo - you can buy me that drink and we can meet for the first time again.

Chapter 13

Sam looked at their reflection in their phone's camera, fixing their messy hair, doing their best to tame it. Their thick hair fell as soon as they removed their hand and Sam sighed, turning off their camera and pocketing their phone. "Here goes nothing," they mumbled to themselves as they reached for the door of Spectrum, memories of last night flashing through their brain. Candycane had assured them that as long as they focused on Holley, they should be able to ignore the majority of the people in the bar. Sam hoped that was true as they had no desire to repeat their rapid exit from the night before and they were anxious enough about meeting Holley without the addition of their gift.

As they walked through the door, Holley waved at them from a table in the back corner of the bar. They had hoped to beat her to the bar to claim a quiet spot. Thankfully it looked like she, too, had wanted somewhere removed from the noise of the dance floor. Sam smiled at her as they walked to the bar and ordered a gin and coke.

Thankfully the bar wasn't that crowded on a Monday night so they only had to filter through a dozen names as they waited for their drink.

They looked back to where Holley was when they ordered, asking the bartender what she was drinking so that they could get her another one. Somehow she looked even more beautiful now than she had when they had run into her earlier. She had traded her Christmas sweater for a short sleeve shirt with a scoop neck, paired with black skinny jeans and boots. Sam was happy to see that she had changed but not dressed up as they had traded their shorts from earlier for jeans and had decided on a short sleeve button up shirt worn open over a solid t-shirt. It gave Sam the sense that this was just a casual drink between acquaintances and that was fine with them. Sure there was a part of them that was hoping the night ended with a kiss, but Sam didn't do relationships and Holley was definitely a relationship girl.

Sam turned back to the bar as the bartender handed them two beverages. They brought their drink to their mouth, taking a large gulp. Why were they so nervous? This was just a drink with a girl that wouldn't amount to anything. If only their rapidly beating heart would get the memo, because Sam felt like they had just run a marathon as they turned and began to walk to the table at the back of the bar. As they sat across from Holley, noticing just how low the scoop neck of her t-shirt fell, they blushed slightly, quickly looking away as to not stare at her cleavage. The sweater she had been wearing earlier was loose fitting and hid the size of her rather large breasts.

Sam took another large swallow of their drink as they tried to compose themselves. The sweater and jeans that Holley was wearing when they walked into her store had been rather misleading. Not only was she absolutely adorable, but her full curvy figure was causing Sam to overheat. They desperately wanted to pull her onto the dance floor, place their hands on her hips, and feel her body rub against them. So why weren't they? Ordinarily that is exactly what they would do if they saw a beautiful woman that they wanted to spend the evening with, they wouldn't think twice about it. Yet here they were tongue tied and unable to even process thoughts as they looked at Holley.

"Thanks for the drink, but I was the one who was supposed to be buying you a drink, remember?" Holley said, smiling at them as she picked up the glass bottle and sipped on her hard cider.

"I agreed to meeting you for a drink. I don't remember there being rules about which one of us got to pay for the drink," Sam replied, looking down at the table so that they could stop thinking about her full red lips on the mouth of the bottle. "Um, you look really nice. Not that your ugly Christmas sweater wasn't stunning, but it didn't do you justice." They looked up at her as they finished speaking just in time to see the color rise in her cheeks as she blushed at the compliment.

"Thanks. You seemed pretty set on it being September so I figured I should save my blinking rudolph sweater for our second date," Holley laughed.

Sam found the tension leaving their body and their heart began beating normally as the sound of her melodic laugh filled their ears. "I thought this was just a drink," Sam said smiling.

"I guess I was hoping that it might be more," Holley said, looking away.

"Why don't we see how the drink goes and go from there?" Sam asked. "After the last few days, I'm not ruling anything out."

"You wanna talk about it?" Holley asked.

"Just the normal birthday stuff. Spoke with my mother on the phone and was reminded of all the reasons that I'm choosing to live a life of sin and what a disappointment I am. Someone slipped something into my drink because I was too distracted to notice and I ditched my best friend at the bar because I was freaking out. Pretty standard," Sam answered.

"That sounds terrible. Birthdays are supposed to be a celebration," Holley replied.

"Meh. They happen every year. I will live. I'd rather talk about you. Why don't you tell me why you love Christmas so much?" Sam asked.

"We can talk about me later. Right now, we're having a do over for your birthday. So I'm buying you a drink and we're dancing because that is why you go to a bar on your birthday, so you can have free drinks and dance with strangers," Holley answered, laughing as she stood and extended her hand to Sam.

Sam took Holley's hand and she pulled them from their seat, dragging them towards the bar. "What is your shot of choice?" she asked when they reached the counter.

"Promise not to laugh?" Sam asked.

"Ugh, it is something basic like tequila isn't it?" Holley asked.

"No," Sam replied, wrinkling up their face in disgust. "I hate tequila."

"Then what is it?" Holley asked, raising an eyebrow. "You don't strike me as a vodka person, since you were drinking gin."

"Peppermint schnapps," Sam answered, their cheeks reddening with an embarrassed blush. "I know. I know. People don't shoot schnapps. They mix it with things."

Holley smiled at them as she ordered four shots of peppermint schnapps. "That is the most unique answer I have ever gotten to that question. I like it," she said as she handed a shot glass to Sam. "Happy Birthday, Sam. Here's to, wait, how old are you?"

"Twenty-five," Sam answered as they raised the glass and tilted it back.

"To twenty-five," Holley said as she threw back a shot glass. "Wow, that burns. And clears your sinuses. You seriously enjoy drinking that or were you just trying to come up with something absurd?"

"I love peppermint. You get used to the burn and it leaves you feeling refreshed instead of an aftertaste of regret," Sam answered.

"Alright. Well here's to new experiences," Holley handed Sam another shot before picking up one for herself. "Here goes." She grimaced as the peppermint liquor hit her throat, forcing herself to swallow it.

"You didn't have to drink another one if you hated it that much," Sam said, laughing at her. "You want me to get you another cider to wash it down with?"

"Already ordered," Holley said, turning and grabbing a fresh bottle.

"So now do I get to find out why you love Christmas?" Sam asked.

"Nope. Now we dance," Holley answered, walking backwards onto the dance floor, beckoning Sam to join them with her hand not holding her drink.

Sam scanned the dance floor, quickly taking in the names and status of each of the people dancing before bringing their attention back to Holley. She was swaying her hips to the music as she sipped her drink, her eyes fixed on Sam. Despite their concerns about what might happen if they danced with her, Sam couldn't keep themselves from joining her and placing their hands on her hips as they pulled her close to them.

Dancing wasn't something that had ever been one of Sam's strengths. To say they had two left feet was kind. As such Sam's idea of dancing normally involved them standing and barely swaying as their partner danced in front of them. But here they were facing Holley and following her lead as their bodies moved as one to the beat of the music. Holley was a fantastic dancer, moving effortlessly to the music as she ran her hands along Sam's ribcage, driving them wild.

As Sam felt their temperature begin to rise, they found themselves fighting their physical urges to move their hands from Holley's hips and begin exploring her body. Fearing that they might mess up their chances to get to know her, Sam pulled back from her as the music changed and the dj began playing throwback hits from the nineties. Thankfully if Holley noticed that Sam was uncomfortable, it didn't show. Instead she started over dramatically and comically doing the cabbage patch, causing Sam to laugh as they joined her.

They danced and laughed until the bar closed. As they walked out of the bar, Holley looked at Sam and smiled. "I had a really great time tonight. Happy Birthday, Sam. I hope that I can see you again," she said.

"Wait. I thought you said something about a date. I had a wonderful time having a drink with you, and if you would let me, I would love to continue this and officially make it a date," Sam said.

"It's one in the morning. You want to go on a date now?" Holley asked.

"I know a great diner that has the best cheese fries in the city and a menu that includes over thirty different milkshake flavors," Sam answered. "So, yeah. Would you like to have a late night snack while we maybe get to know each other a little?"

"That is quite possibly the most adorably awkward way anyone has ever asked me on a date," Holley replied, smiling at them.

"So, that's a no, then?" Sam asked, pouting a little.

"Are you kidding? You had me at cheese fries. It is a definite yes," Holley answered.

Chapter 14

Chas's Cafe was a tiny diner a few blocks from the apartment that Sam and Faith had shared when they were in college. The twenty-four hour diner was a favorite for college students craving coffee and sugar to fuel late night study sessions or satisfy drunken cravings. Sam and Faith frequented the diner while in school and Sam had continued to visit Chas's at least once a week to check out the flavor of the week on the milkshake menu.

"Sam," the woman standing behind the counter called out as Sam walked in with Holley.

"Hey, Chas. How's it going?" Sam asked.

"You didn't come in on your birthday. I still owe you a shake," Chas replied. "And who is your friend?"

"Chas, this is Holley," Sam answered. "We are kind of on a first date." Sam whispered the last of what they said, hoping that Holley wouldn't hear.

Chas winked at Sam. "I got you. Sit anywhere you like. I will be right over with menus," she said.

Sam thanked her and led Holley to a corner booth, sliding in across from her once she sat. "I hope you are hungry. I didn't expect Chas to be here this late, but she won't let me leave until I'm completely stuffed," Sam explained.

"I get the feeling you come here frequently. I have been here for almost three years and I have never heard of the place," Holley said, looking around the diner. "It's cute."

"It is pretty popular with the college kids," Sam replied. "You've only been here for three years? What brought you to the city?"

"I moved here for a job, a job I hated, but I sort of fell in love with the city, so I stayed," Holley answered.

"And then you stumbled into a job at a Christmas store?" Sam asked.

"No. Then I opened a Christmas store. The Christmas Claus-it is my shop," Holley answered, smiling proudly.

"Oh. Wow. That's great. It looked like a cute little shop from what I saw. Though I confess I was more interested in the shop owner than the products within," Sam replied.

Holley blushed and smiled at Sam. "I feel as if I should perhaps be offended since you didn't look around my shop, but it is hard to be upset when you say something like that," she said. "I would love to show you the store sometime, though."

"Oh, um. Yeah that would be nice. Maybe when it is a little closer to Christmas. I mean it isn't even Fall yet," Sam laughed.

"It is never too early to start buying Christmas decor," Holley replied. "When do you put your tree up? You aren't one of those after Thanksgiving people, are you?"

"Actually I'm more of the kind of person that doesn't put up a tree," Sam answered. "I don't really celebrate Christmas."

"What? How can you not celebrate Christmas? It is the most magical day of the year!" Holley said, looking at Sam with a look of confusion. "Why wouldn't you celebrate the holiday?"

Sam sat there looking at Holley, who looked like someone had just taken a pin to her balloon. How were they going to explain their views on Christmas to someone who still believed in the magic of the holiday? They opened their mouth to try to say something, but they were interrupted as a plate of french fries covered in four kinds of melted cheese was placed on the table.

"Christmas! I should have known it was you. Chas seems to think you never eat. Don't you have some fancy job these days?" a tall thin guy wearing an apron stained with grease, asked as he placed two menus on the table.

"Oh, hey Trevor. Good to see you. Tell Chas thanks for the fries," Sam said, picking up the menu. "And um, I will have a chocolate covered candy cane shake, but Holley might need a little time with the menu."

"What's the featured flavor this week?" Holley asked.

"Apple Pie," Trevor answered.

"That sounds like a good September flavor. I will have that," Holley said, handing the menu back to Trevor. Once he had walked away, she looked at Sam with a raised eyebrow. "Christmas? He called you Christmas. Care to explain that? Since you don't even put up a tree."

Sam sighed. "He called me Christmas because that is my last name. I'm Sam Christmas," Sam answered.

"Wait, really?" Holley asked, trying not to laugh.

"Yeah. Really. It's hysterical. I know," Sam said, folding their arms and frowning.

"That wasn't why I was laughing. It just seems odd that you of all people wouldn't celebrate Christmas," Holley replied, reaching for a fry. "Look, I feel like we took a bad turn there. Let's eat some of these amazing fries and start over. My name is Holley, Holley Daye. Nice to meet you."

"Holley Daye? And you wonder why I don't like Christmas? How was childhood not awful for you?" Sam asked.

"Oh, it was terrible. Kids can be awful, but I decided to embrace my name rather than miss out on the incredible feeling I get during the holidays," Holley answered. "You can't have a problem with Christmas just because of your name. There has to be more to it than that."

"It isn't the only reason. The holidays were never good times when I was growing up. They mostly just served as a reminder of what I didn't have, not in a material way, but the things that matter like a stable family life," Sam answered. "Most holiday seasons I didn't even know if I would have a place to call home as my mother had a tendency to move in with men who would inevitably leave her in December and we would find ourselves living in a motel until she found someone else."

"That's heartbreaking. You never did any Christmas activities with your mom?" Holley asked.

"No. She hated Christmas because it made her think of my father, so she was happy to ignore the season," Sam answered. "All except for the religious part. She got sober when I was eleven and found Jesus, dragging me to church multiple times a week and to every Christmas service she could find."

"That part of the holiday can be good, too. Though for me the magic lies in the spirit of giving and the kindness of strangers that Christmas brings. It is a time for family and laughter, a time to make memories and spend with the ones we love," Holley said.

"That is a nice idea and all, but the only memories I have of Christmas are painful ones," Sam replied.

"Maybe it is time that changes. It is never too late to experience the real meaning of Christmas," Holley offered.

"Can we maybe talk about something else for a little bit?" Sam asked as Chas appeared with milkshakes.

"Chocolate candy cane shake? Must be for my favorite elf," she said with a warm smile as she placed it in front of Sam. "And apple pie for, Holley. Do you two need anything else? A refill on fries perhaps?"

"Yeah. That would be nice, Chas. Thanks," Sam answered.

As Chas walked away, Holley tasted her shake, letting out a satisfied moan. "This is the best milkshake I have ever had. There is no way that your Christmas themed concoction can be better than this," Holley said, pushing her shake across the table for Sam to try.

"I don't know. This shake is almost enough to make me believe in Christmas magic," Sam laughed as they traded shakes with Holley.

An hour passed as Sam and Holley shared their milkshakes and ate two more plates of cheese fries. "I don't want this night to end, but it is getting really late and I know we both have work in the morning," Holley said after finishing her shake.

Sam pulled their phone from their pocket to check the time and noticed several missed calls and texts from Faith. "Wow, when did it get to be so late? I can't believe it is almost three. Do you live far from here?" Sam asked.

"I'm on the other end of the city. You?" Holley replied.

"I'm only a few miles from here, actually, but we can get a cab and I can ride with you, if you want," Sam offered.

"No. That is ok. You are so close to your home. You don't have to see me home. I had a really great time tonight and I would love to see you again," Holley said as they walked out of the cafe. She reached out a hand to flag down an approaching cab.

As the cab pulled over to the curb, Sam reached out and grabbed Holley's hand, pulling her towards them as they leaned forward and pressed their lips against hers in a quick chaste kiss. "Have a good night, Holley. Thanks for the birthday drink. I hope we can do this again soon," Sam said, backing away from her and smiling as she stepped back toward the cab.

Sam watched the cab drive away, touching their lips and smiling. How had such a simple kiss been so electrifying? They could still feel her lips on theirs, her full soft lips that had yielded to their kiss as soon as their mouths had met. Sam turned and walked from the diner, choosing to walk the two miles back to their apartment. It had been a crazy couple of days, but for the past few hours, all Sam had thought about was the gorgeous woman that they were spending time with. Her laugh and her infectious smile had silenced the constant noise of the list filtering through their brain.

Sam did not do dates. Sam did not do relationships. And Sam didn't do crushes, but as they walked home all they could think about was Holley and when they could see her again. If last night had been the worst night of their lives to date, tonight might just have been the best. As they pulled their phone back out to text Faith and tell her about their night, their phone vibrated as a new message came through.

Can't stop thinking about that kiss. If the cab hadn't been there, I wouldn't have let you walk away so easily. Thanks again for an amazing night.

Chapter 15

Sam hadn't slept, not really. They got home close to four in the morning to find Candycane still very much awake, waiting on a full report of Sam's evening. By the time they had satisfied the elf's curiosities, it was almost five. Two hours later, half an hour before their alarm would have gone off, Faith called demanding to hear all about Sam's date.

As a result, Sam was sitting in their cubicle at work, coffee in one hand, staring at their monitor while fighting to keep their eyes open. They had spent the first part of their morning dodging their fellow accountants as they were too tired to process who was naughty or nice. As that information had started hitting their brain, it had instantly given them a headache and that added to their lack of sleep was causing Sam to be irrationally angry.

Candycane had wanted to accompany them to the office but Sam managed to talk her out of it as there wouldn't be a good explanation for her being there. The compromise was for her to get a phone so she could contact Sam if needed. This had been something that Sam had hoped would take the better part of the day, but apparently being an elf had perks and a quick visit to the North Pole was all Candycane needed to have a working cell phone.

Sam massaged their head and silenced their phone as another message from Candycane dropped in. She had spent the morning texting Sam every minute to ask how they were doing and make sure that work wasn't overwhelming them. Sam worked in a relatively small department and typically only saw twelve to fifteen people when they were at work, all of whom they had already seen for the day, making it easy for Sam to ignore their naughty or nice designation. Although Sam had assured the elf that they were fine, she continued to check in, causing Sam's phone to vibrate until it fell off of their desk. Sam rolled their eyes as they picked up their phone and sent a quick message to Candycane, letting her know that they were turning off their phone so they could focus on work and that they would call her if they needed her. They threw their phone in their desk drawer as they did their best to look at the numbers on their screen.

Without the constant distraction of their phone, Sam was able to get their work done in a few hours, leaving them with three hours in which they had little to do but sit with their thoughts. Sam tried to think about the events of the past few days, their new gift and the trip to the North Pole, but without the distraction of people filtering through their brain, there was only one thing or rather one person that they could think about, Holley Daye.

She was the reason that they were exhausted today, but as they thought about her they couldn't help but smile. Holley was everything that Sam would normally avoid. She wasn't a one night stand or just a pretty distraction. Holley had made Sam feel alive in ways that they hadn't in years. They could still hear her laugh and taste her lips as they thought back to last night. She had texted them that she wanted to see them again, which wasn't completely new for Sam, but they didn't usually feel the same. They wanted to see her soon, but they didn't want to seem overly eager and they weren't entirely sure how dating worked since they hadn't tried to date anyone since junior year of college.

Faith would know what to do, well maybe. She also hadn't dated anyone since Freshman year of college as that was when she met Xavier. Shit, Xavier. Sam opened their drawer and grabbed their phone as they remembered X's birthday dinner. Was that really tonight? As they looked down at their phone's screen, they saw that Faith had called twice and texted half a dozen times. Clicking on the messages, they groaned. It was definitely tonight. So much for the nap that they had been looking forward to.

Sam quickly skimmed the texts from Candycane, clearing their phone of notifications. No messages from Holley, they noticed. Sam frowned. Why would there be a message from her? It wasn't as if they had texted her. In fact they hadn't texted her since before their date yesterday. What if it was their fault that she hadn't sent them anything? They desperately wanted to talk to Faith about this but today was Xavier's day and that was all that Faith would be focused on.

Sam powered off their computer and packed up their belongings, preparing themselves to leave work. As they walked from their desk towards the stairs, they called Faith. The location of X's party was going to be an issue. They had no doubt of that, and they would definitely need Candycane if they were going to survive the evening.

With the okay from Faith to bring their elven companion, Sam stopped at the store to buy a card for X before heading home. As a rule, Sam hated shopping for birthday cards, mostly because they hated celebrating birthdays, but Faith celebrated everything and they had been roped into X's celebrations from the very moment that Faith met him. So, buying X a card had become somewhat of a tradition, one that Sam still loathed, but a tradition.

Luckily for Sam, the store only offered one card that matched what they had been looking for so they were in and out and on their way home before the long line of people at the pharmacy could draw their attention. Their head hadn't stopped hurting and Sam was really not in the mood to have to process all of those people especially since they would find themselves surrounded by children in just a few hours.

Thus far the majority of people that had crossed paths with Sam had been adults, and where they still provided Sam with information for the list, Sam was aware that the only names that really mattered were the names of the children. That information would be filtered into the list that Wyatt would end up with when it was time for him to deliver presents. It was also a list that Candycane had explained to him was constantly changing as children bounced between naughty and nice much more frequently than adults, meaning that it was possible for their designation to change while Sam was looking at them. This was something that Sam was very much not looking forward to.

As they reached their apartment, Sam wasn't sure what they were less excited about, the large crowd of people that they would soon be forced to be around or the birthday celebration. They desperately wanted a few moments of peace to prepare themselves for the evening, but as they pulled their key from their pocket, their door flew open in front of them. "Welcome home, Sam! Tell me all about your day. How did it go? Any headaches?" Candycane bombarded them with questions as they entered their home.

"Yes, a massive migraine and I just want to lay down for a few minutes and forget about everything," Sam answered, setting down their bags and collapsing on their couch.

"Oh no. I was afraid that might happen. Processing the list takes a lot of your brain's focus and making yourself concentrate on other things, such as work or very specific interactions like your date last night are bound to be taxing especially early on as you learn to use your gift," Candycane answered. "This is why I should have been with you today. I could have given you something for your headache hours ago."

"I took headache meds twice. Nothing is working," Sam groaned. "I'm perfectly capable of taking care of myself. I have been doing it for twenty-five years."

"Are you sure about that?" Candycane asked, handing Sam a mug filled with a hot liquid.

"What is this?" Sam asked, inhaling the vapors from the top of the mug smelling peppermint and lavender. "It smells like body wash."

"Headache cure. Drink," Candycane instructed.

Sam lifted the beverage and took a tentative sip. Despite the smell, the drink tasted like warm peppermint milk and instantly put Sam at ease. They could feel the stress of the day lift from their shoulders and the pain in their head began to lessen. "How?" Sam asked as they took another drink.

"Magic?" Candycane answered with a shrug. "Old elven recipe, just the right mix of herbs and flavors to soothe the mind."

"This is amazing. Do you have any idea how much money you could make if you sold this?" Sam asked. "My headache is completely gone."

"Perhaps, but that is not why we do the things we do. This is a gift to you," Candycane answered. "Speaking of gifts. You sent me a message about a birthday party. I wanted to get a gift but I was unsure of what would be appropriate since I did not know who the party was for."

"Oh. I got a card. We can both just sign that and buy his game card tonight," Sam said, reaching in his bag and retrieving the card.

Candycane took the card from him and frowned as she looked at the large number eight on the front of the card. "You want to give an eight year old a gift card?" she asked, shaking her head.

"He isn't eight, not really," Sam answered. "He is twenty-seven. We're celebrating the birth of his true self, the anniversary of when he started his transition."

"Oh. I see. So we're going to a not birthday party for a not child at a place for children?" Candycane asked.

"It is a birthday or at the very least a day that deserves celebrating just as much as a birthday, if not more. And who said anything about it being for kids?" Sam replied.

"Well you said games, food, and fun. Why wouldn't I assume it was for kids? Adults in your world don't really play games," Candycane answered.

"I mean we aren't playing hopscotch and candyland." Sam answered. "But I assure you that both kids and adults love Shooter's."

Chapter 16

Shooter's Shenanigans was an arcade, restaurant, and bar that featured everything from pinball to bowling to skeeball to games of chance. It was a favorite location for children's birthday parties, bachelor parties, dates, and groups of people wanting to watch various sporting events at the bar. Ordinarily it was one of the few places outside of Chas's that Sam looked forward to going to. But that was before they had unlocked their gift.

Now they found themselves standing in a bathroom stall, hyperventilating while Candycane did their best to try and calm them. They had walked into Shooter's behind two bus loads of kids and at least one large group of young men wearing fraternity sweatshirts.

The rush of information that hit Sam as they tried to process all of the naughty and nice names had made the room appear to spin causing them to stumble and start to fall. Candycane had acted quickly, stopping their fall and leading them to the bathroom. "Come on, Sam. Deep breaths. In and out. Just focus on breathing. You can do this. I'm right here with you," Candycane said, rubbing their back as she tried to soothe them.

"I, I can't. There, there's too many of them," Sam said as they tried to control their breathing.

"You just need to focus on those that are closest to you. It isn't possible to process so many names at one time, especially for someone who has just unlocked their magic," Candycane explained.

"But how? There are so many people. And there are kids that are bouncing from naughty to nice. I can feel it trying to rewrite the data in my brain. How do I ignore it?" Sam asked.

"You can't ignore it but you can learn to limit how much you let in at once. It starts by pulling your focus to those closest to you. If you really concentrate, it will block out the information coming from the people in the background," Candycane explained.

"You make that sound so easy. With all the noises and lights here, it is really hard to only look at what is right in front of me," Sam replied.

"I never said it would be easy, but you have to try. This won't be the only time that you will be in a situation with lots of people," Candycane said, pulling out her phone and sending a text message.

"Who are you texting? You didn't even have a phone until today," Sam asked.

"Sam, where are you? You can't stay in here all night," Faith called from outside of the stall. "CC? You guys still in here?"

"Over here, Faith," Candycane answered, opening the door to the stall and walking out.

Faith walked over to the stall and looked at Sam, who was leaning on the wall as they tried to make the world stop spinning. "Hey, look at me. You are going to be alright. I can't imagine what it must be like to see what you are seeing, but I know that you can overcome it. You have never let hardships stand in the way of you living your life.

And tonight is not the night that is going to begin," Faith said. "Sam Christmas is the toughest, most resilient person I know."

"Thanks, Faith. Can we walk together perhaps? I think I will be alright once we get to the bar. It was just a lot as soon as we entered and I wasn't prepared for it," Sam replied.

"Of course. X got us a table. He is excited to meet CC," Faith answered.

"Wait. How did you explain Candycane to him?" Sam asked.

"I told him you met her at work. Don't worry. Your secret is safe with me," Faith answered, smiling at Candycane.

"That is much appreciated, Faith. I'm looking forward to meeting your other half as well," Candycane replied.

"Good. Because I do not want to spend the night in the bathroom and I'm sure X is ready to challenge Sam to a skee ball tournament" Faith laughed.

"You mean he is ready to lose at skee ball," Sam said, exiting the stall and walking past their friends to the door.

An hour later, Sam had adjusted to things and was standing beside Xavier while the two of them played skee ball. "And that is another one in the 100 which makes 510 for me. Sorry birthday boy, but you just can't beat me," Sam said.

"It is unfair how good you are at this," X complained as he stepped back from the game. "I'm going to go get a beer, and then we're going to play something I can win at."

"Alright. I'm gonna play a few more rounds," Sam said, hitting the button to start a new game.

"This one taken?" a sweet voice beside Sam caused them to drop the ball in their hand short as it dropped into the ten point spot.

"No, it is free," Sam said, turning to look at the person standing beside them. "Holley? What are you doing here?"

"A six year old's birthday party," she answered. "You?"

"A friend's party," Sam replied. "It is nice to see you. I wanted to message you but I wasn't sure if it would be too soon."

"How are you so adorable?" Holley asked. "I had a great time last night. I thought that was obvious."

"Yeah I thought you did, but I was afraid if I messaged you too soon, you would think there was something wrong with me," Sam answered. "It had been a while since I had gone on a date."

"Really? I find that hard to believe. Incredibly attractive humans don't tend to stay single, especially ones with lips as soft as yours," Holley said, causing Sam to drop the ball in their hand to the ground.

A flustered and embarrassed Sam crouched down to retrieve the ball. "I could say the same for you. Beautiful women are rarely single, especially ones with a body like yours," Sam said, biting their lip and looking her over as they stood.

"Maybe we should either play these games or take this somewhere else, because if you look at me like that again, I'm really going to want to kiss you again," Holley said, looking at Sam's mouth.

"Sam! Hey. We're gonna do cake. You can bring your friend," Faith yelled from the bar.

Sam looked towards the bar and then back to Holley and sighed. "I gotta go. I totally get it if you don't want to deal with my friends, but there is cake," they said with a hopeful smile.

"I already had cake, but seeing you made me stay when my friends left, so I could maybe have another piece of cake," Holley said.

Sam tentatively extended their hand towards her, waiting for her to take theirs. As she grabbed their hand and their fingers intertwined, Sam started walking towards their friends, a huge smile on their face. As they walked toward the bar, Sam pointed out their friends to Holley, letting her know who each of them were. "So the girl with the blue hair is Faith. She's my best friend and we are here celebrating her partner's birthday of sorts. He is the tall thin guy with the red and blonde dreadlocks and as Faith says, milk chocolate complexion. Then there is CC, the tall thin blonde with impossibly pale skin. I'm pretty sure your skin is darker than hers. She is my roommate. We work together."

"Hey, just because you were blessed with a slightly darker shade of pasty white, doesn't mean you have to make fun of those of us who can't go out in the sun for fear of bursting into flames," Holley laughed.

Faith took no time welcoming Holley to the table, smiling at Sam as she did. "So, are you the one responsible for my cranky friend here smiling for a change?" Faith asked, putting her arm around Holley.

"I'm not cranky, Faith," Sam insisted, causing everyone to laugh.

"Clearly," X agreed.

"We came over here for cake, not for abuse," Sam said, crossing their arms and rolling their eyes.

"Come on dude, that is mild after what you did to me over there at skee ball," X laughed.

Holley spent the next hour and a half playing games and hanging out with Sam and their friends. Leaning on a basketball game, she watched as Xavier finally found a game that they were better than Sam at. A yawn escaped her as she tried to cheer them on, and Sam handed the ball in their hand to Candycane as they caught sight of the yawn. "Hey, why don't you show him how it is done? I saw you over here earlier, hitting every basket," Sam laughed. "You look exhausted, Holley. How about I take you home?"

"No. No. You can stay with your friends. It is fine. I'm not used to being out late," Holley replied.

"It's cool. You two go. I will make sure CC gets home, alright," Faith said from beside X. "It was nice meeting you, Holley."

"You too, Faith, all of you. Thanks for including me in your night. Happy birthday, Xavier," Holley said, grabbing Sam's hand as they started to walk to the door.

Sam was once again hit with a wave of new information as they approached the entrance. The late hour had greatly reduced the number of children, making it easier for Sam to process the names as they walked past people to the doors. A large group of college students were standing outside of the bar talking as they waited for cabs, causing Sam to turn away from them and walk quickly in the opposite direction.

"Where are we going, Sam? I assumed we would be waiting for a ride," Holley asked as they left Shooter's behind them.

"It is a beautiful night. I know you are tired, but I thought maybe we could walk a little. There is something I would like to show you," Sam answered.

Chapter 17

As the noise of the bar faded behind them, Sam led Holley a few blocks to the north before turning and heading east towards the river. As they continued to walk the large buildings of the city began to disappear behind them. Sam turned a block away from the river and led them to an old pedestrian bridge that crossed over train tracks that had laid dormant for decades.

"Um, where are we?" Holley asked. "I have never been back here before, and no offense but it seems a little sketchy."

"I used to come here all the time when I was in college. Trust me it is worth it. You just have to be careful climbing the stairs," Sam answered, walking over to the bridge and looking up at it.

"Wait, you want to climb those and go up there? This bridge looks like it hasn't been used in fifty years," Holley replied.

"Yeah. I'm sure. Just follow my lead, okay?" Sam asked, releasing her hand and beginning to ascend the stairs.

Holley followed them as they stepped around broken boards and missing stairs. She tripped over the last step as she reached the top and fell into Sam's arms. They looked down at her and smiled, concern in their eyes. "Hey, you alright?" they asked.

"Nothing injured except for my pride," Holley answered, standing upright, but not letting go of Sam's arms. "Thanks for catching me."

"I couldn't let you fall and miss seeing this view," Sam said, leading her towards the center of the bridge and looking out over the river with the city in the background.

"Wow, it is beautiful," Holley said.

"Yes, it really is," Sam said, looking at Holley. "Just about the most beautiful thing I have ever seen."

Holley turned to face them and blushed as she realized that they were looking at her and not at the skyline. "Hey, you didn't bring me up here to look at me," she said, turning back to look at the city. "I bet it looks amazing once the city puts up Christmas lights."

"You would think about Christmas, wouldn't you?" Sam shook their head. "But you are right, I brought you here so you could see Richfield in a way I figured you had never seen it. Seeing you enjoy this view was even better than I had imagined. This is my favorite place in the city. It makes all of the noise and clutter of the city fade away. I love living in the city but I have never fully been comfortable around so many people. But here, it is just my city. There is no one else, no noise, no ugliness, just me and the city lights reflecting on the river," Sam explained, leaning on the railing and looking out across the water.

"And you chose to share it with me?" Holley asked. "Why? What makes me so special?"

"Faith was right as much as I hate to admit it. I haven't smiled like this in a very long time. When I'm with you, I feel happier than I can remember ever feeling. I wanted to try and bring you somewhere that would maybe give you some of the joy that you have given me," Sam answered.

Holley grabbed Sam's hand and pulled them to her, her free hand reaching behind their neck and pulling them down to meet her lips in a kiss. It began as a soft innocent kiss but as Sam wrapped their arms around her waist, her lips parted. With the cityscape behind them, they shared a passionate kiss, only separating when the hoot of an owl landing in the rafters caused them to jump. "Um, wow. I hate to end this, but perhaps it is time we head home. I could stay out all night with you, but we really do both need to rest," Holley said, stepping back from Sam.

Sam tried their best to fight a yawn as they opened their mouth to speak. "It looks like you are right. Thank you for letting me share this with you," Sam said, taking Holley's hand as they walked back to the stairs.

"Thank you for sharing it with me. I wasn't looking forward to spending my evening at a child's birthday party. I almost didn't go, but I'm so glad that I did. You managed to make tonight one that I will not forget for a long time," Holley said.

"That makes two of us," Sam said as they reached the main road and flagged down a cab.

After Sam had safely seen Holley home, they took the cab to Faith's apartment. There was something about this woman that was causing them to rethink their entire outlook on life and they needed their friend to help them make sense of things. Sam knocked multiple times before Faith finally answered the door.

Wrapping her silk robe tight around her body, Faith pulled the door open enough for Sam to enter. "You do remember that it is X's birthday, right?" she asked, looking back to the bedroom.

"I do. I'm sorry. I just. I needed to talk to you, and I didn't think I would be able to sleep until I did," Sam explained. "And you wouldn't have answered if you were still being intimate."

"Alright. I wouldn't have, but he just fell asleep, so you cut it a little close," Faith said walking to her kitchen and filling two glasses of water. "Here, sit. Tell me what couldn't wait until morning." Faith handed Sam a glass of water as she walked to her dining table and sat.

Sam sat down across from her and took a sip of water. "She is going to ruin me, Faith. I can't stop thinking about her and I hate not being around her. I can still feel her kiss on my lips, but it is fading and I need it again," Sam answered.

"So, you like her. Like you actually like her. There is nothing wrong with that, Sam. She seems like a lovely woman and she makes you smile. There is nothing wrong with dating her and seeing where it goes," Faith answered.

"But, I don't date people. It only ends in pain. You know I don't believe in love and romance," Sam argued.

"You also don't believe in Christmas and Santa Claus but you know for a fact that those are real now. Would it be that weird to think that you were wrong about love, too?" Faith asked.

"Yes. It would be. Because unlike Christmas, I have had actual experiences with how hateful and deceitful women can be. Love exists only to cause pain," Sam answered.

"My cynical friend," Faith said, shaking her head at Sam. "Love is beautiful. I know. I found it and I live with it every day. You can't be afraid to open your heart to the possibility."

"But what happens if I open my heart just to have it crushed?" Sam asked.

"You can't keep yourself from potential happiness because you are afraid of getting hurt. Live in the now. If she makes you happy, which I know she does, pursue this. You would be doing yourself a disservice if you didn't," Faith replied. "Now I'm going to go back to bed, cuddle into the love of my life, and go to sleep. I trust you can let yourself out."

Faith stood and walked to her bedroom without waiting for Sam to reply.

A disservice? What if continuing to see her opened them up to a hurt like they had never known? But what if she continued to fill their heart with happiness? Sam couldn't remember being this happy ever. Maybe Faith was right. Maybe they should give this a shot. Sam's phone alerted them to a text message as they exited Faith's apartment building.

Good night, Sam. Thank you for two of the best nights I have had in a very long time.

Sam smiled as they looked down at their phone. Holley's beautiful smile with her sparkling eyes and dimple popped into their head, as they typed out their reply.

Good night, beautiful. Your gorgeous smile and delicious kisses will be all I'm thinking about as I close my eyes tonight.

Sam was all smiles as they walked home. This woman was most likely going to break their heart and shatter any remaining hope that love might actually exist, but whatever happened between now and then, Sam was pretty sure it would be worth it. Tomorrow they would have to spend time with Candycane when they were done with work so that they could work on perfecting their list gathering skills, but they would have to find time to see Holley because that was all they wanted to do.

Over the next several weeks, when Sam wasn't working either for Mercer's or the metaphorical man in the red suit, they could be found with Holley. Lunch dates, nights in watching movies, evenings at the Spectrum, and many trips to Chas's Cafe had filled the remainder of September and Halloween was fast approaching.

Halloween was one of the only holidays that Sam tolerated. Pumpkin carving, hayrides, and apple cider had always made October one of Sam's favorite months. There was a great farm just thirty minutes outside of the city that not only had an incredible pumpkin patch but also a fantastic corn maze. Sam hadn't been there for years and was greatly looking forward to spending a Saturday with Holley in the crisp fall air.

Or at least they had been, until Faith reminded them that a pumpkin patch the Saturday before Halloween would be full of children. Sam had mostly avoided large crowds of kids since Xaveir's birthday. Candycane and Sam had been slowly going to places like the park, the mall, and the library so that Sam could be around kids and start to collect information without overwhelming them. Sam tried to argue that once they adjusted to the people at Shooter's they were fine, but Faith was quick to remind them that the majority of the children left an hour after they got there.

As a result, Sam's date day with Holley turned into a group trip so that Candycane and Faith would be there if Sam had a similar experience to the one they had when they entered Shooter's Shenanigans on X's birthday. The only positive about this was that Xavier had a car so they didn't need to rent one for the day. Sam kept reminding themselves that was a positive as they sat between Candycane and Holley in the backseat with their knees in their chest. Being that they were the tallest of the three in the back, it had made little sense for them to sit in the middle, but Candycane wanted to be able to look out the window and even though Holley was the shortest of the three, Sam couldn't make her squeeze into the middle, so chivalry had them sitting with their long legs pressed against the seat and their knees touching the back of the center console. Were it not for Holley's fingers intertwined with theirs, Sam would have spent the ride grumbling, but instead they were smiling as they listened to Holley and their friends laugh and chat as they rode to the farm.

Chapter 18

Much as they were enjoying the company of their friends, Sam was hopeful that at some point they would get some alone time with Holley. Over the past month, she had become incredibly important to them and they wanted a chance to tell her just how much she meant to them. The plan had been to do it on the hayride, but as they pulled into the full parking lot, Sam doubted that would provide the privacy they were seeking.

Instinctively, Sam squeezed Holley's hand as their heart began to race the moment that they were able to see the large quantities of children running around. This had perhaps been a mistake. It definitely wasn't going to be the romantic day they had planned. Instead Sam was pretty sure they were going to spend the whole day on the verge of a panic attack, looking for the exit.

"Are you alright, Sam?" Holley asked, giving their hand a reassuring squeeze as X parked.

"Um, I will be. I'm just going to need a minute. I don't do that well in crowds," Sam answered.

"They'll be fine. Why don't you and X go get us a wagon so we can all go pick out pumpkins?" Faith suggested. "We'll be right there."

Holley kissed Sam's cheek before stepping out of the car and following Xavier. Faith hopped into the back seat, taking Holley's spot and grabbing Sam's hand. "Alright, Sam. When we leave this car, I want you to focus on the ground. Candycane and I can guide you through the entrance and past the bounce houses and slides," Faith explained.

"Normally I would say that is a bad idea because of all the names that are going to be missed, but if it can get us in without Sam hyperventilating, I'm all for it," Candycane agreed.

"Look, we need the data. Maybe just having the two of you with me when we walk through will be enough. If you can both just talk to me like you did at the mall, I will try to record what I can," Sam answered. "Right now I pretty much just want to get out of the car and make sure I can stand."

"Oh yeah, right. Sorry about that. We weren't all gifted with such long legs," Faith said, sliding out of the car so that Sam could follow.

Sam stretched as they stepped out of the car. "Some of us were not meant to ride in the back seat of a hatchback, but I do appreciate X offering to drive," Sam said, looking towards the farm. "I guess we should do this. I don't want Holley thinking I'm having an anxiety attack or anything."

"It was really very cute how concerned she looked when she walked away," Faith said. "You two seem to be getting pretty serious."

"We're just having a good time. I don't know how serious it is yet, but I like her. I really do and I don't want to scare her off today," Sam said as they started walking.

MAKING THE LIST

"Hey. You got this and we are here for you to help you through it," Candycane said reassuringly as she threw an arm around Sam's shoulders.

"Yeah. We will get through this together," Faith said, throwing her arm over Sam's other shoulder as the three of them walked through the gate.

The farm was incredibly crowded and there were children of all ages running from the slides and inflatable castles that surrounded the entrance. Sam could feel their breathing speed up as names began to flood their brain. "If so many of these children are naughty, how is there even a need for Santa Claus anymore?" Sam asked, scanning the crowd.

"Most children don't stay on the naughty list. They just have bad days, but eventually they end up back on the nice list. But, sadly, some children are just mean," Candycane answered, watching a child shove other children so that they could get to the front of the line for the tallest slide.

"Yeah. Kids are awful," Sam said, shaking their head. "I'm probably the worst Christmas ever."

"No. You might not be on board with everything Christmas has to offer, but you understand your duty and you are trying your best. You are going to be a great Christmas. I know it," Candycane said as they exited the play area and headed for the pumpkin patch.

"Hey, we got two wagons because Holley said she needs to get a bunch for her shop," Xavier explained when they met up.

"I just want to have a few for the front of the store for trick or treating," Holley said.

"That is a great idea. Why don't you and Sam look for those and the rest of us can go pick out pumpkins over here," Faith offered, winking at Sam.

"Thanks Faith. That sounds like a great idea," Sam replied, taking the wagon's handle and pulling it toward the back of the patch where there were significantly less people.

"So, if I get four of these for the front of the shop, you are going to help me carve them right? Because you are the one who said I needed to embrace the other holidays," Holley asked.

"Yeah. Totally. I love carving pumpkins and the more we have the more seeds we get. I roast a mean pumpkin seed," Sam replied.

"I look forward to trying them," Holley said, reaching out and grabbing their hand. "Any chance you could come over tonight so we can work on them?"

"Yeah. I should be able to. I just have to make sure it is alright with Faith and CC, but they already crashed our date, so I think they will be okay," Sam laughed.

Pawning Candycane off on Faith for pumpkin carving had not been as easy as Sam had hoped, but after they promised that they would attend Faith's Halloween party, she had conceded. When Xavier dropped them off at Holley's apartment, Faith hopped out of the car and gave Holley a hug. "Thanks for letting us join you today. It was so much fun. I hope you will be joining Sam at my party next week," Faith said, sticking her tongue out at Sam before releasing Holley and getting back in the car.

"A party?" Holley asked as the car drove away.

Sam looked over the box of pumpkins they were carrying and sighed. "Faith throws a costume party every year. She has been bugging me to go. But we really don't have to if you don't want to," Sam answered.

"No. That would be fun. As long as you want me there with you," Holley said as they walked into her apartment.

"Of course I want you there," Sam said, putting the box of pumpkins on her kitchen table. "Can I talk to you before we start with the pumpkins?"

"Oh boy. This sounds ominous," Holley said, slumping down onto her couch.

"What? I didn't mean for it to come out that way. I'm sorry," Sam said, sitting next to her and reaching for one of her hands. "Holley, this past month has been incredible. I never thought I would find anyone that I wanted to spend time with like I do with you. When we are together, nothing else matters. All of the stresses of the outside world just melt away. I told you that I hadn't been on a date in a long time when we started talking. A long time didn't really do the amount of time justice. Before we went out, it had been almost five years since my last date. Something about you made me change my outlook on dating, and it is starting to make me change my opinion on relationships. Holley, I haven't asked anybody this in a very very long time, but I don't want to see anybody else. I don't want to think about you seeing anyone else and I don't want to lose what we have because I'm afraid." Sam paused and reached for Holley's other hand, swallowing hard as they looked her in the eyes. "Will you be my girlfriend?" Sam asked, looking away almost as soon as the words had left their mouth.

"Yes. Yes. Of course I will be your girlfriend. I don't want to date anyone else, either. Being with you this past month has been nothing short of amazing and I can't wait to see what the future holds," Holley answered, pulling on Sam's hands and bringing their gaze back to her. Once they were looking at her again, she leaned forward and kissed them. "Now I believe we have pumpkins to carve and Halloween costumes to discuss," Holley said as she pulled away from them.

After a debate that Sam had lost, they helped Holley carve four pumpkins with a Christmas twist. There was a skull wearing a santa hat, a ghost that said ho ho ho instead of boo, one that said Merry Halloween, and a last one that featured a cat with reindeer antlers. "These jack-o-lanterns go against everything that carving a jack-o-lantern is for," Sam grumbled as they stood back and looked at them.

"They are perfect!" Holley beamed as she hugged them. "Thank you for helping me. I know we have a party, but do you think you will be free to hand out candy with me?"

"CC will probably want to come, too. Is that alright?" Sam asked. "We don't get a lot of kids in our apartment and she loves seeing the kids in their costumes."

"All the help we can get. From what I have been told it is a pretty big event. Most of the businesses hand out coupons and flyers for sales which helps bring people in. I printed off my calendar of holiday activities that I'm planning on hosting at the store to hand out with the candy," Holley answered.

"Holiday activities?" Sam asked.

"Yeah. Making ornaments and Christmas cards for example," Holley answered.

"If you aren't careful, CC is going to live at your store," Sam laughed.

"If it means you will be there, I don't mind at all. I mean she is welcome without you, but I know you don't like Christmas and I just think that if you spent it with someone who could show you just how magical it can be that you might change your mind," Holley replied. "Please, give me a chance to warm your cold grinchy heart."

"Fine. Show me what Christmas is about, but please can we get through Halloween first?" Sam asked, pulling a tray of freshly roasted pumpkin seeds from the oven.

"Deal. Now, about Halloween costumes," Holley smiled at them, walking over to Sam and kissing them. "I have an idea and it is something I really want to do for the shop, but it could carry over and we wouldn't need to get new costumes," she said, looking up at them and batting her lashes.

"Why do I feel like I'm not going to like where this is going?" Sam grumbled, wrapping an arm around her waist and pulling her to them. "What do you say we table this discussion for the night and focus on more enjoyable activities?" Sam leaned down and met her lips in a heated kiss. All thoughts of Halloween and costumes drifted away as Holley led Sam back to her bedroom.

Chapter 19

By the time Halloween rolled around, Sam was spending almost every night with Holley. They knew once November hit they would have to designate time to spend with Candycane, who in the week since they had asked Holley to be their girlfriend, they had barely seen, but tonight she would be spending the entire evening with them. Sam glanced at their watch, four thirty. Sam promised Holley that they would meet her at her shop at five to get ready for the trick or treaters. It would take them at least fifteen minutes to get to Old Town. They powered down their computer and texted Candycane. She was meeting them out front and knowing her, she was already there.

The quick reply confirmed what Sam had feared and they quickly headed to the elevator to meet her. When Sam stepped outside, they saw Candycane leaning on a light pole dressed in the same red and green elven outfit that she had been wearing when they met. "I told you that you would have time to change at the shop," Sam said, flagging a cab so that they could quickly get off of the street.

"I haven't been able to wear my clothes since I have been back here. I jumped at the opportunity," Candycane answered.

"Look in December, people won't think that is so weird. But it is Halloween, almost two full months until Christmas. People don't expect to see a Christmas elf walking around the city," Sam said. "I don't want people being unkind to you."

"Awww. You care. Thanks, Sam. You also don't want to be embarrassed walking around talking to an elf," Candycane said, laughing.

"What is so funny?" Sam asked.

"Holley still hasn't told you what your costume is, has she?" she asked.

"No. Why?" they questioned.

"Oh. No reason. I just think that you are gonna be less than pleased," Candycane replied.

Pleased was definitely something that Sam was not as they stepped out of the bathroom in Holley's store. Holley and Candycane couldn't help themselves from laughing at the frown on Sam's face. "You are the grumpiest Santa Claus I have ever seen," Holley said.

Sam was dressed in a full Santa suit complete with padding for the belly and a white beard and was standing with their arms folded, scowling. "When you said you had costumes that were Christmas themed, I didn't think you meant Santa Claus. Of all the things," Sam replied.

"You look adorable, and it will make sense once I put mine on. You will see," Holley kissed them on the cheek as she walked by on her way to the bathroom. When she reappeared she was wearing a red dress with a white apron and a red bonnet above a white wig. "Every Santa needs a Mrs. Claus," she said, smiling at Sam.

"You two are the cutest!" Candycane squealed with excitement.

"Mrs. Claus, you owe me," Sam said with a huff. "Also, you still look beautiful. I look ridiculous."

"I think you look great. And I think the kids are going to love getting candy from Santa," Holley replied.

"The kids are not what I'm worried about. Faith is never going to let me hear the end of this," Sam mumbled as they followed Candycane and Holley to the front of the store.

The kids should have been what Sam was worried about. Holley was right, even on Halloween, children's faces lit up when they saw Santa Claus. Sam spent the night with a long line of children waiting to talk to them, not just to say trick or treat but to tell them how good they had been all year and what they wanted for Christmas. Given that Sam was able to see that at least a third of the children they saw that night were most definitely not currently on the nice list, it was difficult to smile at all of them as they handed out candy.

The pounding headache they were fighting was also making it hard to focus and keep a smile on their face. Thankfully Candycane had remembered to bring some of her magical tea with her and kept offering it to Sam whenever she could tell things were getting to be too much. Sam was incredibly relieved when they ran out of candy and the last of the children wandered away. "Wow, that was much busier than I'd anticipated," Sam said, standing and stretching. "You ready for a party? I know I could use a drink."

"Somehow I have a feeling that you are going to end up being on the naughty list, Mr. Claus," Holley smirked at them as she walked towards the door. "I need to close everything up. You two are welcome to hang out inside while I do," she said, entering the shop.

"This place is AMAZING. How have I not been here before?" Candycane asked, walking the aisles and looking at the decorated trees.

"I told you she would never wanna leave," Sam called to Holley as they walked around the shop with Candycane.

"CC, you are welcome, anytime. I could use some help around here, if you are looking for extra work. I know you already work with Sam, but if you wanted some extra money for the holidays," Holley offered, walking over and joining them.

"Seriously? I don't know if I could find time, but I would love to help you here," Candycane answered, a huge smile on her face.

"Awesome. Just let me know. I think I'm all set if we're ready to go," Holley said, grabbing Sam's hand and frowning at the beard that was in it.

"My face got hot. You do realize that it is still in the seventies out there and you have me in this fake fur suit with this thick beard. I need a cold drink so badly right now," Sam said, moving the beard to their other hand so that they could hold hers.

"Lucky for you, you are even more adorable without the beard," Holley leaned up and gave them a quick kiss on the lips. "But the beard goes back on when we get to the party. Faith deserves the full effect."

As Sam and Holley entered Faith's apartment, Sam instantly regretted their costume. Faith ran towards them, squealing with excitement. "I never thought I would see the day," she laughed. "Sam Christmas in a Santa suit. Holley, I don't know what you did to them, but don't stop."

"We were marketing at her store, Faith. Don't get too excited," Sam answered.

"Too late. Already there." Faith answered. "And I have a little present for you, Santa. Follow me."

Sam rolled their eyes but followed Faith to the kitchen where she produced a bottle of peppermint schnapps and a pair of shot glasses.

"Thanks, Faith. In all the years that we have hung out, I don't think you have ever gotten me schnapps for a party."

"Yeah, well you know the look you get when you buy that crap in October?" Faith laughed. "I wasn't really sure what CC would drink, but I figured that she might have tastes similar to yours."

"Funny, Faith. Really funny. I don't drink like an elf," Sam said through gritted teeth. "You gonna take one of these with me?" Sam opened the bottle and filled both glasses.

"Oh why not? Here's to my good friend, Santa," Faith said, lifting her glass and throwing it back.

"You are enjoying this far too much," Sam said as they lowered their glass. "You get ciders? Holley will want one."

"I didn't forget your girlfriend," Faith smiled. "I really like saying that." Faith handed a cider to Sam.

"I'll take one of those, too." Sam reached for another one. "And, I'm kinda liking saying it, too, but don't let it go to your head," they said.

"Are you kidding? I'm taking complete credit for your new outlook on love and Christmas. That birthday toast had some serious power in it," Faith laughed.

"Whatever you did to get this one to give dating a chance, I thank you, Faith," Holley said as she joined them. "As for the Christmas thing, I think they have a long way to go, but I intend to help them find the holiday spirit."

Sam opened their cider and took a large gulp. "The only spirits I want to talk about right now contain alcohol. No more talk of Christmas. It's October," Sam declared. "Happy Halloween!" Sam raised their bottle for a toast.

"Happy Halloween, Santa. Tomorrow your season begins," Holley said, clinking her bottle with theirs.

Chapter 20

Holley had been right when she said that Santa's season was upon them. Sam spent the morning of November first nursing a hangover while they sat in a theater listening to Mercers' executives excitedly talk about new products and goals for the holiday season. Each employee was handed a Mercers' gift bag featuring a smiling Santa Claus standing in front of a Mercer's department store when they entered and the C.E.O. was currently standing center stage going over the contents of the bag. Sam sighed as they watched the people around them put on the red and green elf hats that featured elf ears on the side and the Mercers' logo on the front. Along with the hat, each of them had also been gifted a green t-shirt with red writing on it that said "Santa Shops at Mercers." Sam rubbed their pounding temple as they watched people pull the t-shirts over their existing clothes.

Watching so many naughty people get excited about cheesy corporate advertising disguised as festive holiday clothing was only adding to the nausea Sam was fighting. They had lost track of how many shots they had done the night before as they had tried to keep up with Candycane, who much to their annoyance had been wide awake, looking no worse for the wear this morning. Sam pulled out their phone and sent a quick text to Holley to check on her. She was still sleeping when Sam left for work so they had left her to rest in their bed. They smiled as she sent a quick response complaining about how happy Sam's roommate was in the morning.

"Hey Christmas, this stuff should be right up your alley, right?" the accountant sitting to Sam's right, joked, reading Sam's smile as an invitation to start a conversation.

"Because my last name is Christmas. Wow, I've never heard that one before, Lawrence." Sam answered, rolling their eyes before returning their attention to their phone and sending Holley another message. They wanted to make sure she was feeling better than they were and needed to confirm that they were meeting her with Candycane after work to help her decorate the store. Their phone vibrated shortly after with a message from Holley.

CC is already at work with me as she was much more alert than I was this morning and she had the day off. I can't wait to see you, cutie. Sorry you are feeling so bad. When you get here you can tell me where it hurts and I will kiss it and make it better.

She was quite possibly the cutest person in all of existence. Sam could almost feel their headache start to lessen as they thought of Holley, her kind eyes, soft touch, and sweet kisses. They took a moment to send a reply before trying to focus on the remainder of their meeting.

Your kisses make everything better.

After putting their phone away, Sam couldn't focus on the presentations about new toys and the gifts of the season. Their thoughts constantly returned to Holley. Sam had been positive that they hated the idea of relationships, but they were very much enjoying having a girlfriend. How someone who loved Christmas as much as Holley did could bring them so much happiness they weren't sure, but their heart was more full than it had ever been..

The meeting seemed to last forever and by the time it was over Sam had more than their fill of Christmas for one day. The last thing they wanted to do was decorate a store for the holidays, but they promised Holley they would help her. You can do this for her, they told themselves as they stepped out of the cab in front of the Christmas Claus-it.

"Hey. Is that Santa Claus I see?" Holley asked, laughing as she walked over to Sam and pulled them into a quick embrace, giving them a kiss on the cheek.

"I'm afraid Santa has returned to the North Pole or maybe he is shopping at Mercers," Sam sighed, placing their gift bag on the counter.

"Santa would never shop at Mercers," Holley said, frowning at Sam.

"He would. I have a shirt to prove it. Look," Sam replied, gesturing to their bag.

Holley pulled the shirt, hat, and Mercers' catalog from the bag. She groaned as she opened the shirt. "No wonder you hate Christmas. This is not what the holiday is about," Holley said, returning the items to the bag and placing it on the floor behind the counter.

"I spent the entire day watching presentations that tell a different story. Christmas is about commercialism. Mercers will make over half of their annual income between now and New Years," Sam answered.

"But Christmas is about spending time with the people who matter the most to us. It is about making memories that will last a lifetime and it is about giving. Not just giving presents that you buy at the store, but handmade gifts, food, and your time, volunteering to help those less fortunate than you," Holley countered.

"Your Christmas sounds really nice and all, but I don't think that version still exists," Sam said.

"Of course it does," Candycane said, as she walked up behind them. "You just haven't had the chance to see it. Working for Mercers has made you see a side of Christmas driven by money and greed, but that is the exact opposite of what the holiday is supposed to be."

"I get what you are trying to say, both of you, but Holley, you own a Christmas store. Are you not also making money off of the holiday?" Sam asked.

"I know you have been in here a few times, but I don't think you have ever really looked around. The items here are hand made, many of them by me, or they are second-hand items and factory rejects from big box stores that I try and salvage so that they don't just end up being added to the overflowing landfills. And yes, I charge for them, but I also have free family activities from now until Christmas, because the real magic of the holiday is in the memories not in the presents," Holley answered.

"I didn't mean anything by that. I don't think you are anything like the evil empire I work for. I just have a hard time seeing the idealized version of this season that you see," Sam said.

"Well, I guess then it is time I started to show you," Holley said. "CC and I have already put up the new displays and posted the calendar of events, so we could call it a night, but I would like to show you some of what I do."

Holley asked CC to watch the front of the store and let her know if she was needed before grabbing Sam's hand and leading them to the shop's backroom. The walls were lined with boxes of merchandise that had the words factory defect in red stamped on them. Sam released Holley's hand and walked to one of the boxes. Opening it, they grabbed an ornament from the box to examine. They held in their hands a beautifully painted village scene with "Tidings of Comfort and Joey" written in script across it. Sam laughed as they read it. "I'm sorry. Comfort and Joey? That's a joke right? Or are there ornaments with other names?" they asked.

"It's an unfortunate misprint and unless you have a Joey in your life it makes the ornament rather useless. I'm not entirely sure how I'm going to upcycle those yet. But I have an easier task planned for the night," Holley answered, walking over to the box that sat on her desk. She opened it to reveal a box of frames shaped like Christmas trees with chipped paint and broken stars on top of them. Holley removed one of the frames and used a blade to pop the rest of the paint out of the frame. "The first part of this project isn't that much fun, but we need to have a blank canvas. It sounds like you had a long day. Why don't you hang out back here and work on this while I close up the shop? Then we can do the fun part."

Holley pulled Sam to them and kissed them before walking out of the room and returning to the front of the store. Sam dumped the frames onto the table before sitting down in front of it. This wasn't Sam's idea of a good time, but they promised Holley that they would keep an open mind. They picked up one of the frames and turned it over in their hand, laughing as they read the label on the back: "Made Exclusively for Mercers." Perhaps Sam would get some enjoyment out of destroying these frames afterall.

An hour later, Holley and Candycane joined Sam in the back, carrying several open rolls of wrapping paper. "How's it going?" Holley asked, putting down the paper and picking up one of the frames.

"I think I'm just about done. I'm curious to see where this is going, but can we maybe order a pizza or something? I'm starving," Sam said, picking up their phone.

"Actually Faith and X are on their way with chinese food," Holley answered. "She texted me and asked if we wanted to join them for dinner. When I declined and told her what we were doing, she asked if they could join."

"That sounds like Faith. What exactly are we doing?" Sam asked.

"We're going to replace the paint with various wrapping papers before sealing them with resin. And we're going to use gift bows in place of the stars. My hope is that these horribly made, cheesy frames will get a new life as a cute, unique, hand-crafted item," Holley answered. "I'm either going to sell them or use them for photos with Santa Claus, which will be happening the second weekend in December."

"Anything would be an improvement on what these looked like before," Sam said. "This looks like it could be fun, though. Show me how we do this."

It was after eleven when they finished pouring the resin in the last of the frames. Faith and Xavier had left an hour earlier, taking Candycane with them. Sam expected that they would follow but they were enjoying going through Holley's stash of wrapping paper scraps to pick out the ones that would be best suited for making trees. Holley looked up from the frames as she finished preparing the last of them and smiled at Sam.

"I would have never imagined that you would take such a serious interest in this," Holley said, gesturing to the table.

"I just wanted to make sure that they looked nice, so you could sell them. And I have never seen so many designs for Christmas paper. I kind of thought they all featured Santa Claus," Sam said. "And how was I supposed to ignore Christmas robots or dinosaurs with scarves on? Where do you even find these? And a night sky with constellations made of snowflakes? Come on. I had to use that one."

"I'm glad you like my paper selection. Those are going to make for some interesting trees, but they are definitely fun." Holley shook her head and laughed. "Here I pictured you as the type to wrap gifts in paper that said bah humbug," she teased.

"Gifts? Try gift cards. You don't have to wrap those," Sam replied.

"Gift cards are so impersonal. You don't really get everyone gift cards, do you?" Holley asked.

"What's wrong with letting people pick out their own presents? I'd rather get something I want or need." Sam answered.

"That so isn't the point," Holley huffed. "You're supposed to buy gifts that make you think of the person."

"I normally avoid shopping this time of the year. Which makes gift cards the easy way to get something for the few people I actually care enough about to buy a present," Sam said.

"You don't have to buy the gift. You can always make one. Like these," Holley replied, pointing to the frames.

Sam yawned as they opened their mouth to argue. "Alright, we can discuss this later. Tonight was more fun than I had expected. I'll give you that. It's been a rough few days and if I actually expect to be able to work tomorrow, I need to sleep." Sam said.

"It's late. My place is closer than yours. Why don't you just crash with me tonight?" Holley asked.

"Sounds good. You know I won't pass up a chance to curl up with you. I have plans with CC tomorrow night, so I probably won't see you," Sam replied. "I sure don't sleep much when I'm around you." Sam laughed.

"I never said anything to suggest that we would do anything else. I, too, haven't slept for what feels like weeks," Holley replied. "Let's get out of here and try to get some sleep."

Chapter 21

Despite both of them agreeing that they were going to Holley's to sleep, they were awake until close to three in the morning, talking and exchanging passionate kisses. Sam cursed their alarm clock as it blared just three and half hours after they had fallen asleep. They looked down at Holley apologetically as they kissed the top of her head and slid out from underneath her. Sam never missed work, but as they got dressed in the dark in Holley's bedroom, they were very tempted to call in sick. But they were already taking a half day so that they could meet Candycane to work on the list.

"Do you have to leave? It is so early," Holley grumbled as she opened her eyes.

"Unfortunately I do. Go back to sleep. At least one of us should get some rest," Sam said, walking over to her and giving her a quick kiss. "Last night was better than I had expected."

"You weren't that bad yourself," Holley replied with a smirk.

Color rushed into Sam's cheeks and they found themselves being glad that it was so dark. "I was talking about making frames with you.

I do hope that you will send me a few photos of them once you add the bows today."

"Of course, I will. And yeah, I'm really glad that you helped me yesterday. If you are free on Friday night, I'd really like to show you one of my favorite holiday traditions," Holley said.

"Sounds like a date," Sam replied, leaning in for one more kiss before leaving for work.

Sam was grateful for a short work day as exhaustion was making it hard to focus. By the time they walked out the front doors of the Mercers' building, they were struggling to keep their eyes open. Sam let out a loud exasperated sigh as Candycane came running towards them full of energy. "You wouldn't happen to have any of that energy bottled up in some sort of magic potion would you?" Sam asked.

"You'd have energy, too, if you were sleeping at night," Candycane replied. "Plus I told you that elves don't require as much sleep as humans."

"Can we maybe keep the elf talk to a whisper?" Sam said, glancing around the busy street. "Your kind aren't really common around here."

"Right. Sorry. The best I can do is buy you coffee," Candycane answered, shrugging her shoulders. "I have to ask you something anyhow, so we can stop at a cafe before going to our destination."

"Yeah, where are we going? You never told me," Sam said.

"That's a surprise. First we should caffeinate," Candycane answered, walking towards the coffee shop on the corner.

With a peppermint latte in hand, Sam sat, staring at Candycane. "Are you going to ask me a question or just sit there and fidget? You haven't even touched your hot chocolate," Sam asked.

"Right. Um, sorry. I just don't know how to say it," Candycane answered.

"Just say it. You had no problems talking to me that first night when you showed up at my door. I can't imagine anything that you could say that would sound more preposterous than what you told me then," Sam said.

"I wanna go home, just for a night or maybe a day. I miss my home and," Candycane was cut off as Sam interrupted her.

"Rudolf, you miss Rudolf," Sam said, smiling. "I knew it."

"Tomorrow night he is doing test runs with Blizzard's crew, and before I got my assignment he asked me to help him," Candycane replied. "I don't want to let him or the reindeer down."

"Of course. It's just about returning as a sense of duty. It has nothing to do with you being sweet on a certain reindeer handler," Sam laughed.

"Look, can I go or not?" Candycane asked, wrinkling her face in frustration.

"I'm spending tomorrow night with Holley so I won't be home anyway, if you are trying to go then," Sam answered.

"Yeah. Tomorrow morning actually if you are okay with it," Candycane said. "But if tonight is too rough and you need me to stay, I will stay."

"I don't want to keep you from your life and your happiness. So, you should go," Sam replied. "And why would tonight be an issue? You are making me nervous."

"You'll see. Let's go. I'm hoping to get you acclimated before it gets crowded," Candycane said, standing.

Sam stood and followed Candycane, feeling slightly more awake and incredibly anxious. Sam couldn't figure where they could be going as it was barely November. It had to be too early for most Christmas activities, right? Sam's phone alerted them of a message as they watched Candycane flag down a cab.

Focused on the images of wrapping paper Christmas tree frames, they didn't hear the given destination as they climbed into the backseat of the car. Sam spent the car ride texting with Holley, completely ignoring the outside world. When the cab came to a stop, and they stepped out, Sam's stomach turned into a knot and they felt their airways begin to close. Candycane couldn't be serious. What made them think that a theme park was a good idea? Sam crouched down and put their head in their hands as they tried to calm themselves.

"Sam, are you alright? I know this is scary, but we have to get past this. It will be Thanksgiving soon and then we will have to spend lots of time at crowded events full of children," Candycane said, crouching down to join them.

"Have you ever been to Coaster World? It brings out the worst in people. I'm not sure we will get any usable research here," Sam said, looking up and towards the entrance.

"From what I have learned about amusement parks, that sounds par for the course. But any research is good research and we have to practice with large groups of people. Come on, Sam," Candycane offered her hand to them to help them stand as she rose to her feet.

Sam stood and followed her into the park. Coaster World was a small amusement park that was open year round that featured seven roller coasters. The coasters were all grouped close to each other in Thrill Seekers Valley. Other areas of the park included Little Land, a section of rides for children, and Gamers Canyon which featured carnival games and an arcade. The park had once been named Cowboy World, which was why it was still sectioned off in western themed areas.

"I hope you don't expect me to ride on any of those death traps," Sam said, looking at the brightly colored metal frames that towered over the park. "Someone died on the Heist, that one, the big red one, last year." Sam pointed out the roller coaster. "This park hasn't had a new ride in fifteen years. I wouldn't trust any of those."

"Lucky for you, all we have to do is walk around and observe people. And maybe eat some food. I saw a sign for funnel cake and I'm not leaving here until I've had some," Candycane answered.

"Fine. Let's get you a cake and me a drink and find a good place to sit and watch these unfortunate souls who consider this their idea of fun," Sam grumbled.

With snacks in hand, they wandered into Thrill Seekers Village and sat on a bench that sat between the park's two largest rides. It was incredibly loud, but the noise helped to drown out the one in Sam's head as they were processing significantly more names than they had previously. It also made it so that Candycane and Sam could talk freely as passers by would not be able to hear them.

Aside from there being a lot more nice people there than Sam would have bet on, the first hour was very uneventful. "I need another drink," Sam said, standing. "You want any ... What? What does that mean?" Sam stopped mid question as they focused on a young boy of about ten or eleven who had a black horizontal line above his head instead of text.

"What is it Sam?" Candycane asked.

"That kid. He isn't naughty or nice and he isn't a Christmas because I met the Santas and they didn't have lines above their heads. What does that mean?" Sam questioned, sitting back down.

"I do believe that is what you would look like if you were not a Christmas, Sam. That is the mark of a non-believer," Candycane replied.

"What? I might have been before, but I've been to the North Pole. I've seen reindeer fly. I know Santa is real. I wouldn't call myself a non-believer," Sam countered.

"There is a difference between knowing something exists and believing in it. Many adults no longer believe in Santa Claus as the Santas do not deliver gifts to anyone but children, but most of them believed at one time and still believe in the magic of Christmas," Candycane explained. "That is something that you and that child do not believe in."

"So, he just doesn't get gifts, then?" Sam asked.

"There is a special list for the non-believers, especially if they are children. The Keeper of the List will monitor him closely," Candycane answered.

When they left two hours later, Sam was still asking Candycane questions regarding the handling of those who didn't believe. "People can change. Just as they can go from naughty to nice and back. And not believing in the nonsense of a commercial holiday doesn't make someone a bad person. That just seems really unfair. What if he never bought into the whole Christmas thing? Does that mean he never received a gift from Santa? Wouldn't the Santas want to bring him something to try and change his belief? Why shun the non-believers?" Sam asked, sitting in the cab on the way home.

"A non-believer has to make that change on their own. It can't be forced. You should know that better than anyone with as much as Faith has tried to make you celebrate Christmas," Candycane answered. "Don't worry. There are instances where those who don't believe have a change of heart."

Chapter 22

A change of heart? That phrase along with the experience from the park had kept Sam up most of the night. Everything about the non-believers being shunned had not sat well with them. If anyone had tried to show Sam the magic of Christmas when they were young, they might not have grown up to loathe the holiday the way that they did. There was definitely something fundamentally wrong with this system. As a new Christmas that had reluctantly accepted their duties, Sam doubted anyone would listen if they complained, but they were making a note to discuss it with Wyatt or Peter if they ever had the chance to return to the North Pole.

It was eerily quiet in Sam's apartment this morning with Candycane leaving last night to return home and prepare for her date with Rudolf. Sam was actually growing accustomed to her large breakfasts in the morning and sighed as they settled for a bowl of cereal, the kind with sugar coated flakes and marshmallows, and a coffee. Their phone blared to life as a text message came in, making Sam smile as they read it.

Good morning, cutie. I missed you last night. Hope you had fun with CC and hope you are ready to experience the real meaning of Christmas tonight.

What could Holley possibly mean by that? Sam was pretty sure that Candycane and the Christmas Council had already explained all of that to them and there was no way that was what Holley was planning on showing them. Whatever Holley had in mind would have to wait until after work, which was going to make for an incredibly long day.

Sam expected a tough work day with too much on their mind to concentrate. They didn't expect to walk into an emergency meeting brought on by the financial projections they made that morning. As they put together their numbers to share with the board, Sam wished they weren't so thorough. Based on recent retail trends and the shift in consumers' desires to purchase handmade items from small businesses, Sam's math was forecasting returns well under the numbers that Mercers was hoping to hit.

Sam had little to do with how Mercers would attempt to overcome and change this. They simply had the unfortunate job of being the one to present it. As tempers began to flare and panic started to set in on the faces surrounding them, Sam felt a pang of guilt. It was their job to discover things like this but they never felt good about it. Mercers had overcome challenges like this in the past and it wasn't the first time that Sam had questioned their Christmas projections. This was what Sam had grown accustomed to for the holidays over the last several years. Christmas, at the core, was about making money. It was going to take something pretty incredible to make them think differently.

Their destination with Holley was only a few blocks from the Mercers building so she had suggested meeting them there. Sam was called into their boss's office just as they were packing up their desk to leave. They sent Holley a quick text to let her know they would be a few minutes late before meeting with their boss. Sam had been waiting for this all day. If Sam's findings kept Mercers from losing money this holiday season, there would be a possible promotion in their future. They had heard that before, so Sam didn't expect anything to come of it. They were still sitting at the same desk in the same cubicle that they had started at almost four years ago. It was nice to hear that their boss had been impressed with their findings, but as he continued to drone on about the important work they were doing, Sam found themselves fidgeting and watching the clock.

When their boss paused, waiting on input from Sam, they lied and said they had nothing new to offer on the topic and asked if they were done. Their boss frowned slightly, but smiled when Sam explained that they were meeting someone and they were already late. He thanked Sam once more before dismissing them. Sam practically ran to the elevator for fear that he would think of something else to say.

Holley was sitting in the lobby, flipping through the Mercers' Christmas catalog. She looked up at the sound of the elevator, a huge smile forming on her face as she met Sam's gaze. "Hey, I'm really really sorry," Sam apologized. "I was stuck talking to my boss. It has been a pretty long day. We have time for dinner before we go, right? I sort of worked through lunch."

"There will be food there, but we can grab a snack on the way. We just need to hurry. They will be starting soon," Holley said, standing and walking to Sam. She leaned in for a quick kiss as she reached them. "I saw a hot dog stand on the way. My treat. Can't have you wasting away on me." Holley laughed as she poked them in the side. "With all the sugar you consume, I don't understand how you are so skinny."

"Living on stress and caffeine will do that to you," Sam answered with a shrug.

"Maybe I need to try your diet," Holley laughed.

"Why would you think that? You are perfect just the way you are," Sam said, putting an arm around her waist and pulling her to them. "Come on. I believe you wanted to show me the meaning of Christmas." They exited the building and followed Holley's lead as she turned and they headed east.

A short walk with a detour for hot dogs brought them to the Richfield Community Center. Sam had lived in the city for a little over six years and had never once visited the center. A poster on the door advertised an event for "Holiday Heroes." There was a picture of a collection box full of wrapped presents on the flyer. In bold text at the bottom it read, "Get your donation box today!"

"Holiday Heroes?" Sam asked as Holley opened the door.

"Yes. Tonight you're going to become a hero," Holley replied.

"But I left my cape at home," Sam joked, as Holley took their hand and led them to a large room full of people.

Sam gasped as they looked around the room. Lucky for them the room was decorated with images of children and families receiving gifts from heroes. The images had captured pure joy and gratitude on the faces of the people and it was very moving. That, however, was not what caused Sam's reaction.

Sam found themselves surrounded by nice people. There wasn't a naughty person to be found. Was that even possible? Sam didn't think there was that much good in the city or the world for that matter.

"It really is amazing, isn't it?" Holley whispered, squeezing their hand.

"Yeah. Amazing," Sam agreed, following Holley to a pair of empty seats.

As Sam listened to the presentation about the purpose of Holiday Heroes and the many ways that people could help, they felt a warmth inside their chest. If Sam's mom had given their information to a group like this when they were young, they might have experienced the wonder of a Christmas morning. What these people were providing for families was so much more than material items. Holley said that Christmas was about the kindness of strangers and giving but Sam didn't understand that until this moment.

"I want to thank each of you for coming out tonight. For us to have another successful season, the real work begins now. Boxes are in the foyer for those of you interested in taking those and setting them up. If you are staying to make ornaments, tables are set up in the kitchen," the man presenting said, returning the microphone to the stand.

"That is what we are doing," Holley explained. "Making the ornaments for the hero trees. I'm putting one up in the store and taking a box as well." Holley's face lit up, her dimple on full display, as she jumped from her seat and grabbed Sam's arm.

"How could I say no to that kind of excitement? Bring on the ornaments," Sam said, standing and following Holley to the kitchen.

Ornament making consisted of gluing information regarding the needs of a family onto a fun holiday shaped piece of paper. Ornament shapes included snowmen, stockings, and Christmas trees. The completed ornaments were bundled in stacks of twenty-five and placed in envelopes. Those envelopes were available for people to take so they could place the ornaments on trees for people to take.

Sam had seen hero trees before but they had never paid attention to them. The idea of buying presents for a stranger when they didn't even want to buy presents for their friends seemed strange. Now, though, after spending an hour reading the lists they were putting on the ornaments, Sam wanted to be a hero for several families. As they thought about that an idea came to them.

"Holley, if someone wanted more information on this so they could present it to someone, who would they talk to?" Sam asked.

"I suppose it would be Mr. Charles," Holley answered, pointing to the man who had given the presentation. "Why?"

"I might have a way to really help out and fix things at work," Sam answered. "I'm not sure, but I need to speak with him. I'll be right back." Sam stood and started to walk away. They had only taken a few steps, when they paused and turned back to the table. Sam ran the few feet back to the table, leaned down and kissed Holley. "Thank you for bringing me here tonight. It has been really rewarding."

Chapter 23

Their excitement over their idea and the foundation had made for a rather late night as they insisted that Holley put up her tree that night so it would be ready when her store opened. Holley couldn't believe her ears when Sam said they wanted to decorate a Christmas tree with her, even if it was a small tree that sat on the counter. She happily took them back to the shop where they spent an hour putting up a tree that should have only taken twenty minutes because Sam wanted to add lights and a tree topper and make sure that it would be impossible to miss so the families in need all got the Christmas they deserved.

The excitement and nerves over their potential meeting with their boss and then if all went well someone in marketing made it almost impossible for them to sleep, making Sam wake well before Candycane the next morning. They weren't sure what time she had returned home or if she even had as her bedroom door was closed. Sam smiled as they thought about the elf. Her arrival had changed their life in ways that they still weren't sure they were happy about, but regardless they had grown fond of her. They hoped her date had gone well or if it was still going on that she was enjoying herself.

Sam grabbed a piece of paper and left a note for Candycane on the kitchen counter so she wouldn't worry when they weren't there for breakfast. They were meeting Mr. Charles for coffee to get a copy of the brochure that Holiday Heroes used when talking to businesses about potentially setting up trees or boxes. Sam hadn't been able to stop thinking about the impact that these gifts had on the families who received them and wanted to help in any way that they could.

Ordinarily Sam took the bus to work, but seeing as they had extra time and really needed to burn some of their nervous energy, they decided to walk the four mile walk to the coffee shop. It would be good for research, too, they thought as they saw the same faces every morning on the bus. They couldn't help but notice how beautiful the city looked in the dim morning light. It was still dark enough that the twinkling of the Christmas lights that hung from most businesses were still visible, making it look as if Sam was walking through a starry sky. How had they missed this for so many years? Fall was still their favorite season with the beautiful colors of autumn leaves, but they couldn't deny that the holiday season really transformed the city.

As the sun began to rise higher into the sky, the lights dimmed and the streets began to fill with people. Sam instantly felt a rush of information flood them as they walked past a busy bus stop. They closed their eyes for a moment as the sudden burst made their head hurt. This was one of the many reasons they had been avoiding walking since they had unlocked their gift. Sam inhaled slowly and opened their eyes. This was something they could do, something they had to do. Sam looked past the people to a store window with a Christmas tree decorated with brightly colored ornaments and festive packages underneath. For reasons they didn't understand, looking at the tree brought them peace and they felt the pain in their head subside. As they continued their walk, they alternated their focus between the people passing by and holiday decor, keeping the overwhelming amount of names running through their brain from causing any sort of panic attack or headache.

Reaching the coffee shop, Sam was relieved that they had figured out how to manage collecting data because this early in the morning the line for coffee was to the door. Sam sighed as they took their place in the back of the line. This might make them late for their meeting. Sam glanced around the shop looking for Mr. Charles. "Sam, over here," a voice called from behind them. They turned to see Mr. Charles sitting at a table with two mugs. "I hope you don't mind, but I ordered for you. I asked Holley what you would like since I didn't have your number."

Sam happily left the line and walked to the table. "Thank you. That was very kind of you and thank you for meeting with me," Sam said as they sat.

"It's my pleasure. I really hope you are successful today. We tried to get a meeting with someone in Mercers a few years ago, but they insisted that they already sent clothing to shelters across the country and thought that was more than enough," Mr. Charles said.

"That program? That is why they don't participate? It's true. Mercers does donate a lot of winter coats, scarves, hats, gloves, and boots to shelters but it is all overflow from inventory that they can't move and a way to try and minimize the loss with a tax write off," Sam grumbled, rolling their eyes. "It's nothing like Holiday Heroes which would give them a chance to give back to the community with very little work on their part."

"Yes, I do believe you might have the fire in you to get them to join us. I can see the spirit of the holiday burning brightly within you. You are a good match for Holley," Mr. Charles laughed.

"I don't know about all of that. I just know that what you and the heroes are doing is an incredible cause and I want to help," Sam replied.

"Well I'm glad to have you on board," Mr. Charles said, reaching for the brochure on the table. "This is what we normally send to businesses regarding the program, but as you are trying to appeal to their business side, I have also provided you with some information on how many families and children we help each year to include the number of gifts that we deliver. I'm hoping that when they see that number, they will want the presents to be purchased at their stores, causing them to set up boxes if nothing else."

"I'm hoping for both boxes and trees, as Mercers sells a lot more than toys," Sam said. "I hate to cut our meeting short, but if I hope to get there in time to talk with my boss before he's in meetings, I need to get going."

"Good luck, Sam," Mr. Charles said, smiling at them. "And remember, even if you fail, you are still a hero."

"Thank you Mr. Charles. I will do my best," Sam replied, standing and grabbing the papers from the table. Sam's phone buzzed as they crossed the street to the Mercers building. They glanced at it as they entered the elevator to see a message from Holley wishing them luck. Sam was sure they would need more than luck if they were going to get Mercers to see this idea as a tood one, but they were counting on corporate greed to win out.

That plan had worked when they spoke with their boss, who didn't even let Sam leave his office when he made a call to marketing. The idea was well received over the phone and a meeting was scheduled in an hour. "I suggest you spend this hour getting everything together to present to them. It will take more than hope and a few numbers to convince them. I'm confident they are only meeting with you because none of them have come up with a solution to the problem you discovered yesterday," Sam's boss said.

Sam wasn't sure what other information they needed as they had plenty of numbers to show what the Holiday Heroes were doing but they headed back to their desk anyway and started researching how partnering with similar organizations had proved profitable for other retailers. By the time the meeting rolled around, Sam was feeling confident that their idea would be well received. They even had looked up similar foundations in states that didn't have Holiday Heroes so that they could offer solutions for the entire company.

Riding in the elevator with their boss, their confidence began to waver and their stomach turned. Last night they had been filled with hope, surrounded by people with kind hearts that had probably always been on the nice list. The manipulative sharks that worked for marketing were likely to all lean towards naughty which would make it much harder to sell them on a charitable act.

The walk to the meeting room did little to calm them as their assumption of the types of people who worked in marketing held true. Sam was walking through a sea of naughtiness as they anxiously balled their fists and tried to control their breathing. Entering the conference room brought a small glimmer of hope as Sam focused on the one person in the room with the word "Nice" above their head. Perhaps they had a chance at this afterall.

Sam had been right that the only nice person in the room would take to the idea immediately. The rest of the room was a much harder sell, some of them showing disinterest as soon as Sam mentioned Holiday Heroes but they didn't let that stop them from launching into the presentation they had prepared showing how profitable it would be if the majority of the gifts purchased for the hero trees and toy drive boxes came from Mercers. In the end, Sam had been able to work out a projection that would not only keep Mercers from taking a loss this holiday season, but could potentially make it their most profitable. That was the turning point that made the room side with Sam.

Sam left all of the information for the organizations with the head of the marketing department and was assured that if possible there would at the very least be boxes in every store by the end of the day. That had gone even better than Sam could have imagined. His boss had been so excited that they gave Sam the rest of the day off with one stipulation, that they find a tree and set up a hero tree on the accounting floor. It was going to be strongly suggested that every member of the accounting team adopt a family.

Sam, who didn't decorate Christmas trees, was about to trim their second tree in two days. This should have annoyed them, but since they could only think of one place in the city to get a tree and decorations, they were more than happy to do it. But first they had to pick up the ornaments for the accounting tree so that they could personally tell Mr. Charles about their success.

They flagged down a cab as they left the community center with two bags of ornaments. They hadn't been able to be the first to tell Mr. Charles as someone from marketing contacted him as soon as the meeting ended. Sam was confident that their idea was well received but they didn't expect them to work that fast. They couldn't wait to tell Holley all about it, but they wanted to surprise her so it would have to wait until they arrived at the shop.

Sam picked up a couple of sandwiches at the deli on the corner before getting in a cab and heading to Old Town. On the ride, they called Candycane to check in and see how things had gone on her date with Rudolf. To their surprise, it went through to voicemail. That was unlike her. She normally answered the moment Sam called. This worried them and they almost redirected the driver so they could check in at the apartment. There had to be a logical explanation. They'd call her again from the Christmas Claus-it and she would answer. If she didn't, Sam could always go to the apartment before returning to work.

As Sam entered the Christmas Claus-it, they were both relieved and annoyed at the sight of Candycane standing behind the counter. She smiled at them as she looked up. "What are you doing here, Sam? Shouldn't you be at work?" Candycane asked.

"I could ask you the same thing," Sam replied. "I'm here for work and to talk to Holley."

"Last I checked, you don't work here, but I do and I also came to talk to Holley," Candycane answered.

"Right. What time did you come home last night?" Sam asked.

"I, um, didn't," Candycane answered, her cheeks turning red as she looked away. "I just came here from Rudolf's this morning."

"Well, I'm glad that you had a good night. You will have to let me know how the test run went later," Sam said as Holley walked out from the back.

"Sam! When did you get here?" Holley asked, walking over and kissing them on the cheek.

"I just got here. I brought lunch. Sorry CC. I forgot you were here today but you can have mine," Sam said, tossing a sandwich at Candycane.

"I can share mine with you, cutie. That was really thoughtful," Holley said. "You want to go eat real quick so I can send CC on a break to eat hers?"

"Sounds like a plan," Sam said, following her to the back.

"What are you doing here?" Holley asked, concern flashing in her eyes. "Did your meeting not go well?"

"Actually it went really, really well," Sam said, smiling. "I'm here to get a Christmas tree for the office, and Mercers has already called Mr. Charles to set up trees and boxes at all of the stores in the city as well as reaching out to similar organizations across the country to do the same."

"Babe, that's incredible!" Holley said, throwing her arms around them in a hug. "I'm so proud of you."

"Thanks. It just made good business sense for them to do it. If people are going to buy new gifts for the hero tree or the donation boxes, why not get them to buy the gifts at Mercers?" Sam answered.

"I'm going to assume that you did it so that more families could be helped this season and not to ensure that Mercers makes a profit this year," Holley said.

"I did, but is it so bad if both things happen?" Sam asked.

"I suppose not. Let's get you a tree. Also, I think you should maybe go out with CC tonight. Not that I don't want to see you, but she could use your perspective I think," Holley said.

Chapter 24

Sam headed back to their apartment after they finished putting up the tree. They were happy to see that there was also a collection box in the lobby of the Mercers building as they left work. Sam thought about returning to the Christmas Claus-it, but Holley had said that Candycane needed to talk and Sam really hadn't spent much time with her that hadn't involved large crowds where it was impossible to talk. Holley had suggested going out, but if Sam really wanted to focus on Candycane, they needed to stay in.

Sam opened their cabinets and fridge, searching for something to make for dinner, with hopes to surprise their roommate. Unfortunately, the only food in the house was the breakfast food that Candycane normally prepared and a collection of tv dinners. Sam really needed to take better care of themselves. They might have a successful adult career, but they still ate like a broke college student. Sam couldn't treat Candycane to a microwaved dinner, especially since she enjoyed the taste of food so much.

Sam pulled out their delivery menus and smiled. Tonight they were going to give Candycane a tour of the best restaurants in the city without ever leaving their apartment. They would start with cheese fries from Chas's cafe and follow it up with an assortment of foods: Italian, Mexican, Thai, sushi, and Indian. For dessert, Sam ordered cupcakes and cookies from two of their favorite bakeries. With food ordered, Sam began warming milk for hot chocolate. They were just putting the finishing touches on the drinks, adding whipped cream and sprinkles, when they heard the key in the door.

"Um, Sam, you order something? There are like three delivery guys following me," Faith's voice called from the doorway.

"Faith? What are you doing here?" Sam asked, walking to the door to collect their food.

"CC texted earlier and I didn't have time to talk, so I told her I would come by tonight," Faith answered.

"Weird. She talked to Holley and tried to talk to you, but not me. I was trying to surprise her with a night in to catch up. I suppose one more doesn't change things. You want a cocoa?" Sam asked.

"Sure. Why not? If I'm gonna hang out with my two favorite elves, I suppose I should join them." Faith laughed.

"I'm not an elf," Sam sighed, shaking their head.

A knock on the door saved Sam from Faith's snarky reply as they opened the door to find Candycane, her hands full with the rest of the food that Sam had ordered. "Um, a little help?" Candycane asked.

"Yeah, Sorry. I didn't expect them to give you the food," Sam said, grabbing bags of food from her and walking to the kitchen. "I made you a hot chocolate and Faith came over. We have a ton of food."

"I see that. Who else is coming?" Candycane asked, grabbing her cocoa and bringing it to her mouth, whipped cream sticking to the end of her nose when she lowered it.

"You have a little something," Sam said, touching the tip of their nose and laughing. "Nobody else is coming. I wanted to give you a taste of what this city has to offer. I feel bad that I've been so busy and we've not had a chance to spend much time together that wasn't for research."

"Wow. I appreciate that Sam. That's really thoughtful of you," Candycane answered. "Holley told me what you did today. I think there might be a scrooge that is starting to feel the Christmas spirit."

"Yeah, yeah. But let's not talk about that tonight. I want to hear about your trip back to the North Pole. Tell me about the test flight and more importantly about Rudolf," Sam replied.

"Wait? The reindeer?" Faith asked.

"The reindeer trainer. He's sweet on Candycane," Sam answered.

"I've known Rudolf for years. We've been friends since we were kids. He asked me out right before Sam's gift unlocked and I had to come here," Candycane explained.

"All I know is that when I met him, he couldn't keep his eyes off of you, so what happened on your date?" Sam asked.

"It wasn't a date. Not really. I was just there to help out with the test flight because Blizzard and the other reindeer are comfortable around me," Candycane replied.

"Fine. How did the test flight go?" Sam asked, opening the bags of food and setting everything on the counter.

"Wow. So much food. This all looks amazing," Candycane said, inhaling deeply. "And smells delicious."

"You aren't getting off the hook that easily. Why doesn't everyone make a plate and then you can tell us all about the flight and what happened after?" Sam suggested.

Sam had purchased a feast and there was little talking about anything other than food as they ate. When finally, they all sat back from the table full, Faith suggested they move to the living room with some of Sam's signature cranberry and gins. Sam made the drinks and Faith grabbed the desserts. "Now, I want to hear all about this guy of yours," Faith said sitting down next to Candycane.

"First off, the test flight was amazing. The reindeer all did so well and it was beautiful up there in the sleigh. It was also incredibly cold. Rudolf had a blanket but we ended up cuddling throughout the flight to stay warm," Candycane said, smiling as she mentioned cuddling with Rudolf.

"That sounds romantic," Faith said.

"Or practical," Sam said, sticking their tongue out at Faith.

"Don't you come in here with your whole love doesn't exist nonsense. Don't ruin this. I have seen how you look at Holley," Faith said.

"It was both romantic and practical," Candycane laughed. "Anyhow, the experience in the sleigh was magical, but the real magic happened after, once we returned to my place for dinner and to warm up." Candycane blushed as she stopped talking and gazed off in the distance.

"What ya thinking about there, CC?" Faith teased.

"I, um. I," Candycane tripped over her words.

"Don't let Faith give you a hard time. You don't have to tell us the specifics," Sam said. "We just want to know if you had a good time and if you plan on seeing him again."

"Hey, some of us want to know the details," Faith said, folding her arms and pouting.

"I'll just say this. After dinner when we were sitting and talking, he kissed me. It was amazing and was followed by a lot more kissing. We ended up falling asleep sitting in front of the fire. When I woke up, I sort of freaked out because I was supposed to be here. I slipped out of his arms and returned here without waking him. And now I'm afraid that he is going to think he did something wrong. I mean I left a note, but what if he hates me for not saying goodbye?" Candycane asked.

"Look, I saw the way he looked at you. There is no way he hates you," Sam answered. "And if you are that concerned, you could always go back tomorrow during the day while I'm at work. Holley still thinks you work with me at Mercers so she will expect you to be there tomorrow."

"Are you sure?" Candycane asked. "I really like him, and I don't want to mess this up. We were friends for so long. This changes everything."

"It's just another way for the two of you to connect. It changes nothing. I think you should go back and talk to him," Faith answered.

"Alright. Enough about me. Can we please talk about what Sam did?" Candycane asked.

"What did Sam do? I feel like I don't even know my best friend anymore. They spend all of their time with you and Holley," Faith said.

"I'm sorry, Faith. You have a key to my place though. You can always come by," Sam replied.

"I can, but you aren't always here anymore. Trust me I'm not complaining about that. I'm very happy that you have found Holley. Now what is this about you finding the Christmas spirit?" Faith asked.

Candycane explained what Holley had shared with them after Sam visited the shop with Sam reluctantly filling the holes in the story and trying to spin it as a business decision and not an act of charity. Faith hugged Sam as they finished the story, squeezing them tight. "Faith, what is this for?" Sam asked, hugging her back.

"I'm so proud of you. I don't care what reason you want to give for what you did. You are going to be helping so many people," Faith said.

"If Holley hadn't taken me to their kickoff event, I wouldn't even know that Holiday Heroes existed. She is the one who deserves the credit here. She is determined to make me like Christmas," Sam answered.

Chapter 25

Sam met Holley at her apartment early on Thanksgiving morning without their elven roommate. Candycane decided to go home for the day, despite her curiosity about the holiday. A chance to spend the day with Rudolf beat out her desire to experience Thanksgiving cooking and Faith assured her that there would be leftovers so she wasn't really missing out.

"Where's CC?" Holley asked as soon as she opened the door to let Sam in.

"Nice to see you, too," Sam laughed, entering the apartment. "She's spending the day with family."

"We'll have to make sure to save her some of my sweet potato casserole and corn pudding. She seemed very excited about both of them when we talked earlier this week," Holley replied.

"I'm still shocked that Faith is letting you bring anything. She gets up at three in the morning and starts preparing things," Sam said.

"I can be very persuasive if I want to be," Holley said, smiling at Sam.

"You don't have to tell me. I'm well aware of your powers of persuasion," Sam said, leaning in and meeting Holley's lips in a kiss.

"Good. Then you can help me finish making the corn pudding," Holley said, walking to the kitchen, grabbing an apron, and throwing it at Sam.

They spent the morning cooking while Holley discussed her plans for Friday and Small Business Saturday. Somehow she had talked Sam into working with her both days and she had plans of Santa and a certain elf making a return to the shop. Sam was desperately trying to come up with a list of reasons as to why they should not spend two days in that Santa suit, something that was still going on as they entered the cab to go to Faith's.

"Do you want me to die of heat exhaustion?" Sam asked as they finished their argument.

"If you need someone to help you take the suit off, I believe I already proved how quickly I can do that, or did you already forget about the events of Halloween night?" Holley asked, her eyes running over Sam's body as she bit her lip.

Color poured into Sam's cheeks at the memory. "You bring up some very valid points. I suppose I could suffer if there was a chance at that kind of reward," Sam smiled.

"We can discuss that further later. I promised Faith that we'd get here in time for the parade, which is starting now, so we need to get up there quickly," Holley replied as the cab came to a stop.

"You can watch the parade. I have work to do, remember?" Sam said, throwing their laptop bag over their shoulder before grabbing the insulated bag with the food Holley had prepared.

"You can do that after the parade. There will be plenty of time between the parade and dinner," Holley answered. "You aren't getting out of the full Thanksgiving experience."

Experiencing Thanksgiving was something that Sam had been happily avoiding for years. When they called Faith and asked if Holley could join them for Thanksgiving, Faith had squealed with excitement. She had been trying to get Sam to participate in her Thanksgiving day traditions for years, and with Sam agreeing to actually celebrate the holiday, she decided that this year they would have no choice. There was no way that Sam would refuse when Holley was there.

Faith greeted Sam and Holley in the hallway, running out of the door to meet them at the elevator. "Happy Thanksgiving," Faith said, throwing her arms around Holley first and then Sam. "Here give me that." Faith reached for the bag of food. "And why do you have your computer? Today is about spending time together. It's not for working."

"You know I have to work. I have a report that has to be completed by tomorrow morning," Sam replied.

"Well, if you have to work, you will have to multitask. The parade is on and we have to watch that, all of us, in our matching Friendsgiving sweaters," Faith said as they entered her apartment.

"Matching what?" Sam asked.

"Sweaters," X said as he got up from his chair in front of the television and proudly showed off the orange and brown checked sweater with a three dimensional turkey on the front of it, each of the feathers in the tail, being an actual feather.

"You have to be kidding me," Sam said.

"That's fantastic!" Holley exclaimed. "Are they all the same? I'm not sure that color is going to flatter me the way it does Xavier, with his beautiful brown skin tone, but I absolutely love it."

"Thanks, Holley. I'm sure you will look great in yours, too. As will Faith when she puts hers on," X said, throwing a sweater at Faith.

"Fine," Faith huffed, pulling her sweater, the same one that Xavier was wearing, on. "X picked yours out. I think he is more excited to see you in one of these than I am, Sam."

Faith handed two matching sweaters to Holley, who unfolded hers and started laughing. "I feel a little attacked, but it's fine," she said, showing the sweater to Sam. The sweater or more accurately, sweatshirt, was tan with turkeys printed all over it and featured a large illustration in the middle of a turkey pushing Santa Claus through a doorway with the words "Not yet Fat Man. Today is my day." printed below it.

"This is hideous. Do I really have to wear this?" Sam asked, holding the sweatshirt at an arm's length as if just having it near them was offending them.

Holley pulled hers over her head before snatching the one from Sam's hand and walking over to kiss them. As she broke the kiss, she forced the neck of the sweatshirt over Sam's head. "Yes, you most certainly have to wear it. You agreed to participate in Thanksgiving this year, not just show up for the food.

Sam sighed as they pulled the sweater on properly. "The two of you look so cute. I have one more thing," Faith said, picking up a bag from the counter and tossing it at Sam.

Sam opened the bag to find a trucker hat with a turkey on it with the words "My first Thanksgiving." Sam shook their head. "It is not my first, Faith, and where did you even find this?" they asked.

"You can get anything on the internet. It wasn't the design I wanted, but most sites only printed on infant sizes. And yes, it is your first. You haven't been fully present for a holiday here ever. This year is worth celebrating. Put it on," Faith answered.

"Fine, can we please sit down and watch the parade now?" Sam asked, putting on their hat.

"I never thought I would live to see the day that Sam Christmas wanted to watch the Thanksgiving Day parade," Faith brought her hand to her heart and feigned shock as she gasped.

After the parade, Holley helped Faith with dinner while X and Sam watched football and Sam worked on their report. Dinner was an absolute feast as Faith wanted the day to be one that Sam would never forget in case they never agreed to do this again. There was obviously turkey, stuffing, and gravy, but Faith had also prepared a ham, scalloped potatoes, green bean casserole, and homemade cornbread. With the addition of Holley's sweet potatoes and corn pudding, they were all very full by the time they had finished eating or thought they had finished. Faith had also made pumpkin pie, pecan pie, and apple pie from scratch that she brought out as it appeared everyone was finishing with the main course.

"If somebody wants to roll me to the sink, I'll gladly wash dishes. You really outdid yourself, Faith," Sam said as they finished the last of their pie.

"We have a dishwasher, and much as I would like to take you up on that, Holley told me that the two of you have plans. I don't want you to be late. Thank you both for coming. Holley, you are coming back afterwards to pick up your casserole dishes and leftovers, right?" Faith asked.

"Of course. We will be back. Thank you for including me and for understanding," Holley answered. "Happy Thanksgiving, Faith and Xavier. I'm really glad that I have the two of you in my life."

"We're grateful for you, too, and for you helping to find Sam's holiday spirit. Happy Thanksgiving. I hope you have a good time tonight," Faith replied as she walked toward them to give them both a hug.

Chapter 26

"Want me to try and get a cab?" Sam asked as they exited Faith's apartment building.

"No. We can walk there. It isn't far," Holley answered. "So, how was your first Thanksgiving, Sam?"

Sam sighed and rolled their eyes. "I'm not sure I'm a fan of you and Faith ganging up on me, but it was nice. I enjoyed it. Thank you for coming with me," Sam answered.

"I'm so glad you asked, and I'm really excited to share my favorite tradition with you," Holley replied. "I think it is the perfect way to really start the Christmas season."

"Hey, today is about turkey, not Santa Claus," Sam laughed, gesturing at their sweater.

"This is still a Thanksgiving activity. It just embodies what I think is so wonderful about the entire season," Holley said, as she stopped in front of a homeless shelter.

"Um, what are we doing here?" Sam asked, tentatively.

"This is our destination. We are going to serve Thanksgiving meals. It's incredibly rewarding and I've been doing it since I was a child," Holley answered.

"That's really admirable, but I don't think I can go in there with you," Sam said. "I'm really sorry."

Holley reached for Sam's hand, grabbing it and squeezing it reassuringly. "What's going on, Sam?" she asked.

"I just. I can't," Sam said, looking away as they wiped their eyes that were damp with the onset of tears.

Holley pulled them into a hug. "Sam, you don't have to do this, if you don't want to, but please talk to me. What's wrong?" she asked.

Sam stepped back from her embrace and took a deep breath. "Do you remember when I told you that I spent most holiday seasons moving and living in hotels? That wasn't always the case. There were many nights spent in shelters, wondering if we were going to find somewhere to live or what our next full meal was going to be. My mother struggled to keep a job and we didn't always have money to stay in a hotel. This is why I hate the holidays. It just brings up so many terrible memories," Sam answered.

"Sam, I'm sorry. I had no idea, and I understand why you wouldn't want to go in there, but this is your chance to help others who are going through a similar situation to what you experienced. It could help to heal some of your pain around the holiday. I'm not forcing you to join me, and I understand if you try and have to leave, but for me giving back and helping those in need has always been an act that brings me joy and inner peace. And I will be right there with you, if it gets to be too much," Holley replied.

"I can try," Sam said. "I don't promise anything, but for you, I will try."

"Don't do it for me. Do this for you. I really think it might help," Holley replied, taking their hand. "But, only if you think you are ready. I won't be upset if you think you can't do it."

Sam squeezed Holley's hand and took a step towards the shelter. "With you by my side, I think there is little that I can't do. Let's go serve some turkey," Sam answered.

Inside the shelter there were rows of tables set up with place settings and many of them were already full with people waiting for dinner. Sam paused as they entered and looked around the room at the families. There were so many children seated at the tables, many of whom were nice. Sam hoped that they would have homes by the time Christmas rolled around so that Wyatt could find them. Sam tried to focus on the goodwill in the room as the names began to flood their brain.

"Are you okay, Sam?" Holley asked as they had yet to start walking again.

Sam shook their head and closed their eyes before focusing on Holley. "Yeah, I'm alright. Looks like everyone is ready to eat. Where do we go to get them some grub?"

"Come on. Mr. Charles should be in the kitchen. I think he will be happy to see you," Holley answered.

"Sam!" Mr. Charles exclaimed, running over and hugging Sam and then Holley. "It is so good to see you both. "Happy Thanksgiving."

"Happy Thanksgiving to you, Mr. Charles. How are the donations coming along for Holiday Heroes?" Sam asked.

"The donations have been rolling in since we placed boxes and trees in Mercers. I'm not sure what you said to make them change their minds, but the results are already incredible and the holiday shopping season officially starts tomorrow. We're going to be able to help more families and children than we ever have," Mr. Charles answered.

"That's incredible. I'm so happy that it's been so well received. I hope that it's able to help some of the families that we're serving today," Sam said.

"We always drop off gifts at the shelters for families that spend their holiday here," Mr. Charles answered. "This year, we will be able to give more because of our Christmas angel." He pointed at Sam when he said angel.

"Oh, no. Holley is the one to thank. I wouldn't even know that Holiday Heroes existed if it wasn't for her," Sam said.

"Take some credit, Sam. Getting Mercers to participate was your idea, and I'm so proud of you," Holley said, leaning in and kissing their cheek.

Sam started to blush and turned away. "So, about the hungry people in the other room," Sam said, changing the subject. "Should we maybe take them some food?"

Holley and Sam helped to serve hundreds of Thanksgiving Day Meals that evening. Sam, who had known what it felt like to feel the hopelessness of being without a home, saw hope and joy on the faces of the people they served. It filled them with warmth and they understood what Holley had meant about this being a selfish act. As they left the shelter and walked back to Faith's apartment, Sam could not stop smiling.

"Holley, thank you for talking me into joining you tonight. That was an incredible experience. Those families, I thought being around them would be heartbreaking but they were all so thankful for what we were doing and happy to be spending the time together. It was amazing and heartwarming. I never experienced things like that when I was in that situation and I'm glad we could provide it for those families," Sam said, feeling tears in their eyes for the second time. They wiped their eyes, and smiled at Holley. "Don't worry. These are good tears."

"Sam, this is what the holidays are supposed to be about. It's about spreading love and kindness. It's about giving. This is why I love the Christmas season. And I'm so happy it was a good experience for you," Holley said.

"So far your idea of the holidays is one that I could learn to enjoy," Sam replied. "I want to do more for the shelter. I'm going to talk with Mr. Charles, but those kids deserve a real Christmas. They should get to see Santa and tell him what they want for Christmas and they should get those gifts."

"Sam, that's a tough thing to promise. There is no guarantee that the same families will show up for Christmas. But, it is admirable and I think if anyone can make it happen, it's you. I'm sure Mr. Charles would love to hear your ideas," Holley said.

"I don't know if I have ideas, necessarily. I just don't want to see those kids grow up with the same cynical world view that I have. There's a lot of good in this world and they should get to see that instead of the ugliness," Sam explained.

"That's beautiful. I want to be able to help you give that to those families," Holley said, pulling them to her and giving them a deep passionate kiss.

"Um, hi," Sam said, as the kiss ended. "What did I do to deserve that?"

"Just being you. You have a huge heart, Sam Christmas. Getting to know you and experiencing your giving nature and kindness has been a true gift and I cannot wait to spend this Christmas season with you. Happy Thanksgiving, Sam," Holley replied.

"I still think that you are more responsible for that than you know. You have opened my eyes to a lot of things that I didn't know existed and you have shown me a different side of Christmas and the holidays, one that isn't so material. I look forward to what this season has to offer. Happy Thanksgiving, Holley. I'm incredibly thankful to have you in my life," Sam said, as they continued walking.

As they entered Faith's apartment building, Sam smiled at the Hero tree in the lobby. They hated the holidays and everything they stood for, or at least they thought they did. The past month had really begun to change their feelings as they were learning a new way to view the season. Holley's idea of what Christmas truly meant was starting to make Sam second guess themselves and their thoughts on the holidays. That wasn't the only thing that Holley was making Sam second guess. The more they got to know Holley, the less they hated the idea of relationships and love.

When the elevator doors opened on Faith's floor, Sam grabbed Holley's hand. "I know we were planning on spending some more time here, but I'd kind of like to get our things and head home. I still unfortunately have some work to do, and I'd like to spend some one on one time with you. Show you just how thankful I'm for you, if you know what I mean," Sam said.

"I'm not sure how I can refuse that offer," Holley said, pulling Sam to them as they exited the elevator and kissing them again. "I just hope that your work can wait until after you have given thanks."

Chapter 27

Sam sat in Holley's apartment in the very early hours of the morning finishing their report. They crept from her room, once she finally fell asleep. It was harder than they wanted to admit leaving her to work. Much as they hated to admit it, Holley was stealing their heart. They wouldn't say that they were in love, but they could see it leading to that, which was an idea that really terrified Sam. As they completed their financial review and hit send on their email, they pulled out their phone and texted Faith.

I think I might be in trouble. I promised Holley I'd work with her tomorrow and then I think I have to go to the mall with Candycane, but can we meet up after? I need to talk.

Sam expected Faith to be asleep, but their phone rang before they were able to set it down. "Hey, Faith. Why aren't you sleeping?" Sam asked as they answered their phone.

"Probably for the same reasons you aren't sleeping," Faith giggled. "I know you didn't think I would just ignore that text, especially when

I'm pretty sure I know exactly what kind of trouble you think you might be in."

"If you think you know and you know why I'm awake, you also know that I'm not where I can talk, so why did you call?" Sam asked.

"Because I wanted confirmation, and now I have it. You're in love," Faith teased.

"I'm not. I just need to talk about things. So can we do that tonight?" Sam asked.

"Sure. I'm always here for you and your delusions. Come over when you're done with the mall," Faith replied.

"Thanks. I'm gonna go back to bed now. Wipe that silly grin off of your face and go to sleep," Sam said.

"Good night, Sam. Stop being afraid of love. It isn't as scary as you think it is," Faith said before she hung up.

As Sam walked back to Holley's bedroom, they knew that they were falling for her. They really hoped that their dislike of the Christmas season and the many typical traditions that went with it didn't mess things up with Holley. She was opening their eyes to a whole new world when it came to love and to the holidays, but Sam was incredibly nervous that something would happen to mess all of it up. Christmas had never been kind to them and they weren't sure why that would change now.

"Hey cutie. Where'd you go?" Holley asked as Sam got back into bed.

"I had to finish my work. Sorry. I didn't mean to wake you," Sam said, kissing her as they cuddled back into her.

"I was afraid you had run away so you didn't have to be Santa," Holley laughed.

"You can't get rid of me that easily. It's a good try, but you promised a reward if I was a good Santa," Sam answered, kissing her again.

Holley returned the kiss, opening her mouth to Sam as their tongue met hers. When she pulled away, breathless, she looked at them and shook her head. "As much as I want to see where that kiss might lead, we both need to get some sleep. Tomorrow is going to be a very busy day," Holley said.

Sam wasn't sure what they were expecting when Holley suggested it would be busy in the shop on Friday, but it wasn't this. There were people standing outside of the Christmas Claus-it waiting for Holley to unlock the door. The plan had been for Candycane to man the register while Holley helped people shop and Sam played Santa Claus for any of the children who entered. Instead, Sam spent the bulk of the day, helping to load Christmas trees, blow molds, and other holiday decorations in cars. Candycane, much to her delight, spent the day beside Holley carefully wrapping fragile ornaments and packaging them. While Holley was hardly able to walk from the register due to the constant line. By the time the shop closed, all three of them were exhausted.

"Well, you think tomorrow, Santa is actually going to get to sit and listen to what the kids want or do you expect it to be another day like today?" Sam asked as Holley locked the door.

"I hope tomorrow goes closer to plan because I scheduled a wreath making event tomorrow and I have had a lot of interest in it. Plus I think I sold almost all of my trees today, which I had not expected," Holley answered.

"That's a good thing, though," Sam said. "It was a really great day. People really like your store. You should be proud."

"I am. I just wasn't expecting to have to spend the night doing inventory so I could figure out what I need to order," Holley said.

"I wish we could stay and help, but," Sam started to explain.

"But, you and CC have plans and I wouldn't dream of keeping you from them. I'll see you both in the morning. Thank you for everything today," Holley said, walking over to Sam and giving them a quick kiss.

"Thanks, boss. Appreciate it," Candycane said. "Come on, Sam. Let's head home and change."

Back at the apartment, Sam asked Candycane how her trip home had been. "So, things good with you and Rudolf?" they asked.

Candycane blushed at the question. "I think so. He slept over again, but this time he was awake when I left and kissed me goodbye," she answered.

"I told you that he wouldn't be mad at you," Sam said. "He likes you too much to let something silly keep him from having a shot."

"Yeah, well I rather like him, too. But enough about that. How was Thanksgiving?" Candycane asked.

"It was really nice. I'm going to head over to Faith's when we're done at the mall if you want to come for leftovers," Sam answered.

"I would love that, but that wasn't what I meant. It just seemed like there was a little something going on between you and Holley. It felt a little different, the way that you look at her and she looks at you. I don't know. I was just wondering if anything had happened," Candycane said.

"Not sure what you mean. But it was kind of a crazy day today. I didn't expect to have to process so much information. It got a little overwhelming a few times, but I tried to use Holley as my means to ground myself so maybe that was what you saw," Sam guessed.

"Maybe. We're definitely going to be around a lot more people here in a moment. Are you ready for it?" Candycane asked.

"I have to be, don't I?" Sam replied. "Time's ticking. It'll be Christmas before we know it."

"True. But, I don't want you to overdo it. Let me know if it's too much, ok?" Candycane asked.

"You'll know. Come on. You ready? I'm pretty sure you've never experienced anything like a mall on black Friday," Sam answered.

As Sam expected, the mall was absolutely packed, wall to wall people with lines reaching the entrances of most of the stores. Their head was flooded with names as soon as they entered. Sam briefly leaned on the wall as they did their best to maintain focus, finally pulling their attention to a much smaller sample of people so that they were able to walk with Candycane. They made several laps around the mall, before finding a table in the food court so that they could grab a snack and a drink.

"I'm not sure that today was a good day to gather information. Black Friday brings out the worst in people. I think the naughty to nice ratio is close to three to one," Sam laughed.

"You could be right. I had someone push me out of the way in the line to get a drink. I've never seen people behave like this," Candycane replied.

"Yeah. People as a whole are pretty terrible, though," Sam said. "You ready to get outta here and get some turkey?"

"That sounds like a really good idea," Candycane agreed.

Chapter 28

Candycane was well into her second plate of Thanksgiving leftovers when Faith grabbed a bottle of wine and headed to the couch with Sam. "Alright friend, if it isn't the scary word that starts with the letter L that has you all worked up, what is it?" Faith asked.

"I never said it wasn't that word. I said I wasn't in love," Sam corrected.

"She didn't say it, did she?" Faith asked.

"No, why? Did she say something to you?" Sam asked.

"No. Of course not. I just got worried. She's a keeper, Sam. I don't wanna see you mess this up," Faith replied. "I can see it in your eyes. Don't sabotage this."

"I don't want to either, Faith. I really do like her, a lot. I could be starting to fall for her, and that terrifies me," Sam said.

"Why? She's perfect for you," Faith said. "She is beautiful, not in the skinny "I could be a model" way that you normally date, but truly beautiful. She challenges you, but doesn't want to change you. She just brings out the best in you. What's wrong with falling for her?"

"Because every single time I let my guard down and let someone in all the way, something happens and I end up alone. This never ends well for me," Sam answered.

"This is exactly what I'm talking about. Do not sabotage this. Get out of your head. Isn't there enough in there right now? You really have room for unnecessary doubt?" Faith asked.

"How can you say it's unnecessary? I really really like her. I'm afraid to lose her," Sam countered.

"That sounds an awful lot like love to me, but you are gonna have to figure that out on your own. Don't get in your head on this one. Let your heart take control," Faith said.

"I'll try, but something always happens. Always. What if I'm too much like my mother? What if I'm not meant for lasting relationships?" Sam asked.

"Um, you know damn well that isn't true. You haven't seriously dated anyone since Simone and that was junior year. Your mom would have been with at least ten people in that amount of time," Faith replied.

"Okay, you have a point there. I think I'm just scared to fall, and it's happening, Faith. I can't picture my life without her already and it's only been a few months. Is that crazy?" Sam asked.

"I knew I wanted to marry X after our third date. When you know, you know. Stop stressing about it and just enjoy the ride," Faith answered. "If it is meant to be, it will be."

"Thanks, Faith. I probably should get CC home. We have to be back at the Christmas Claus-it early tomorrow. Holley had a record sales day today and I can only imagine what tomorrow will bring. She almost sold out of Christmas trees. Can you believe that?" Sam laughed.

"Good for her. You getting a tree this year? I imagine Candycane would like one," Faith asked.

"Um, I hadn't really thought about it," Sam answered with a shrug. "I guess if I decide to, I know where to get one."

"That you do," Faith laughed. "Good luck tomorrow. And I'm here if you need anything."

Sam and Candycane met Holley at the Christmas Claus-it at eight in the morning, two hours before the store was to open, so that they could help restock the shelves and prepare for the day. Holley was right, a lot of her stock sold on Friday and the shelves were rather empty even after restocking. As Sam tried to help bring product to the front, they found a small stack of Christmas trees that looked forgotten as dust covered the boxes.

"What's with the dusty trees in the corner?" Sam asked.

"Those trees are broken. The lights don't work or they are missing the base or there is a broken branch," Holley answered. "Nobody wants a broken tree."

"I do," Sam said. "Whichever one you think we can salvage, I'll buy it. CC and I need a tree," Sam replied.

"You really want to buy a broken tree?" Holley asked.

"Actually, I'll buy all of them. I'm going to see if we can put up a few trees in the shelter, spread some holiday cheer," Sam answered.

"That is an incredible idea. You don't have to buy them. I can donate them. I'm sure I have lights and ornaments, too," Holley replied.

"I was thinking that we could possibly make ornaments for the trees with the children at the shelter, if the shelter is alright with it. I'm calling them tomorrow," Sam suggested.

"I love that. I would really enjoy that and I'm sure the children there would, too. For someone who hates Christmas so much, that is quite a holiday gesture," Holley said, smiling at Sam.

"I'm just trying to help people in a way that I wish someone had helped me when I was younger," Sam replied. "Let's not make it something more than what it is. I think we have a wreath workshop to set up and a store to open."

Holley walked over to Sam and wrapped her arms around them, pulling them close to her and giving them a quick kiss. "Alright, Ebenezer, of course it has nothing to do with Christmas spirit. Whatever you say,"

Sam opened their mouth to argue when a loud crash from the store caused them to jump. "Oh, no," they sighed. "Everything alright out there, CC?" Sam yelled.

"I might have broken a shelf. I think everything is still sellable, though," CC called back. "I hope," she added as she started to pick up the ornaments that had fallen.

"Why don't you let me take care of that, so you can get ready for your event?" Sam offered as they walked back out to the shop floor.

A few hours later the Christmas Claus-it was full of people, shopping and making wreaths while children visited Santa. Sam managed a quick break around noon to grab food for all three of them and make a quick call to the homeless shelter because they were too excited to wait for tomorrow. The person they spoke with seemed excited to hear Sam's ideas and scheduled a meeting for Sam with the director for the next day. When Sam returned to the shop, they stopped and watched Holley helping a customer attach a ribbon to the wreath she was creating. They couldn't help but smile as they watched Holley. She was radiating happiness and it was reflecting back in the smiles on the faces of those gathered around the table.

Holley looked up at them and they pointed to the bag of food in their hand before walking to the back with it. "CC, give me a few minutes to eat and I'll swap with you," Sam called to the elf who was dealing with a long line of customers. Sam had avoided shopping and really going anywhere in the days following Thanksgiving for years. The constant flow of people entering the Christmas Claus-it paired with the trip to the mall yesterday had confirmed the reasons why, but despite it all, they were finding themselves enjoying the time spent with Holley and Candycane in the shop. Sam took a bite of pizza as they leaned back in their chair, enjoying a few moments of peace.

The quiet would be short lived as Candycane poked her head in the backroom to let Sam know that there was a customer there asking for them. As far as Sam knew, the only people who knew they were at the shop were Holley, Candycane, Faith, and X, so they were unsure who could be asking to see them. Sam set down their pizza and sighed as they stood and put their Santa beard back on, not wanting to cause doubt in the minds of any of the children they had spoken with. Walking back into the shop, Sam quickly scanned the space, collecting names for the list, stopping their scan as they came across a person that provided them with no information as they had no indication of their behavior above their head. When the person in question turned to face them, Sam recognized him immediately.

"Wyatt!" Sam called, walking towards the man, who was wearing an ugly Christmas sweater featuring Santa Claus wearing a Cowboy hat. "Great sweater. What are you doing here?"

"I heard a rumor that a certain skeptical Christmas was beginning to embrace the magic of the season. I had to see it for myself," Wyatt answered, smiling at the sight of Sam in a Santa suit.

"I'm helping my girlfriend out. Don't get too excited," Sam replied, nodding towards Holley who looked up at them and smiled.

"You managed to score a woman like that? I'm impressed. Not only is she beautiful, but you can't get any nicer than that," Wyatt said.

"I don't know how I did it either. She's incredible and she loves Christmas so if anyone is to blame for me having any kind of changed outlook on the season, it is her. I'm not promising a change in outlook, but she has opened my eyes to things about the holiday that aren't completely awful," Sam replied.

"That's good to hear. I won't keep you, Sam. I just wanted to drop by and say hello. Candycane tells me you are doing well and learning to cope with things. I'm sure I don't need to tell you that the next few weeks are critical for collecting names," Wyatt said.

"Yes, we are on our way to a crowded mall later tonight. I won't forget my duty," Sam answered. "Good seeing you, Wyatt." Sam shook Wyatt's hand, before turning back to see Candycane beaming with pride. "Alright, CC, go get some food. I'm tagging in, and then maybe you can relieve Holley. She was supposed to end that class over an hour ago, but people keep showing up for it."

"You got it. I'll be as quick as I can, Santa," CC giggled, as she ran to the back.

The rest of the work day flew by as the shop stayed busy past closing time, the last of the customers checking out twenty minutes after six. They were all exhausted as they were finally able to lock the door. "That had to be another record day," Sam said as they flipped the closed sign.

"It was definitely a busy one. I wouldn't have been able to do it without the both of you," Holley said. "I know you probably have plans, but I would love to take the both of you to dinner as a thank you."

"That isn't necessary," Candycane said. "But, I do think that the past few days deserve celebrating, and I would be happy to postpone our plans to do that."

"Really, CC? Are you sure?" Sam asked. "I'm not complaining. I just want to be sure."

"I think with how things went today that it will be just fine, and Holley earned it," Candycane answered.

"She definitely did. I'm so proud of you, beautiful. It was an amazing couple of days," Sam said, pulling Holley into a hug.

"Thank you. Let's go celebrate and see if I can talk either of you into coming back with me tomorrow," Holley laughed.

Chapter 29

Much as Sam wanted to accompany Candycane and Holley to the Christmas Claus-it for another day, they had a meeting with the director of the homeless shelter. Planning for meetings was something that Sam excelled at and they had spent the night writing a proposal for Christmas at the shelter. However when it came to presenting their ideas, especially to strangers, Sam found it hard to find their words. For this reason, they asked Faith to go with them.

The shelter was a short walk from Faith's apartment so Sam took a cab to their friend's home to meet for breakfast before heading to the meeting. Faith read over Sam's proposal while they ate, not speaking until she read the entire thing. When she was done, she looked at Sam and smiled. "Christmas at the shelter, I love it! I'm not sure what you have done with my best friend, but I'm glad you have found the Christmas spirit," Faith said.

"I have found the desire to help people, in particular children who deserve to know happiness and have a reason for hope. I was in their shoes and I know how hard it can be to find a reason to keep going. A simple gesture like this would have meant the world to me back then. I just want to help these kids smile again," Sam replied.

"Well this plan of yours sounds like one that will bring a lot of smiles. I'm proud of you, Sam," Faith said.

"Shouldn't you save that for if the shelter goes along with my ideas?" Sam asked.

"No. I'm proud of you for just having the idea and having the courage to share it with the shelter," Faith answered.

"Um, thanks. If we're gonna get there on time, we should probably head out," Sam said as they stood and walked their plate to the sink.

As they walked to the shelter, Faith asked Sam about Holley and how they were dealing with their feelings for her. Sam continued to avoid the terrifying l word, but they did say that watching her work, seeing her in her element for a few days, definitely cemented that they had strong feelings for her. That revelation led to Faith obnoxiously singing that Sam was in love for the rest of the walk, which resulted in Sam speed walking to the shelter.

Sam paused when they reached the shelter and turned to Faith. "As incredibly catchy as that tune of yours is, can you maybe give that a rest so we can meet with the director?" Sam asked.

"Of course, but don't think we are done talking about Holley," Faith said.

"Fine," Sam grumbled, as they opened the door to the shelter and entered. Sam stopped suddenly, causing Faith to run into them. Standing before them was a tall slender woman with light brown skin, hazel eyes, and long black hair that she wore in tight braids. Sam inhaled deeply, the familiar scent of jasmine causing a flood of memories to run through their brain. "Simone?" they asked as the woman smiled at them.

"Sam!" the woman exclaimed. "When I saw your name come across my desk, I thought that it had to be some sort of mistake. The Sam Christmas I know would never inquire about helping the shelter for the holidays. And yet here you are with Faith beside you. Almost makes me feel like we're in college again."

"Well we aren't in college anymore, Simone and Sam has changed a lot since then," Faith said.

"They sure look the same," Simone said as she looked over their body appreciatively. "Actually, Sam, you look incredible."

"Thanks, Simone," Sam said, blushing as they looked at the only woman that they ever thought they loved. "You still look pretty great, yourself."

Faith rolled her eyes and elbowed Sam in the ribs. "Yeah, Yeah. We've all aged really well. It isn't like college was that long ago. We didn't come here to reminisce. We came to discuss Sam's ideas for the shelter, so could we maybe focus on that?" Faith asked.

"Whoa, easy there Faith. No need to go all mama bear on me. I'm a married woman now," Simone replied.

"Because being attached stopped you before," Faith countered.

"Alright. Alright. There's no need to bring up the past. We've all grown up and moved on. It's nice to see you, Simone. Faith is right, though. We came here for a reason. Let's see if we can do something for the kids who have to call this place home for the holiday," Sam said.

"Yes. I'm excited to see what you have come up with. My office is this way," Simone answered, walking down the hallway.

Sam read the nameplate on Simone's desk as they entered her office. "Reynolds? You married Terrance?" Sam asked, as they sat.

"Yes, Sam. I did. It was always the plan. Terrance and I started dating at fourteen. We were meant to be together," Simone answered.

"I thought we weren't dwelling on the past," Faith said, shaking her head. "Your complicated history isn't going to keep you from listening to Sam's proposal is it?"

"Of course not. We don't have a complicated history. It's actually rather simple. Sam never told you?" Simone asked.

"That you left them heartbroken to run back to Terrance? Yeah I heard all about it," Faith answered.

"I thought we weren't reliving the past," Sam said, trying to stop the conversation.

"You told Faith that I broke up with you?" Simone asked. "That is a very loose interpretation of events. I asked you if you loved me and you said you didn't believe in love. I'm not sure what you thought I was going to stay for after that."

"Sam, seriously?" Faith looked at Sam and shook her head in disappointment. "I'm sorry, Simone. I've been rude to you and clearly you don't deserve that," Faith said.

"It's fine, Faith, really. I'm very happy with Terrance. I really do believe that I would have ended up with him. Sam just expedited the process," Simone said. "Now about Sam's ideas for the shelter, how are we going to bring some Christmas cheer into this place?"

Sam and Faith spent the next hour discussing decorating the shelter and having multiple activities for the children throughout the month leading up to Christmas. Simone loved all of the ideas and not only gave the plan her stamp of approval but told them that they could decorate as early as that night if they would like to. Sam agreed to return with trees and decorations almost before Simone had finished speaking. Simone printed up a quick volunteer agreement for Sam to sign and asked them to get back to her with dates for the events once they had a chance to figure out which days worked best for them before escorting Sam and Faith back to the foyer.

MAKING THE LIST

"I'm sorry I have to cut this short, but I have an important call. It was very nice seeing both of you again," Simone said, turning and walking back towards her office.

Sam was still excitedly talking about festive decorations as they exited the shelter with Faith. "Holley is going to be so incredibly excited. I have to head over there and tell her. You want to come with?" Sam asked.

"Sure, I'll come with. We aren't gonna discuss the fact that Simone is the director of the shelter? I have held a grudge against her for five years because she broke your heart when you were the reason that the two of you broke up. We aren't gonna talk about that?" Faith asked, scowling at Sam as she flagged down a cab.

"Telling Simone I didn't love her was the hardest thing I have ever done. You know how much love terrifies me. And I knew deep down that she still loved Terrance. She would have never chosen me long term. I did what I did to protect my heart," Sam said.

"And seeing her today didn't upset you?" Faith asked.

"I mean it was weird, but no. I've moved past that," Sam answered. "Besides I was much too worried about the kids having a Christmas to dwell on such things."

"So it isn't going to be a problem, then? You aren't going to let this mess things up with what you have with Holley, right?" Faith asked.

"Why would Simone mess things up with Holley? They are two very different women and my feelings for Holley are completely different than what I felt for Simone. I'm a different person now," Sam answered.

"Good. Just checking. Because if you pull that kind of crap with Holley, I might not forgive you," Faith threatened.

"Holley and I aren't even remotely ready for that kind of conversation yet. I'm sorry I never told you the truth about what happened with Simone and I. Can we move past it and try to celebrate the fact that we're going to be trying to make a depressing place a little bit brighter for families in need?" Sam asked as the cab came to a stop in front of the Christmas Claus-it.

Chapter 30

Holley, Candycane, Faith, Xavier, and Sam returned to the shelter with two trees and several boxes of decorations a few hours later. Holley was so excited about the idea that she closed the shop two hours early so they could try and have the decorations up by the time the shelter opened its doors for dinner. Both trees were up and Xavier and Sam were hanging lights from the ceiling when Simone returned to the shelter.

"Well, this is already looking much more festive," Simone said, smiling up at Sam before walking over to the tree that Holley, Faith, and Candycane were decorating. "Faith, it's nice to see you again. Who are your friends?"

"Simone, I didn't expect to see you tonight. Isn't your workday over?" Faith asked.

"Yes, it is. I actually came back to offer my help with the decor," Simone replied.

"That's great. We still have to get the other tree ready before dinner," Holley said, extending her hand towards Simone. "I'm Holley and this is CC. Thank you so much for allowing us to do this."

"Holley is the owner of the Christmas Claus-it, the shop that donated all of these items, and she is Sam's girlfriend," Faith explained.

"It is a pleasure to meet you, Holley, and CC. I'm the one who should be thanking you. This is a really great gesture that I think the patrons of the shelter will really appreciate," Simone said, shaking Holley's hand.

"CC and Faith, if the two of you can finish this tree, Simone and I can start on the other one," Holley suggested, handing a pack of tinsel to Faith.

"Of course, boss," CC laughed.

"You sure you don't want to finish this one?" Faith asked. "I could help Simone with the other tree."

"I'd like to talk with Simone more about the activities that Sam suggested," Holley explained. "You two can help us when you finish this one."

"Everything alright, Faith?" CC asked once it was just the two of them at the tree.

"There's a history with Simone and Sam and I don't trust her," Faith said. "I should after what I learned this morning, but I can't get past the things that she did to Sam."

"Sam doesn't look too bothered by it," CC said, nodding towards Sam who was walking towards the other tree.

Sam walked over to Holley and wrapped their arm around her waist, pulling her to them as they kissed her on the cheek. "Simone, I see you've met Holley. She's the one who is really responsible for all of this," Sam said.

"Nonsense, Sam. This was your idea," Holley said, handing a string of lights to Sam. "You mind untangling these for me, cutie?"

Sam blushed and took the lights from Holley. "I'm gonna go test them first. If they don't work, I think X and I had a few strands we didn't use," Sam said, turning and walking away. They could hear Simone and Holley giggling behind them. Sam wasn't sure why but Simone and Holley talking made them nervous. It occurred to them that they had never been in a situation where they had an ex and a current girlfriend in the same room as Sam hadn't been in a relationship since Simone.

"How you holding up, bud?" Faith said, pulling Sam from their thoughts.

"I'm fine. Why wouldn't I be fine?" Sam asked, way too defensively to actually be fine.

"Yeah, that is kind of a disturbing development, huh?" Faith asked, nodding towards the tree.

"Is it, though? Why is it bothering me?" Sam asked.

"I don't know. Because you don't trust Simone? That's why I don't like it," Faith answered.

"She's married, Faith. I've just never been in a room with two people I've been in a relationship with before. It's a strange feeling, even if one of them ended a long time ago and the other one is new and so much more than the first one ever was," Sam said.

"Hey, those lights ready?" Holley said, walking up behind Sam and wrapping her arms around their waist.

"Yeah, just finished with them. I think the doors are about to open. Let's get this tree finished," Sam answered, turning and walking with Holley.

The looks on the faces of the children that walked in as the shelter doors were opened to the public filled Sam with warmth. The majority of the children were "nice," reminding Sam that they wanted to ask Wyatt how he delivered gifts to kids without homes. The thought of them not receiving presents paired with watching the families finish eating and start to find their cots for the night pulled at Sam's heart and they grew sad as they remembered many nights spent the same way.

"You alright, Sam?" Holley asked as she noticed the change in their demeanor.

"It's been a long day. I think I'm just tired. Can we get out of here for the night, maybe?" Sam asked.

"I'm going to head home, myself. What you all have done is truly amazing and I cannot wait to see how the kids react to the events you have planned. Thank you again, all of you," Simone said, walking over to Sam and hugging them. "I'm really proud of you, Sam."

"I'll call you tomorrow so we can finalize the dates and times for the events, Simone," Sam said as they all walked to the exit.

"Sounds like a plan," Simone replied. "Good night." She walked to her office as the rest of them exited the shelter.

Faith invited everyone to go back to their place since it was so close, but Holley declined, saying she was ready to go home. Sam, who really wasn't in the mood to socialize, eagerly agreed to join Holley. It really had been a very long day, physically and emotionally exhausting, and they wanted nothing more than to curl up in bed with Holley and go to sleep.

Unfortunately for Sam, Holley had questions that she had been waiting to ask when the two of them were alone. When they entered Holley's apartment, she headed to the kitchen and began preparing two large mugs of hot chocolate. "Sam, what we did tonight was really magical. It meant a lot to those families. You should be proud of yourself," Holley said.

"It did look like they enjoyed the decorations, didn't it?" Sam asked, smiling.

"It really did. I'm glad that Simone was open to the idea," Holley said. "She went to school with you, Faith, and Xavier?"

"Yeah," Sam nodded. "That's how we all know her. I dated her for a while," Sam answered.

"You dated her?" Holley asked. "She's gorgeous, like supermodel pretty. Did she look like that when you dated?"

"Yeah," Sam shrugged. "Why?" they asked.

"Because if you can score women that look like her, why are you with me?" Holley asked.

"Holley, you are beautiful, way more beautiful than Simone. You have to know that," Sam replied.

"I know I have a pretty enough face, but my body has nothing on hers," Holley countered. "She's so thin. I've never looked like that and never will."

"Look, I know when I first saw you, you were in a sweater and jeans so I couldn't really see your body, but when we went on our first date and you wore clothing that showed off your curves, it was really hard for me to behave that night, okay. Maybe I haven't shown you enough, but I'm really really fond of your body. You are a beautiful, sexy woman, Holley. Sure, I dated Simone and yeah she is pretty, but you are gorgeous. To me there is no comparison between you two. You win every time and that is without adding what an incredible person you are on the inside," Sam said, walking over to Holley and wrapping her in a tight embrace as their lips met hers.

When they broke the kiss, Holley looked up at Sam breathless. "Thank you, Sam. Plus-sized women aren't for everyone. I know this, and hearing that you dated someone who looks like Simone is a little intimidating, but when you kiss me like that, I feel like I'm every bit as pretty as she is," Holley said.

"Prettier," Sam said, pulling her to them and kissing her again. "Why don't you let me show you just how much I enjoy your body?" Sam began to pull at Holley's clothes as they kissed her.

"How about we take this to the bedroom?" Holley asked, pulling Sam's hands from her body. She laughed as Sam stuck their bottom lip out in a pout as she stopped them from undressing her in the kitchen. "You are far too adorable, Sam Christmas." She grabbed their hand and led them to her room.

Sam lay awake while Holley slept peacefully on their chest. Sam lazily traced patterns on her back as they lightly ran their fingers over her skin. They weren't sure why they weren't sleeping as they had been absolutely exhausted when they left the shelter, but when they had tried to sleep their brain had refused to let them. All Sam could see when they closed their eyes were the children in the shelter, their bright smiles and eyes full of wonder at the Christmas decor. The idea that those children would miss out on the wonder of the holiday was eating at Sam.

They knew what it was like to watch the kids at school show off their new toys after Christmas when they never received gifts for the holiday. It was hard enough to spend every night wondering where they were going to sleep and if they were going to eat without the reminder that they weren't special enough for Santa to remember them. As Sam's own memories collided with their thoughts about the children they had seen that night, tears ran down their face. Sam couldn't let those kids miss out on the magic of Christmas. It was something that Sam had denied themselves for years because of their experiences as a child and something that they were just beginning to allow back in their life.

Holley shifted slightly and they looked down at her and smiled. Holley was opening their world to so much more than they had ever imagined possible. She was the reason for their new outlook on the holiday. Even with their birthright, Sam would never have experienced the true spirit of Christmas without her. Sam still wasn't entirely sure that they were capable of love, but if anyone could change that, it would be Holley. As they looked down at her, Sam knew that they would have to do something to show her just how much they appreciated everything she was doing for them. She had planned out a bunch of activities for them over the next few weeks and Sam couldn't wait to see what that would bring, but somehow they would have to find a few surprises for her as well.

Chapter 31

The last few days of November were incredibly busy days for Sam at work as they had to run numbers for all of the stores to see how successful the partnership with organizations like Holiday Heroes was going. As a result, Sam worked long days often well into the night so they were not able to spend time with Holley. They were barely able to squeeze a few hours in with Candycane sitting in the mall watching kids push and shove while in line to meet Santa.

By the time they returned to their apartment on November thirtieth, they could barely keep their eyes open. Sam was so tired in fact that they didn't see the box in front of their door until they tripped over it, trying to enter their apartment. "You alright, Sam?" Candycane asked, reaching down and picking up the box. "Not sure what this is, but it has your name on it."

Sam took the box from Candycane and walked to the kitchen to open it. "Thanks Candycane. Sorry I was grumpy at the mall. Work has just taken a lot out of me the past few days. Teaming up with the charity organizations seems to be incredibly profitable which is great but it isn't sitting right with me anymore. I mean I'm grateful that there are more gifts being purchased, but I don't really care if Mercers makes money off of it now. It would be different if they were using that increase in profits to give back, but I know they won't," Sam grumbled as they grabbed a knife to open the box they had placed on their counter.

"It's alright. I appreciate that you have still made the effort to put the work in for the list. I know you would rather be with Holley," Candycane said. "Perhaps if the profits are enough, you could recommend that Mercers do the right things and give some of it back?"

"I can try, but all they care about is profit. I have no doubt that if this continues this may well earn me a promotion," Sam sighed as they shook their head.

"Is that not what you wanted?" Candycane asked.

"Yeah. I guess, maybe. Look, I'm tired, too tired to have this conversation. I'm gonna open this and go to bed," Sam answered.

"Alright, Sam. I'm here if you change your mind. Good night," Candycane replied as she walked to her room.

Sam opened the box to find an advent calendar and a note from Holley. The calendar featured an image of Santa's workshop with 25 numbered squares on it that contained chocolate mint truffles. Sam examined the calendar and fought the urge to open the first door and try one of the chocolates. They set the calendar on the counter and placed the empty box next to the trash can, as they picked up the note and walked to their room to escape temptation. Sitting on their bed, they unfolded the note, smiling as they read it.

Sam,

I wanted to make sure that you got the full Christmas experience and I figured you never had one of these growing up. I hope you enjoy the chocolate and the countdown to my favorite day of the year. I know I can't wait to count down the days with you.

• *Holley*

After signing her name, she had drawn a heart, which Sam was currently tracing with their thumb. This was possibly one of the most thoughtful gifts anyone had ever given them. Sam wasn't completely sure what the heart at the end meant, but it had definitely touched theirs. They could not wait to see her tomorrow and thank her for the kind gesture. She was the only thing on their mind as they closed their eyes and drifted off that night, sleeping peacefully for the first time in days.

Sam jumped out of bed as their alarm went off December first. Their dreams had been full of images of Holley and the two of them spending time together, ice skating and looking at holiday displays in store windows, both things that Sam was planning on doing with her for her birthday. When Sam walked out to the kitchen, they opened the first door on their advent calendar and popped the truffle in their mouth.

"Hey, you are gonna spoil your appetite," Candycane scolded as she placed a plate of french toast in front of them.

"Think of it as an appetizer," Sam laughed. "I had to open it. Isn't that the point of advent calendars?"

"You could have waited until after breakfast," Candycane shook her head at them. "Do you know what you and Holley are doing tonight?"

"I don't. Are we still meeting for lunch? I'm going to try to leave work early, so I figure we can have lunch and then I'll head over to the shop and surprise Holley," Sam replied.

"Only if you can get away. If not, it's fine. I was just hoping we could get some work in on the list early so that I could go visit Rudolf tonight," Candycane said.

"You got it. I'll be there. Where are we meeting, again?" Sam asked.

"I was thinking we would just go to the mall. I know kids will be in school, but I figure the younger children will still be there," Candycane shrugged.

"Sounds like a valiant effort, at least," Sam laughed. "I'll meet you at the food court." Sam shoved the last of their french toast in their mouth as they stood and walked to get their coat. "Hate to eat and run, but if I'm gonna meet you for lunch, I gotta get there and start working."

The mall was busier than Sam had anticipated for a random Wednesday afternoon. Apparently the onset of December had caused panic for many of the mothers who were pushing strollers loaded with shopping bags through the food court. Sam had never really experienced this aspect of the holiday, at least not from the perspective of the consumer. Sam had spent the last several years analyzing shopping behaviors and trends each holiday season for work, but all of that data came from numbers on a screen.

"I'm shocked there are as many people here as there are. I guess this will have been a more successful lunch than I thought it would be," Sam laughed.

"I think we should meet here for lunch at least three times a week until Christmas," Candycane said. "It is only going to get busier."

"Yeah," Sam agreed as they brought their hands to their temples and massaged lightly. "I think I've had about enough of it for today, though. And you have a date to prepare for."

Candycane blushed as she stood. "Fine, but tomorrow night we have to go somewhere with lots of people so try and prepare yourself for that. This is the most crucial time of the year," Candycane said.

"Yes. Got it. Don't forget Saturday we have lunch with Santa at the shelter. I'm going to need an elf, so don't go running off with Rudy never to return," Sam laughed.

"Rudolf. He hates that nickname. And you aren't getting rid of me that easily, Sam," Candycane replied as they walked out of the mall.

Sam stopped at a flower stand outside and purchased a Christmas bouquet made up of red roses and white carnations before walking the few blocks to the Christmas Claus-it. They weren't sure what the proper thank you was for the calendar, but this seemed like a good start. Sam stopped outside of the shop and watched Holley interacting with a customer through the window. Even in this element, in an ugly holiday sweater with her hair back in a messy ponytail as she demonstrated Christmas lights, she was gorgeous. How had they gotten so lucky?

Holley glanced up at them as they walked through the door, her dimple appearing as she smiled at them. "I will be right with you," she called to Sam, returning her attention to the customer she was helping.

Sam waited patiently for the woman to leave before walking over to Holley and giving her a quick kiss. "Hey there, beautiful. I got my calendar and just wanted to say thank you," Sam said, handing her the bouquet that they had been hiding behind their back.

"These are beautiful. I'm a hot mess who has been running around here all morning because apparently there are tons of people in this city who wait for December first to start decorating," Holley replied. "Thank you for these. Now please tell me that you are going to stay and help me get through the rest of this day."

"I was so looking forward to racing back to my cubicle, but if a better offer was to come along," Sam said, smiling at Holley.

"If I have to prove to you that spending time with me is better than crunching numbers, I think you should maybe go back to your cubicle," Holley replied.

"I assure you that spending time with you is much better than work," Sam said, wrapping their arms around Holley's waist and pulling her to them as they met her lips in a deep passionate kiss. When they pulled away, they looked at her and smiled. "So, what exactly can I do for you?"

"When you kiss me like that, I can barely think," Holley replied, breathlessly. She glanced towards the store as the door chime sounded. "Could you head out and watch the register while I put these incredible flowers in some water?"

Sam spent the rest of the day helping Holley in the shop. As they watched her work, they found themselves falling more and more for the woman. Her smile was infectious and Sam loved watching her work, so much so that they were almost sad when the last customer left and she asked them to lock the door. "You really are passionate about the things that you sell, aren't you?" Sam asked as they walked back to the register.

"Of course I am. I love Christmas and I only sell products that I would use in decorating. These items are more than just lights and ornaments. They bring the magic of the holiday into people's homes. This is important," Holley said. "And tonight, you are going to see just how important. We're decorating your apartment."

"We're what?" Sam asked. "I figured we'd be baking cookies or watching holiday movies at your place."

"I know CC is out of town for the night and I thought it would be a nice surprise for her when she got back and it gives us a chance to spend some time together. Besides, you did buy a tree from me and you have yet to put it up." Holley answered. "I'll make eggnog."

"Spending the night alone with you is more than enough to make me agree, but if you insist on eggnog, I'm not going to say no," Sam replied.

Chapter 32

That night Holley helped turn Sam's apartment into a space that a Christmas elf could happily call home. As they decorated she told Sam of her childhood and how she celebrated the holidays with her family. Sam was amazed at how she seemed to glow as she talked about picking the perfect tree and personal ornaments for each of them every year. When they had finished putting the tree up, she handed a box to Sam. Inside was an ornament with the words "Believe in the Magic of Christmas" written around Santa's face.

"I thought this could be your first ornament to celebrate the first Christmas that you actually celebrated," Holley said.

"That's really very sweet, Holley. Thank you. I've never had my own ornament or my own tree or anything for Christmas, really. Faith has given me gifts over the years, but because she knows me they have always just been practical things that I needed. This is the first gift I've ever gotten that was really a Christmas gift," Sam said.

"I have a feeling that you are going to have a lot of firsts in the next few weeks, Sam. Christmas really is a magical time of year and I can't wait to show you all of it," Holley replied. "Now, where should we hang the mistletoe?" Holley held up a fake sprig of mistletoe, nibbling on her bottom lip as she held it above her head.

Sam leaned in and kissed her, grabbing the mistletoe and walking to their bedroom. "I think that belongs in here," they called out as they entered the room.

Holley and Sam were almost asleep when they heard the door to the apartment open. Sam jumped out of bed and quickly pulled on a shirt and shorts so that they could witness Candycane's reaction as she turned on the light. When they entered the living room, they saw the elf standing in front of the tree with a huge grin on her face and tears in her eyes. "It is beautiful, Sam. Absolutely beautiful," she said without looking from the tree.

Holley walked into the room with a blanket wrapped around her. "We thought it would help with the feeling of homesickness you were having. Sam told me that your family goes all out for the holidays. You deserved a tree," she said.

"Do you really like it?" Sam asked.

Candycane turned and threw her arms around Sam in a hug. "I love it. Thank you so much," she said, looking over Sam's shoulder at Holley. "Thank you, both of you. This is the sweetest thing."

"I'm really glad you like it," Holley said. "Sam's coming over Friday night to get ready for the Santa lunch at the shelter. We could use an extra hand if you're free."

"You mean it?" Candycane asked.

"Of course. Being away from family this time of year is really hard, especially if it's the first time you have been away from them," Holley said.

"Thank you. Now I fear I woke the two of you. It's late. I will be there Friday. Good night," Candycane said, walking past them to her room.

Friday night they all met at Holley's to make cookies for Saturday. They spent several hours baking a variety of Christmas cookies, including a large selection of sugar cookies that they cut into Christmas trees, stockings, and reindeer. These they left undecorated as Candycane decided that she would like to set up a cookie icing station for the kids. Both Holley and Sam loved that idea, but it made Holley decide that they needed to make two more kinds of cookies to replace the sugar cookies for the trays that they were planning to set up on the tables. When all was said and done they had made chocolate chip, gingerbread, shortbread, snickerdoodles, and cake batter crinkle cookies, which they dyed green to be grinch cookies.

It was well after midnight when they were done baking and as the sugar wore off, the late hour became apparent as exhaustion overcame them. "CC, I'm sorry it's so late. I guess time got away from us. You're welcome to crash on my couch if you're too tired to go home," Holley offered.

The next morning, Candycane and Sam left for their apartment, by way of a crowded Christmas market full of children. "How is it that you managed to find an opportunity to work on the list this early in the morning?" Sam grumbled as they walked through the mass of people, names filtering through their brain.

"Because it's my job, Sam. What we're doing today is important, but it's taking us away from the list when we could be collecting names, so this is my solution," Candycane answered.

"Fine, but I'm really going to need coffee before I let you dress me up as an elf. I'm still mad that Simone went out and hired a professional Santa. I'm a perfectly good Santa," Sam said.

"You'll make an exceptional elf, too," Candycane answered. "I visited Bobbin's personally to get you an outfit for today. I think you're going to love it."

A few hours later, Sam and Candycane arrived at Holley's, fully dressed in their elf attire. "Oh my gosh. The two of you look amazing!" Holley exclaimed as she opened the door. "Sam, you are the cutest elf I have ever seen."

Sam rolled their eyes and looked back at Candycane. "CC was in charge of our costumes," Sam replied, their hands pulling on their red and white striped suspenders. They were wearing red pants and a bright green shirt with red buttons as well as green shoes with curled toes and a long green hat with a red and white pom pom on the end.

"Well, they are fantastic, and I'm jealous," Holley said.

"I could have gotten you one, too, Holley, but you are always so festive. I love your Christmas tree sweater and ornament leggings. It's perfect considering you plan to make tree decorations with the kids," Candycane said. "This is going to be a great event."

"I really hope so. I want today to make a difference in the lives of these kids. I feel like my life might have turned out differently if someone had taken the time to do something like this," Sam said. "Let's get the cookies and craft supplies and get to the shelter. I want to make sure we get everything set up and ready to go."

The shelter decorations had been updated to include red and green table cloths on all of the tables as well as a fancy armchair for Santa.

There were stations set up throughout the shelter for ornament making, cookie icing, and letters to Santa. That was the table that Sam was working at as they had plans to personally deliver the letters to Wyatt to ensure that these children still had a Christmas despite not having homes.

Simone had done an outstanding job advertising the event and there was a line waiting outside of the shelter when they opened the doors. The lunch ended up lasting for four hours as families rotated in, eating the provided meal and allowing their kids to participate in all of the activities, including meeting Santa. As the event came to an end and they started to clean up, Simone walked over to Sam to congratulate them.

"Sam, this was an incredible success. Thank you so very much. I know that the kids really enjoyed it. And I think that you did, too," she said, smiling at them.

"It was a really rewarding day. Thanks for letting us do it," Sam replied. "I'm sure Holley had a great time, too."

"She's a really great one, Sam. I don't know if she's the one responsible for this change in you, but I think that if you had been the same person five years ago, I might have walked away from Terrance. Don't let your fear of love mess this one up. I see the way you look at her. Don't be afraid to tell her what she means to you," Simone said, giving Sam a hug. "Merry Christmas, Sam. I hope to see more of you here in the future."

"Everything alright, Sam?" Holley asked, walking over after Simone walked away.

"Yeah. She was just saying thank you. I think today went really well. Did you have fun? The trees look like they got a lot of new decorations," Sam replied.

"They all seemed to really enjoy themselves. I was hoping we could come back and do a story hour. Maybe give all of the kids a book and read a few Christmas stories?" Holley suggested.

"You should talk to Simone about that. That sounds like a really good idea. I'd love to help you with it," Sam said. "Let me know what Simone says." Holley walked off to find Simone and Sam finished gathering the letters to Santa, placing all of them in their shoulder bag to deliver to Wyatt the next morning.

Sam wanted to go tonight, but Candycane had quickly told them that they would have to wait for the morning for several reasons, one of which was that Wyatt would not be available until the morning. That however wasn't the main reason for Candycane insisting they stay. That reason was the Christmas movie marathon that Faith had invited all of them to a week ago, a marathon that both Candycane and Holley were looking forward to.

Holley returned to help Sam and CC with the rest of the cleanup of their stations with a huge smile on her face. "I take it your chat with Simone was successful?" Sam asked.

"It was. She can't wait to have us all back," Holley answered. "You both ready to head to Faith's? I saved a box of cookies."

Faith and X had prepared a spread of movie watching snacks that were set up on the dining table along with an ice bucket full of hard ciders for everyone to enjoy. As everyone filled their plates with food, Faith asked about the day, pulling Sam aside to talk to them once she had heard what everyone had to say.

"So, everything was alright with Simone?" Faith asked. "She didn't try anything?"

"I know you don't trust her, but yes. It was fine. We are going back to read stories to the kids. And she even told me not to mess things up with Holley. So I think you can stop worrying about her trying to get me back," Sam answered.

"Well that is good advice. She really does adore you, Sam, and I think you feel the same way about her. Don't take too long to tell her," Faith said.

"I thought I came over here to watch movies, not for relationship advice," Sam grumbled.

"Alright. I'll let it go, but if you mess this up, Sam ..." Faith replied.

"If Sam messes what up?" Holley asked, poking her head around the corner. "Sorry I need to use the bathroom before the movies start. I didn't mean to interrupt your conversation."

"Movie night, Holley. Apparently I have to keep any sarcastic comments to myself so as not to mess up the movie watching experience," Sam said. "I'll save you a seat, cutie." Sam and Faith walked past Holley to the living room.

Sam found themselves enjoying the movies, although the more they watched the more important it made those letters to Santa. The spirit of Christmas and the magic of the holiday was a theme that kept coming up in the films. These were things that were relatively new ideas for Sam, but they were starting to embrace them. By the time the credits rolled on the last film, all Sam wanted to do was head to the North Pole and speak with Wyatt, because there was no way that Sam was going to allow those kids to lose their belief in the magic of Christmas.

Chapter 33

Sam stood in the snow outside of the Santa's residence with Candycane, shivering, despite wearing a coat and boots. It was early in the morning, the sun was still rising, but the lights were on in all of the warehouses. "Wh, wh, wh, why are we not going in?" Sam asked, their teeth shattering.

"Because I wanted you to see how busy they are. Santa Wyatt agreed to meet with you, but he is already at work in his workshop, so we are to wait for him here," Candycane answered.

"Or you could have waited in the foyer," Wyatt said as he walked up behind them. "Come on. Let's get some hot chocolate and discuss whatever this is that you needed to tell me, Sam." He walked past them and into the house, holding the door for them to follow.

They sat in a small sitting room with a fire and a few chairs. Sam emptied the letters from their bag onto the coffee table before sitting down. "These are letters to Santa from children who don't have a home this Christmas. They spend their nights sleeping in a homeless shelter, and home or not, they deserve to get a visit from you on Christmas Eve," Sam explained.

"I agree that they deserve gifts, Sam, and I will gladly deliver their gifts to the shelter if they have not found homes by Christmas, but there is no guarantee that all of them will return to the shelter. I will do my best to locate each of them, though, as I can see how important this is to you," Wyatt replied.

"Thank you. That is more than I had hoped for. I feared that you would tell me it was impossible. That was what my mother used to tell me, that Santa could only deliver gifts to children who had homes and since it was my fault that we spent so many holidays without one, I didn't deserve gifts anyhow," Sam said.

"Your mother was wrong. All children deserve to experience the magic of Christmas. I'm glad to see that you are beginning to feel the spirit of the holiday, Sam," Wyatt answered.

"I am. I've had a lot of help with it," Sam said, looking fondly at Candycane.

"I can't take that credit, Sam. It belongs with Holley," Candycane responded, retrieving her phone from her pocket to check the time. "Speaking of, we really need to go, Sam. I'm going to be late for work, and you are going to be late for your date."

"Right. Thank you for meeting with me Wyatt and for anything that you can do for these kids. I really appreciate it," Sam said, standing and extending their hand to Wyatt.

As soon as Sam released Wyatt's hand, Candycane snapped her fingers, returning them to Sam's apartment. "Sorry to cut that short, Sam, but I'm covering the shop this morning so that you can take Holley to the holiday market," Candycane said.

"The market. I completely forgot. Thanks for remembering," Sam replied. "I owe you one. She's been sad that she hasn't been able to go this year. I think this is going to be a really nice treat for her."

Candycane and Sam arrived at the Christmas Claus-it just as Holley was opening the door for business. "What are the two of you doing here?" Holley asked as they walked in. "Not that I'm sad to see you, but CC you aren't scheduled to work today and I thought the two of you had plans."

"We do have plans," Sam answered. "The plan is for CC to run the shop this morning because we, you and I, are going to the market."

"But, it's Sunday. The shop is going to be busy. I can't leave CC alone to deal with that," Holley argued.

"I'll be fine, boss. I can handle it. You deserve a day off, and yesterday doesn't count," Candycane said. "Go and enjoy the morning with Sam."

"Come on, Holley. I hear that you have to get there early if you want the fresh baked strudels and danishes," Sam said. "Thanks CC. We'll bring you back something delicious to eat."

"You better," Candycane said, as Holley and Sam walked to the door. "Holley, have fun. Don't worry. I have this."

The holiday market was an outdoor festival that happened every weekend starting the Saturday after Thanksgiving. It featured vendors selling homemade pastries and candies as well as crafters selling handmade wares. There were ornaments and wreaths for sale at many of the tables as well as scarves and hats. Vendors also sold toys, soaps, lotions, and other items that could be given as gifts.

Holley stopped at every table, carefully examining the items and chatting with the people who had crafted them. When they left, Sam and Holley each had new crocheted hats and scarves and they had purchased a new hat for CC. They also had found gifts for X and Faith and eaten their way through the market, having tried cakes, cookies, breads, and a large assortment of chocolates.

As they finished shopping and began their walk back towards the shop, Holley paused and pulled on Sam's hand to stop them from walking. "Is something wrong?" Sam asked, turning to face Holley.

"No. It's quite the opposite. This morning was lovely, Sam. This was such a nice surprise. The holiday market is one of my favorite traditions and I was afraid that I wasn't going to make it there this year. Thank you for figuring out a way to take me. This means so much to me," Holley said.

"You've done so much for me, Holley. I just wanted to do something nice for you. I'm really glad I did, too. The market was a lot of fun," Sam replied.

"It really was, but then again everything I do with you is fun," Holley said. "Come on, I suppose we should get this food to CC while it's still warm." Holley started to walk again, not releasing Sam's hand until they were entering the Christmas Claus-it.

"Did the two of you have fun?" Candycane asked.

"We did. It was a really great morning. Thank you. Sam has food for you. I'll take over so you can eat in just a minute," Holley answered as she walked to the back. She put her bags down and walked over to Sam, pulling them to her in a tight embrace and kissing them on the cheek. "Thank you again, Sam. Today was wonderful."

It really had been wonderful, just like every moment that Sam had spent with Holley. The next week Sam spent their nights divided between Candycane and Holley. They worked on the list with Candycane on their lunch break on the days that they were seeing Holley after work, making it the first week where they had worked on the list every single day, which was taking a toll on their brain. Luckily they were getting a break from crowds and the list when they were with

Holley as they had spent their nights in, making gingerbread houses and watching some of Holley's favorite romantic Christmas films.

Watching movies with Holley had given Sam a lot of ideas for her birthday, which they discussed with Faith and Candycane in great detail one night after walking around the mall. "These are great ideas, Sam. I'm just not sure how you are going to do all of it in one night," Faith said, once Sam was done listing off all of the things they wanted to do with Holley.

"If we start early enough, we can get through it, I think. I just want to give her the kind of date night that happens in those cheesy holiday movies she loves so much. Every girl deserves someone that will take them ice skating in front of a large lit Christmas tree, right?" Sam laughed.

"It does sound really romantic. Just make sure you do it your way, though. Don't try too hard to make it from one of the movies. Holley is with Sam, not the guy who runs the Christmas tree farm in the small town in the middle of nowhere," Faith said.

"Faith's right. Those movies are great and full of romance, but you need to give her a night that comes from your heart. Otherwise it will seem too forced and it won't mean as much," Candycane agreed.

"Don't worry. I have something planned for the end of the night that will separate it from the movies," Sam replied. "Just have to work out the specifics, but I'm pretty sure she's gonna love it."

"I can't wait to hear all about it," Faith said.

"Unfortunately her birthday is still a week away. Have to get through pictures with Santa first," Sam said.

Chapter 34

Photos with Santa at the Christmas Claus-it drew a much larger crowd than any of them coud have imagined. Holley briefly considered hiring a professional Santa for the day, but when she had seen how hurt Sam was when they weren't Santa at the shelter, she thought better of it. Sam spent the entire day sitting in a chair while children sat on their knee and told them what they wanted for Christmas. Candycane, dressed in her elf clothes, was there to assist them and make sure that they had plenty of tea to combat the constant flow of information for the list.

The majority of these children were leaning towards the nice list, which fit with what Candycane had said about most kids becoming nice by the time Christmas rolled around. As it was getting close to closing time, a girl who appeared to be around nine reached the front of the line. She was wearing a red dress with a green bow and looked absolutely miserable. Her mother stopped her and fixed her hair before she walked up to Sam. Sam watched the interaction and tried their best to keep a smile on their face, as they knew the girl had no desire to be there. She was only the second non-believer that Sam had come across. Sam never had to take photos with Santa, but they saw themselves when they looked at the little girl. When she sat on their knee and Sam asked what she wanted for Christmas, she responded, "Santa isn't real so it doesn't matter."

"But what if Santa was real?" Sam asked. "What would you want then?"

"An easel and paint supplies, but I won't get them," the girl answered, smiling for her mother and hopping off of Sam's knee.

As she walked away, Sam stood and announced that Santa was going to take a ten minute break. Candycane followed Sam to the backroom to make sure that they were alright, nodding to Holley that they were fine, so she could focus on her customers.

"What happened with that girl?" Candycane asked. "That didn't seem like a normal interaction."

"It wasn't. She's a non-believer. I don't think she has ever received what she really wants for Christmas. I wish there was something that could be done about that," Sam said.

"You may have already done it, Sam. You asked her what she wanted and she answered you, honestly. If Peter decides that she should be on the nice list, she will get her gift," Candycane answered.

"I really hope you're right. I just keep thinking that if I had ever had a real Christmas, things might have been different for me," Sam said,

"I'm sorry that you didn't experience the magic as a child, but I can confidently say that the magic resides in you, Sam. You really have embraced the Christmas spirit," Candycane replied.

"Hey, Santa, everything alright?" Holley said, popping her head in the backroom. "There are a few more kids that just showed up if you are available."

"Yeah, I'll be right out," Sam answered. "Thanks, CC. I don't know how much spirit I have, but I do think I understand Christmas a bit better than I did a few months ago."

Sam and Candycane returned to the sales floor to find Faith and X standing in the line with matching ugly Christmas sweaters on. "We aren't too old to get a photo with Santa, are we?" Faith asked as Sam sat back down.

"There is no age limit for believing in Santa," Holley said. "I was actually hoping that I would get a chance to tell Santa what I wanted for Christmas, too."

"I'm not entirely sure that what you want from Santa is for others to hear," Faith teased.

Holley blushed, turning and walking back to the register. "Looks like someone is trying for the naughty list," Sam said as Faith sat on their knee and X stood behind them.

"Who? Holley? I have no doubt Santa would very much enjoy that," Faith laughed.

"Seriously, Faith. What are you doing here?" Sam asked.

"X and I get our photo taken with Santa every year. How could I pass up getting a picture where Santa is literally my best friend?" Faith replied.

"Fair enough," Sam said. "I have no desire to hear what it is you want for Christmas though." Sam laughed, doing their best to stay in character with a deep chuckle with a few "ho, ho, ho's" thrown in.

After they had gotten a few photos, Holley traded places with Faith and X snapped several pictures of Holley sitting on Sam's knee, including a photo, where Holley pulled Sam's beard down to reveal their face and kissed them. Sam walked to the shelf with the Christmas tree frames they had made displayed on it and picked up the one with the Christmas robots and green and red bow for the star. They handed the frame to Holley. "I think I have need of a frame for the last photo," Sam said.

"Oh really?" Holley laughed. "I thought for sure you wouldn't want any memories of today."

"That last one might be something I'd like to remember," Sam replied, causing everyone to laugh.

"Are you all accompanying us to the store to purchase books for tomorrow night?" Holley asked as she locked the door and closed the store.

"Oh, right. Storytime tomorrow night. I almost forgot. I wish we could attend, but we have plans. I'd love to help buy some of the books though," Faith answered. "Please get pictures tomorrow. I want as many photos of Sam in that suit as I can possibly get. I'm so afraid that Sam Scrooge is going to rear their ugly head again."

"You know I don't think I've gotten you a Christmas present yet, Faith. How's coal sounding? I can put a word in with the big man and get you taken off the nice list," Sam joked.

"Not funny, Santa," Faith replied, sticking her tongue out at them.

"It was a little funny," CC said, smiling. "So, are we heading to the store in the mall?"

"No. There's a bookstore down the street. I already talked to the owner and he agreed to stay open for us to shop," Holley answered. "I can come back and close up after we shop, if you are all ready to go now."

An hour later, they left Once Upon a Tome with bags full of books for the children at the shelter. Sam, Holley, and Candycane dropped the books off before heading back to Sam's apartment. They ordered in and watched Christmas movies until they couldn't keep their eyes open. Sam was the first to head to bed, leaving Candycane and Holley to finish the movie.

Sam had a busy day ahead of them tomorrow and needed to try and get some sleep. They were spending the day meeting someone to help them with their plans for Holley's birthday. They were both excited and anxious about this plan and they were still lying awake with worry when Holley finally came to bed. "Thought you were going to sleep. Was the movie that bad?" Holley asked as she cuddled into them and kissed their shoulder.

"No. I really was having a hard time staying awake. I guess I just couldn't go to sleep without you in my arms," Sam said, rolling onto their back so that she could curl into them with her head on their chest. With Holley sleeping on them, Sam finally was able to find sleep.

The next morning Holley and Candycane went to work at the Christmas Claus-it. Sam went to visit Chas at the diner. They had an idea for a present for Holley that only Chas could help them with. They weren't sure it was going to work but if it did, it would be the perfect gift.

It took Sam and Chas most of the day to get Holley's gift just right, but as morning turned to late afternoon, it finally came together. "Thank you, Chas. I'm sure that she is going to love this," Sam said, looking at their creation and smiling.

"I'm glad that I could help. She seems like a really great girl and you practically glow when you talk about her," Chas replied. "This is for Thursday, right?"

"Yeah. I'll be by Wednesday night to make sure everything is set," Sam answered, pulling their phone from their pocket as their alarm started to sound. "Oh, wow. When did it get so late? I gotta run. See you in a few days! Thanks again." Sam ran out of the door and flagged down a cab to take them to the shelter.

Sam arrived a few minutes after Holley and Candycane, walking in to find them setting up for the event with Simone. "Was starting to think that you forgot about us," Holley said as Sam walked towards them.

"I could never forget about you, Holley. I just got caught up working on something. What can I do to help?" Sam replied.

With the four of them working together, they transformed a corner of the room into a reading nook with a chair set in front of one of the Christmas trees and pillows on the ground in a semicircle. Each pillow had a stack of books sitting on it for the children to keep. Holley had also made sure to get plenty of extras so the shelter could start a small library.

The event was to start after dinner, but many of the children raced over to the corner to talk to Santa as soon as they entered. Sam had agreed to wear the suit one last time and as they watched the faces of the children light up as they spoke with them, Sam was very glad that they had let Holley talk them into it.

Sam, Holley, Candycane, and even Simone took turns reading stories to the children, only stopping when it was time to clean up from dinner and let the families get ready for bed. Holley started picking up the pillows and books that remained as soon as Simone had instructed the children to find their parents. "Holley, you don't have to do that. I think it might be nice if we left that there for the next few nights. The kids really seemed to enjoy it, and I'm sure that I can find a few volunteers to read a story or two," Simone said.

"Are you sure, Simone? I don't mind," Holley replied.

"The three of you have done more than enough. I can't begin to thank you for the light you have brought into this place. It finally feels like there might be some Christmas magic working its way into the shelter," Simone said, smiling at all of them. "I can even feel it when I look at Sam, which is really saying something. I think you are a really positive influence on them, Holley."

"Don't forget all of this started as Sam's idea. I can't take credit for that, Simone. I think Sam has always had the magic of Christmas within them. They were just waiting for it to awaken," Holley said, grabbing Sam's hand and squeezing it.

Sam and Candycane shared a look as Holley finished speaking. She had no idea how close to the truth her words were. "Well, if you don't need us to help with anything, I think I speak for all of us when I say that we're tired and could use some sleep. Thanks again for letting us do this, Simone," Sam said, beginning to walk towards the exit.

"What an amazing night," Holley said once they were outside. "The looks on their faces when we told them that they could keep the books, wow. My heart is so full right now."

"Yeah that was pretty incredible. Sam's gonna have a heck of time trying to top that for your birthday," Candycane laughed.

"But we aren't doing anything special for my birthday," Holley said. "Just meeting some of my friends on Saturday night."

"Which will have to be one amazing night, because you deserve to have one hell of a celebration, Holley," Sam said, leaning in and giving her a quick kiss.

Chapter 35

Candycane kept Sam busy every night to start the week, giving them no time to see Holley. Had they not been so busy planning her birthday, they would have been very annoyed by this, but she was allowing them to have all day Thursday and Saturday night to spend with Holley and forget about the list. Sam was fairly certain that this was because Candycane was planning on visiting Rudolf Saturday night, but since she was helping them, Sam hadn't given her the normal grief that they would have over it. They were really happy that Candycane and Rudolf were doing so well.

"So Candycane, you talk to Rudolf lately?" Sam asked as they ate breakfast Thursday morning.

"You know I've been too busy here to make a trip back that way," Candycane huffed.

"Well, what about Saturday night?" Sam offered.

"He is going to be so busy. Saturday will be one week from Christmas, which means only six days until Rudolf has to have all of his teams ready to fly," Candycane replied.

"Sounds like all the more reason to visit him. I'm sure he could use a hand and a distraction from all of the stress he is feeling," Sam said. "I know I would want to see Holley if I was doing something so stressful."

"You really think that's a good idea?" Candycane asked.

"I do. You should go. Friday night after we're done collecting names. Go. I can help Holley in the shop Saturday," Sam replied.

"We are supposed to be working on the list Saturday," Candycane said.

"True, but there will be plenty of people shopping in Old Town that day and I'll make up for it on Sunday. Promise," Sam said. "And I owe you one for today, anyhow."

"I'm covering today as much for Holley as I am for you," Candycane replied. "Although I'm incredibly curious about this surprise you have planned for her."

"That you'll have to ask her about on Friday," Sam answered. "I gotta get to work and get my reports done quickly so I can kidnap my beautiful girlfriend for her birthday." Sam stood and walked to the door, grabbing their laptop and coat as they exited the apartment.

Sam arrived at the Christmas Claus-it at twelve twenty five, laughing to themselves as they realized the time. Maybe they were becoming a true Christmas after all. They walked through the door to find the store completely decorated for Holley's birthday, balloons everywhere. This had the mark of Candycane and Faith all over it. "Sam!" Holley ran towards them, wrapping her arms around them, and kissing them.

"Look at all of the balloons. CC tells me you had nothing to do with this, but I don't believe her."

"CC is telling the truth. I'm not a big fan of balloons, but she is and so is Faith. My guess would be that they are the ones responsible for this," Sam answered. "It is very festive, though. I almost hate to take you away from it."

"Take me away from it? What do you mean?" Holley asked. "We're open for another five and a half hours."

"That's right, boss. We are. And I am happy to take care of everything here at the shop. You have a birthday to celebrate," Candycane chimed in, trying to usher Holley towards the door.

"Alright. Alright. Let me just go get my things," Holley said. "I'll be right back, Sam."

"I'll be waiting, beautiful. Don't take too long. We have a busy day ahead of us," Sam called as she walked away.

"Where are we going, Sam?" Holley asked as they flagged down a cab.

"It's a surprise. I have planned an entire day of birthday activities for us," Sam answered.

The first stop on the agenda was to the city's botanical garden, which had been decorated with vintage blow molds that made quite a statement even in the daylight. There was also a hall of decorated Christmas trees that featured over fifty trees. Holley had a wonderful time and they both took a ton of pictures of each other enjoying the garden. From there, they made their way to the science museum to visit the exhibit on the science behind Christmas. After the museum, Sam took Holley to dinner at a small cafe that sat across from the Richfield Christmas tree. The tree was a massive pine tree featuring thousands of lights and ornaments, and as they sat and ate dinner, the sun set and the tree lit up, thousands of twinkling lights, blinking in sync to Christmas music.

"Ok, Sam. That was incredibly impressive timing. This has been an amazing birthday. Thank you," Holley said as she looked at the tree in awe.

"Oh, we aren't done yet. This was just the beginning," Sam replied.

"What do you mean we aren't done? You've already done so much," Holley said.

"Consider that the warm-up," Sam laughed. "You ever been ice skating?"

Sam took Holley to an outdoor skating rink that was surrounded by Christmas trees and lights. They skated until Sam's phone began to buzz, alerting them that they needed to move on to the next destination. Sam's last Christmas activity for the night was a trolley ride through some of the suburbs around the city to see some of the largest, tackiest light displays that either of them had ever seen. There was even a stop in the middle of the tour at a hot cocoa food truck where they each got a gourmet hot chocolate. When the trolley dropped them off, Holley was certain that Sam had to be done with their surprises, as it was after ten.

"Sam, I don't know what to say. This was the best birthday I've ever had. It was so kind and thoughtful and all things that I've wanted to do. You are the absolute sweetest," Holley said, pulling Sam towards her and kissing them.

When Sam broke the kiss, they were short on breath. "I almost regret telling you that we aren't done. But, I still have to give you your gift," Sam said, reaching for her hand and walking down the street so that they could enjoy the lit up window displays of the many shops along the road.

"Sam, you know you don't have to give me a present, right? This day has been the best gift," Holley argued as they stopped to admire a window that featured penguins sliding down a snow covered hill on their bellies.

"If you're that anxious, we can cut this part short. I think we've seen enough lights and holiday decorations for one night," Sam said, turning to call a cab over to them.

On the ride to Chas's cafe, Holley couldn't stop talking about all of the incredible things they had done that day. As Sam watched her talk, they were sure that their decision was the right one, even if there was a giant knot forming in the pit of their stomach. They really hoped she liked her gift.

Sam and Holley walked into Chas's and found the booth that they had been in on their first date decorated with a bouquet of birthday balloons. "I suppose you didn't do these one's either," Holley asked as they sat down.

"No, they didn't. I did. Happy Birthday, Holley. Might I suggest the milkshake of the week?" Chas asked.

"Sure. What is it?" Holley asked.

"We are calling it Snowy Honey Day," Chas answered.

"Well that sounds interesting," Holley replied as Chas set the milkshake in front of her.

"I'll leave the two of you, but I do want to know how you enjoyed the shake before you go," Chas said, stepping away from the table.

"Are you not ordering one of your peppermint concoctions, Sam?" Holley asked.

"I. I will, but first I want to see what you think of yours," Sam said.

Holley took a sip of her milkshake and smiled, grabbing the spoon to scoop some of it up so that she could get a better taste. "That is fantastic. Vanilla and honey and just a hint of cinnamon sugar. It's perfect," Holley said.

"Good. I was hoping you'd say that. I created that flavor for you," Sam said. "The flavors reminded me of your lip balm and the scent of your body wash and it's the perfect amount of sweetness without being over the top so it's comforting, just like you."

"Sam Christmas, that is the absolute sweetest thing that anyone has ever done for me," Holley said, getting up and walking to their side of the booth so that she could sit beside them.

"I'm really glad you like it, Holley. You deserved something as amazing as you are," Sam replied.

"Sam," Holley started to say something, and Sam cut her off.

"No, please. Let me say something first before I lose my nerve," Sam said, turning and glaring at the jukebox as Last Christmas started playing. "This has to be the worst Christmas song in the world."

"Hey. What do you have against this song? It's super catchy," Holley argued.

"Because the lyrics don't make any sense. Why did he give his heart to someone who wasn't special in the first place? You don't just give your heart to anyone. They have to be special, deserving, meant for you," Sam said, looking at Holley, "the way that you are meant for me. I love you, Holley. I didn't even know that I was capable of love, but when I'm with you, I know there isn't another word for what I'm feeling. I know it's fast and maybe crazy, but I couldn't wait any longer to tell you. You deserve to have all of me, my heart included."

"Sam," Holley had tears in her eyes as she looked at them. "I love you, too. I have for a while now, but I didn't want to scare you away," she replied as she leaned in and kissed Sam, their mouth opening as hers met theirs.

The world melted away as they shared that kiss. Sam had never felt anything like it before as their heart felt light and free and every bit of tension they had been feeling disappeared. They were kissing the woman that they loved and with kisses like this, they never wanted to kiss anyone else again.

Chapter 36

The kisses in the booth led to a long walk back to Sam's apartment as they had to keep stopping to feel that closeness again. Once they made it back to the apartment, they did their best to sneak back to Sam's bedroom so they didn't wake Candycane. Holley continued to tell Sam how it had been her best birthday mixed with them exchanging declarations of love until they finally fell asleep.

The next morning, Sam woke before Holley and walked out to the kitchen to find not only Candycane waiting for them, but Faith as well. "Good morning to the both of you. This has the feeling of an intervention. What is going on?" Sam asked.

"I don't know, Sam. What is going on? You were super secretive all week about last night's activities and you still haven't told us what happened. I stayed up all night expecting my phone to ring," Faith answered.

"Did you seriously think I was going to call you on Holley's birthday? What do you think we were doing all night?" Sam replied.

"At some point, you had to come up for air," Faith responded.

"Did we really though?" Holley said, walking out into the kitchen. "Good morning CC, Faith. It's a beautiful morning, isn't it?"

"Ok. Spill it. What happened last night?" Faith said. "It's a morning, a morning after which you hardly got any sleep, so why are you in such a good mood? Both of you?"

"Is there a reason this can't wait, Faith? Do you really have to torment my girlfriend with twenty questions the second she wakes up?" Sam asked.

"It's fine, Sam. If either one of them knew what you were planning last night, I could see why they'd be asking," Holley said. "I told them that I loved them, too, and the way they told me and everything about yesterday was absolutely perfect."

"You, what?" Faith asked. "Sam told you that they love you?"

"Oh. You hadn't told them you were planning on doing that, then?" Holley asked, looking at Sam apologetically.

"No, I hadn't because they both would have been insufferable, as you can tell by the fact that both of them look like they are trying very hard not to say things," Sam answered. "Go ahead. Get it out." Sam gestured to their friends.

"Sam. I'm so incredibly happy for you, both of you!" Candycane exclaimed. "I knew it. I've known it. You could just tell, but so happy for you both, really."

"Of all the things you've kept from me over the years, this one stings a little," Faith said. "But, I'm gonna let it slide, because it's about damn time." Sam started to respond, but was unable to get the words out before Faith started singing her annoying song about Sam being in love.

"Don't get too excited about it yet, Faith. They might change their mind after they meet my friends," Holley laughed.

"I'm quite confident that there is very little that will sway them from their feelings. Sam has never been in love before and I was beginning to give up hope. So, Holley, much as I do like you, please know that if you are to break their heart, I might have to break you," Faith said.

"Well, good. Sam won't be the first to receive a threat on their life. Thank you for that, Faith. Though I wouldn't have expected anything else," Holley said, wrapping an arm around Sam and cuddling into them. "My friends are only a fraction as scary as Faith is."

Saturday night Sam and Holley entered The Spectrum to find Holley's friends sitting at the same table they had been at on Sam's birthday. Sam smiled as they remembered sitting at the bar, looking over at her, trying to decide if they should talk to her. "Wow, this brings back a few memories," Sam said.

"Some pretty good memories," Holley said, leaning in and kissing Sam on the cheek. "Come on, let's go meet my friends."

"So this is the reason that we haven't seen you in three months?" a tall thin woman with her long blonde hair pulled back into a ponytail, wearing a flannel shirt and jeans, asked.

"Ramona, don't act like that is completely on me," Holley replied. "You and Haley have something planned every weekend from now until next June and you know it."

"It isn't quite that bad," the shorter woman who had short brown hair and was wearing a black dress over gray tights paired with black boots, replied.

"We are pretty busy though, babe," Ramona said. "So you must be this Sam that we have heard so much about." Ramona extended her hand to Sam. "I'm Ramona and this is my wife, Haley."

Sam shook both of their hands before stepping up to the table to stand beside Holley. "It's nice to meet you both. Thank you for sharing Holley with me."

"So, Holley met you at work, right?" Sam asked.

"Yeah. She worked with me for a few years before she left to open her shop," Haley answered. "Everyone at work used to confuse us because of how similar our names are."

"And Holley met you because fate brought you to her store?" Ramona asked.

"Yeah. That's pretty accurate," Sam answered.

"I was waiting for you to tell us what really happened. Holley has been so mysterious about things with the two of you," Ramona replied. "I think we need a few more drinks so we can get this party started. Walk with me?"

"Yeah. How many shots do you want, beautiful?" Sam asked Holley, winking at her.

"Oh, no. We're drinking my drinks tonight. No shots. Just keep the ciders coming," Holley answered.

"So, Sam, I'm really happy that Holley has found someone, but she hasn't had the best track record with relationships, so I need to know that your intentions are good," Ramona said as they reached the bar.

"I don't know what Holley has told you, but I'm in love with her, so I'm planning on sticking around," Sam answered.

"No shit," Ramona said, laughing. "Well good for her. She hadn't shared that with us yet, but I have no doubt Haley has gotten that out of her by now.

Holley made her friends sound much more terrifying than they actually were. As it turned out Ramona and Haley loved Sam. Holley was right about them always having plans, though and two hours later Ramona was gathering Haley's things so that they could go home because they had to get up early in the morning to drive to Ramona's folks house for the holiday.

"That was short lived. I figured that we'd be here all night, but if you aren't opposed to leaving, I'd much rather spend time with you alone," Sam said once Holley's friends left.

"Sure. We can go back to my place. I wanted to ask you about something anyhow, and it will be easier to talk there," Holley answered.

"So um, what did you want to talk about?" Sam asked as they sat on Holley's couch.

"Well, you know how Ramona and Haley were on their way to Ramona's parents? Well, I know you don't normally celebrate Christmas so I was hoping that meant that you don't have plans and would maybe accompany me home," Holley answered.

"Oh, um. I hadn't even really thought about that, but yeah that makes sense that you'd go home for Christmas. When are you planning on leaving? I normally work all the way up to Christmas Eve, but we can take off as early as the twenty-second if we have plans," Sam answered.

"Wait, does that mean you'll go?" Holley asked.

"Of course I will. After all of your hard work to get me to celebrate Christmas, do you really think that I'd let you enjoy the holiday without me?" Sam replied.

"I can't leave until the night of the twenty-third. I should really stay open on the twenty-fourth but my parents will kill me if I wait to go down until Christmas morning," Holley answered.

"Ok. I will get everything figured out at work on Monday and let you know, but I should be able to get it off. I've never asked before, but I think Mercers kind of owes me right now," Sam said.

Monday morning, Sam walked into the office and asked for time off, something they hadn't done since they had been hired. Their boss told them that it would depend on if they were able to complete all of their reports, including projections for the days that they would miss before they left. That gave them four days to complete the end of holiday report on top of projecting sales for Christmas Eve and running their daily reports on toy and clothing numbers. Unfortunately they weren't full days as Sam had to meet up with Candycane for last minute list work after lunch every day. Which meant that Sam was doing a week's work in two days time.

This proved to be much more challenging than Sam had hoped and they were forced to stay up all night on the twenty-second running numbers at home, so that they could go in and report to their boss first thing in the morning to ask if they could have their time off. They emailed their report as soon as they finished it at four in the morning before crawling into bed to get a few hours of sleep. Their alarm went off almost as soon as they had closed their eyes, causing Sam to curse as they stood.

They inhaled deeply as they stretched, expecting the familiar smell of Candycane's cooking, forgetting that she had gone home to help

Rudolf prepare the reindeer. Damn, they really could have used her cooking this morning. They also needed to talk to her as they wanted to speak to Wyatt about the children in the shelter one more time. They would have to figure that out after work, though, because they needed to get there and show their boss that there was no reason for them to continue working through the end of the day or tomorrow.

On the way to the office, Sam stopped at one of the corner stores and made a copy of the key to their apartment, something they had been meaning to do since Candycane had moved in and they had given her the spare. There was a heart shaped keychain sitting by the register that Sam purchased, sliding the key onto the ring. They laughed at how silly it was as they placed it in their pocket. They'd always found heart shaped things to be as silly as Christmas trees. Their life sure had changed a lot in the last few months, they thought as they walked into the office to present their report to their boss so they could celebrate Christmas.

When Sam finished going over their reports, their boss smiled at them. "Very impressive, Christmas. Very impressive, indeed," he said. "Those numbers are really something. Give me a moment to make a few calls and then I will get back to you on your time off."

Sam sat at their desk staring at their computer and hoping that they would get the answer they needed. As they looked at their monitor, an email notification popped up. Clicking on it, Sam saw that their boss's boss wished to speak with them tomorrow morning in person. Sam sank into their chair in defeat. They had to go with Holley to her parent's house. What could possibly be so important that it needed to wait until the morning? Sam inhaled deeply and stood, walking to their boss's office. "I can't make that meeting," Sam said as they walked into the office.

"Sam, you do realize that the email might say it is an invitation but that meeting is not optional," their boss answered.

"No, I very much think it is optional. I've never asked for a day off the entire time I've worked here and I just ran all of the numbers. I know exactly how much money I made for Mercers this year with my idea to partner with the charity organizations, so I'm going to turn off my computer and walk out the door. The thing is I think that you all need me more than I need you. So, if you aren't willing to give me the time off that I need, you can consider this my resignation," Sam said, turning and walking out of their boss's office.

Chapter 37

When Sam exited the Mercers' building, they felt free for the first time in years. Sam had worked so hard for that company and they had never found joy in any of it. In the past few months, Sam had found happiness in helping others and in working with Holley. Sam thought that working in a stable, well paying job was the answer to living a happy life, but they were barely living before they met Holley. Now they knew that there was so much more out there and the idea of spending even five more minutes in that stuffy building, crunching numbers for a greedy corporation was something that they could no longer do.

Sam began walking back to their apartment to pack, lost in thought and paying little attention to their surroundings for the first time in months. That was how they missed Peppermint standing at the entrance of their apartment building, walking past her and to the elevator. Sam jumped as a hand stopped the elevator from closing and the doors began to open. They opened to reveal Wyatt standing in the foyer. He smiled at Sam as he entered the elevator.

"Wyatt? What are you doing here? Shouldn't you be getting prepared for your deliveries?" Sam asked.

"I should. That's actually what I'm doing. I originally expected that you'd be home on Christmas Eve and I was going to ask you to accompany me when I delivered the gifts to the shelter. Once I learned from Candycane that you were going somewhere else for the holiday, I figured I should stop by and let you know that I will be making a visit to the shelter tomorrow and dropping gifts off for all of the children that sent letters in from there," Wyatt explained.

"Wyatt, that's amazing. Thank you so much!" Sam said. "That means a lot to me."

"No, thank you. Every child should have the opportunity to experience the magic of Christmas. Thank you for making sure that I had these letters," Wyatt said. "Merry Christmas, Sam. I hope you have a wonderful holiday."

Sam and Holley left for her parent's house late on the twenty-third, not arriving until almost midnight. Holley's parents were both still awake, waiting for them to arrive, welcoming them in with cups of hot chocolate as they asked them to sit and join them for a quick chat. Sam was terrified that this chat was going to be full of disapproval of their relationship. They had been very pleasantly surprised when instead Holley's parents had welcomed them into their home and simply wished to get to know them a little better.

After a short conversation, Holley and Sam took their things to her room to turn in for the night. Holley curled into them as she got into bed, looking up at Sam and smiling. "I'm so glad you are here with me.

Tomorrow will be very busy, but I think you will find it enjoyable," Holley said, leaning up and kissing Sam. "Good night, love."

Sam lay awake for about an hour before they finally were able to sleep. Sam would have never imagined a world where they would be at their girlfriend's house to celebrate Christmas. The last few months had really changed their thoughts on a great many things. They were both excited and nervous to give Holley her Christmas present. They also hadn't told her about work yet, but they figured that was a conversation that could wait until they returned to Richfield. Right now they just needed to be present with Holley and enjoy Christmas.

Christmas Eve began with a very early wake up for breakfast with Holley's parents and Holley's best friend since childhood, Marie. Over pancakes and coffee, Holley and Marie laughed and reminisced about the past. Sam enjoyed listening to the stories, especially since they didn't have memories like that with anyone. They had more than their share of great moments with Faith, but they never had any close friends before college.

After breakfast, the kitchen turned into a cookie baking factory with Holley's mom keeping each of them busy whipping up various batters. They baked for hours, making everything from sugar cookies to shortbread to peanut brittle. When all was said and done, they had eight different types of cookies, peppermint bark, and the brittle. Once the baking was done, they packaged them in small tins, two of each cookie per container.

"Alright, what are we doing with all of these cookies? Not that I didn't enjoy making and tasting all of them," Sam asked as they finished packaging them.

"We deliver them, of course. First though," Holley's mom produced three gift bags, handing one to each of them.

"Oh, you are in for a real treat, Sam. Mrs. Daye picks out the absolute best festive attire," Marie said, reaching into her bag and pulling out a sweater with blinking lights on a Christmas tree and a hat shaped like a tree.

"Those are fantastic, Marie," Holley said as she opened her bag to reveal a sweater covered in christmas bows and beanie with a giant christmas bow where the pom pom should be. "Open yours, Sam."

Sam's sweater had the words "Believe in the Magic of Christmas" around Santa's face. Their hat was a normal Santa hat with the word "Believe" on it. "This is pretty perfect, Mrs. Daye. Thank you," Sam said, pulling on their sweater.

"I am so glad you all like your sweaters. Now off to the nursing home with the cookies, all of you. You can take my car, Holley," Mrs. Daye said.

"You aren't coming this year, Mom?" Holley asked.

"No. I need to stay here and work on dinner. I want to make sure we have a proper dinner before we open gifts tonight," she answered.

"Mom, we normally just grab a pizza. Why change that?" Holley asked.

"Because this year, it isn't just us. Sam deserves a Christmas Eve dinner," Mrs. Daye replied.

"You really don't have to go to that trouble," Sam said.

"It isn't any trouble. Now go on. The residents are waiting for you," Holley's mom answered.

On the ride to the nursing home, Sam learned that this was a Daye family tradition since Holley was a small child. Marie joined in when she was ten and hadn't missed it since. This was the first year that Holley's parents were not going, but Sam was with them instead so they would be able to successfully deliver the cookies. The home had three main corridors and each of them took a bag full of cookie tins and walked down a hallway, knocking on the doors and delivering cookies to the residents.

As Sam made their way down the hall, they exchanged small conversations with the residents, wishing them a Merry Christmas and wishing them well. The residents were each very thankful and Sam was rather enjoying the experience. When they reached the last room, they knocked a few times before finally hearing a small voice say they could come in. Sam walked in to find a woman in bed. She smiled at them as they entered and motioned for them to come sit beside her. Sam placed the cookies on the table beside her and sat down.

"Thank you, child. This is a very kind thing you do. Your mother must be so proud of you," the woman said.

"I'm not so sure about that," Sam replied.

"How could you say such a thing? Taking time out of your holiday to visit a stranger and bring them a moment of happiness is a very admirable thing," she said.

"Perhaps, but my mother and I don't really talk," Sam explained. "She has no knowledge of the things I do."

"That's very sad. Here you are wishing me a happy holiday when you could be calling your mother to do the same. I don't know what your reason is for keeping her at a distance, but when you get to be my age, you think about the mistakes you made and are left alone with nothing but regret. If I can offer you one bit of advice in return for your kind gesture, it is to call her. Do not let yourself end up like me, living out my days wondering what if," she said.

"Thank you for your wisdom. Merry Christmas," Sam said, standing to leave.

"Will you call your mother?" the woman asked.

"I'll consider it," Sam answered as they walked out the door. The woman's words echoed in their brain as they met back up with Holley and Marie in the parking lot.

When they returned to the Daye's home, Marie said her goodbyes as she had to return to her family. Sam grabbed Holley's hand as they watched her drive away. "So, she seems pretty great," Sam said.

"Yeah, we've been through a lot together. I suppose rather like you and Faith. I think of her like a sister, honestly. I'm glad you got to meet her. She didn't threaten you too badly, did she?" Holley asked.

"Oh, no. Ramona was actually much scarier," Sam laughed.

"Good. So, we have a little time to kill before dinner," Holley said, pulling Sam close to her. "You want to go change clothes?

"What? Are you kidding? Your mom totally nailed it with this sweater. I'm wearing this all night, but if you need someone to help you change," Sam offered. They cursed as their phone began to ring, pulling it from their pocket to read Mercers on the caller id. "I gotta take this call. I'll meet you inside when I'm done."

"Okay, love," Holley kissed Sam on the cheek before walking away.

Sam answered the phone expecting to hear their boss's voice, so they were quite shocked when there was a woman on the line. "Sam Christmas, this is Mallory Thorne, head of accounting for Mercers. I would like to wish you a Merry Christmas. I do hope you are enjoying it with your family. Also, I wish to apologize for the behavior of your former boss, Mr. Edwards. He has since been relieved of his post, a post that I would like to offer to you," Mallory said.

"I, um. Wow. That would be quite a promotion," Sam replied.

"Yes it would and it would come with a very significant raise as well. What do you say, Sam?" she asked.

"Miss Thorne, I am flattered, really I am, but I meant it when I resigned yesterday. I've discovered things that are more important in life than money and I can no longer continue to work at Mercers. I have to do something more meaningful, something that I can be proud of, something that helps others and makes my heart full. Thank you for the opportunity, but I have no intentions of returning to work there," Sam answered. "Now, I have to return to my holiday. Merry Christmas, Miss Thorne." Sam hung up the phone and walked back into the house. The first time they quit it had been an impulse. This time it seemed more final and they felt a weight lift from their shoulders. Sam had been a bit unsure about the decision, but now they were sure that it was the right choice.

They were still smiling as they walked back into the house and met up with Holley in her room. "I take it that was a good call?" she asked.

"Um, yeah. I was going to wait to tell you when we got back home, but Mercers offered me a promotion," Sam answered.

"Babe, that's awesome. Congratulations," Holley said, throwing her arms around them in a hug.

Sam pulled back from the hug and looked into Holley's eyes. "I turned it down. I quit," Sam said. "With everything that I've learned the past few months with you, I couldn't keep working there. I want to do something that gives back and helps people."

Holley pulled Sam into an even tighter hug. "You really have found the Christmas spirit, Sam. I'm so proud of you. And if you are looking for work in the meantime, I know this little Christmas shop that could use some help," Holley laughed.

"Thanks for understanding. I would love to work for you," Sam replied, leaning in as their mouth met hers in a deep passionate kiss, only pulling away when Mrs. Daye yelled that dinner was ready.

Chapter 38

After dinner, the Daye's sat down to watch Santa Claus is Coming to Town and Rudolf the Red-Nosed Reindeer, having enjoyed the classic films with Holley since she was little. When the movies ended, Mr. Daye lit a fire and turned the lights on the Christmas tree. Christmas carols played as they opened presents. Sam and Holley agreed to save their gifts to each other for Christmas morning, but they exchanged gifts with her parents.

Sam received a beanie crocheted by Mrs. Daye and a bottle of Peppermint Schnapps. They hadn't expected to be included at all and thanked both of them many times. Because Holley had told them gift cards were terrible gifts, Sam brought pie and ice cream from Chas's cafe, wanting to bring them some of their favorite things. After they finished opening gifts, they all had ice cream and chocolate pie. As was tradition, they stayed up until midnight so they could wish each other Merry Christmas before going to bed.

Once back in Holley's room, she pulled out a box and handed it to Sam. "It isn't anything big, but I think you'll like it." Sam opened the box to find two framed pictures. The first was the Christmas tree frame that Sam had picked out with the picture of Holley on their knee, kissing them. The second photo was a wooden frame with a photo of the city at night taken from the old bridge that Sam had shared with her.

"I love them. Thank you, Holley. This photo of the city is incredible. When did you take this?" Sam asked.

"I walked back over there the night that you and CC talked about things. I was falling for you and just needed to clear my mind. I didn't plan on ending up at the bridge, but fate brought me there and it was so beautiful that I had to take a picture. I didn't plan on it being a gift for you at the time, but I figured you'd like it," Holley answered.

"I'm not really sure that my gifts are half as good as yours," Sam said, handing her a gift bag.

"I'm sure that whatever this, will be perfect, just like you, Sam Christmas," Holley said, leaning in and kissing them before reaching into the bag. She pulled out a small box and opened it to reveal a clear Christmas ball with a business card from The Spectrum, a hard cider cap, and a peppermint inside.

"That's a memento from our first drink together. All of those items are from the bar that night. I kept them because I wanted to remember the evening," Sam explained.

"I love it," Holley said, retrieving the last item from the bag. She opened the box and pulled out the heart shaped keychain with the key to Sam's apartment. "Is this what I think it is?"

"The key to my heart?" Sam asked with a cheesy smile on their face.

"Is that what it is?" Holley asked. "I thought I had already unlocked that."

"You have," Sam agreed. "It's just a key to my place. You're there so often I thought you should have one. That way you can come over whenever you want and stay as long as you want."

"Are you asking me to move in with you, Sam?" Holley asked.

"I, um, I mean. I just, um. We spend almost every night together anyhow. I just thought. It's too soon isn't it?" Sam replied.

"Yes, Sam. Yes, I'll move in with you," Holley answered, pulling Sam to her to kiss them. They spent the next few hours discussing their plans for when they returned to Richfield until they fell asleep in each other's arms.

***

When Sam woke Christmas morning, Holley was already awake, making breakfast with her mother. Sam walked into the kitchen, kissed Holley on the cheek, and wished her and her mother a Merry Christmas before stepping outside to make a phone call.

Sam took a few deep breaths before they dialed the number they had blocked back in September. "Hi, Mom," Sam said as their mother answered the phone. "I just wanted to call and wish you a Merry Christmas." Sam was on the phone with her for less than ten minutes, which was long enough for her to start to disapprove of Sam's choices, but they told her about Holley and they wished her well, ending the call before it turned into a fight. The woman in the nursing home had been right. They were glad that they called.

Turning to walk back to the house, Sam jumped as they found Peter standing behind them. "Wh, what? How? What are you doing here?" Sam finally asked, as they stumbled over their words.

"I have a proposition for you, Sam," Peter answered. "I know it's Christmas, and I don't wish to take you away from your celebration, but seeing as you are currently without a job and I'm without a predecessor, I was wondering if you might consider being the next keeper."

"You want me to do what you do? I've only collected names for one year. Are you sure I would be qualified?" Sam asked. "I didn't even believe in any of this a few months ago. I'm sure there is someone else that would be a better candidate."

"I'm quite certain that you are more than qualified, perhaps even more than I was when I took the job, but I know it's a big commitment and a lot to think about. I don't need an answer today. I will visit you again after the New Year and we can talk about it further. Merry Christmas, Sam," Peter said, nodding at Peppermint, who had just appeared beside him. She smiled at Sam as she snapped her fingers and they disappeared.

Sam glanced down at their phone as they started to walk back towards the house, smiling as they saw a text message from Candycane. They sent a quick response to her wishing her and Rudolf a happy holiday and sent Faith a short message to let her know they would call her later as they entered the house. They had a lot to think about and a lot to talk to their friends about, but all of that could wait until after they had spent their first Christmas with Holley.

"Everything alright?" Holley asked as Sam walked back into the kitchen.

"Everything is perfect," Sam said, smiling as they wrapped an arm around Holley, and walked to the kitchen table to sit down for breakfast. As they ate with Holley's family, Sam wasn't sure that they had ever been more at peace. They had spent so much of their life hating Christmas for so many reasons, but Holley had shown them what the real meaning of the holiday was. She had given them hope and awoken something within them. She had opened their eyes and their heart. As Sam looked at Holley, they truly believed in the magic of Christmas.

The Story Continues in Checking It Twice

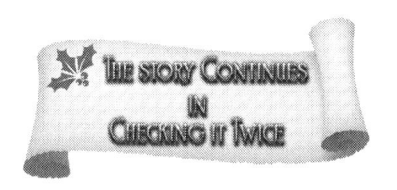

Acknowledgements

Jen - Thank you for helping me when I was stuck and letting me bounce ideas off of you. And as always thank you for your support.

Ashley - For reminding me that writing this was possible and always having faith in my abilities.

My Family - Thank you for instilling a love for the holidays and the true meaning of the season.

About the Author

Aiden Murray (he/him) is a genderqueer author writing books with LGBTQIA+ inclusion and non-binary protagonists. Knight of Elysia is his first novel. A barista by trade, Aiden has always had a passion for writing. A lover of fantasy stories and cute romance stories, Aiden struggled to find books with characters that represented him. Pulling from his love of fiction, role playing video games, and his own experiences, he began writing.

When not making coffee, playing video games, or writing, Aiden enjoys spending time with his wife visiting antique stores and artisan shops. Both he and his spouse adore the holidays and try to experience the magic of Christmas throughout the year. Fueled by caffeine, Aiden can typically be found with a cup of coffee in hand for +5 Intellect.

More by Aiden Murray

Quests for Elysia Series:
Knight of Elysia
Princess of Elysia
Hunter of Elysia
Battle for Elysia

The Wolf of Grimm Street

Made in the USA
Middletown, DE
10 July 2024

57016775R00154